I0596665

Previous Books by Marc A. Cirigliano

Guido Cavalcanti, *The Complete Poems*
The Complete Lyric Poems of Dante Alighieri
Melancolia poetica
The Fundamentals of Snowboard Carving and Racing
Scrape Exchange
Bleak Clarity (co-authored with Bruno Chalifour)
Fly Like the Wind

A Restless Spirit

The Last Months of Manfred von Richthofen

Marc A. Cirigliano

for william & travis

Preface

My title here, *A Restless Spirit*, is Manfred von Richthofen's own self-appellation in his wartime autobiography, *Der rote Kampfflieger* (*The Red Battle Flyer*), where he referred to himself as "*…einen so unruhigen Geist.*" For someone who, along with Oswald Boelcke and Max Immelmann, defined the idea of the new type of warrior, the battle flyer—what we today call the *fighter pilot*—Manfred's last nine-and-a-half months were a time of personal tumult, struggle and suffering.

It was such for everyone involved at home and away on each side of the war. In fact, my wife Lindy's grandfather, Richard Winslow Breck, Sr. was a doughboy in France during the summer of 1918. On his way walking to, of all things, a pickup baseball game, he and a comrade were strafed by a German plane. Granddad Breck went one way, while his friend the other. The pilot, a pretty good shot, saw to it that Granddad had to have his right leg amputated in an Entente field hospital the next day.

The war was, at the level of everyman and everywoman, a string of moments filled with suffering and disfigurement, both physical and psychological. In particular, the insidious damage of combat caused PTSD and TBI are just beginning to be understood for the permanent injuries and disabilities that they are.

This is my third novel in as many years, preceded by *Scrape Exchange* and *Fly Like the Wind*. It is part of what has evolved as a series based on themes informed by Buddhism. I come to regard the ideas of cooperation, self-development, conflict resolution and peace as essential components of the human experience.

Readers who want a quick look into the actual historical life of Manfred von Richthofen can easily consult Manfred's own autobiography, now free online, *Der Rote Kampfflieger*, translated by J. Ellis Barker as *The Red Battle Flyer*. Of further interest is Manfred's mother Kunigunde's wartime diaries, *Mein Kriegstagebuch*, translated with an accessible historical introduction by Suzanne Hayes Fischer as *Mother of Eagles*.

Deb Morrow and Blanche Warner were each generous with their time and energy in reading the manuscript and offering substantive suggestions. My wife Lindy, mother-in-law Nan Huy and family friend Lynne Wiley encouraged me to press forward with the task of completing my work. The lads at the World War I website *The Aerodrome* answered historical questions with intelligence, enthusiasm and alacrity when my own research came up short. Duane Delamarter was wonderful in creating my cover. Above all, my publisher, Ed Indovina, was gracious throughout this entire process.

Any errors or omission are my own.

Chapter One

"Let's hope for fifty-eight," Menzke said as he helped Manfred von Richthofen pull up his large, baggy flying   overalls over the waist of his leather jacket.

"And fifty-nine and sixty!" Manfred quipped as he cinched his belt around the baggy pants that would have made him look like a circus clown if he weren't Germany's top flying ace.

"As you wish, sir," Menzke replied.

"The battle is in the mind, Menzke. In the mind," Manfred tapped his head.

"No doubt, sir."

"You know--good to fly and get away from all   that paperwork!" Manfred had a bit of the imp in his eye.

"With rank comes responsibility, sir," Menzke, Manfred's orderly, retorted.

Manfred chuckled as he put on his leather helmet and gloves before ascending into his Albatros D.V.

"Here," Menzke, Manfred's orderly, handed his cockpit belt to Manfred over the flying ace's shoulder.

"Give Fritzi a hand," Manfred said as he clipped his belt into place.

Menzke went around the front of biplane to help Fritzi, Manfred's mechanic, spin the prop. Manfred nodded to both of them and they gave the prop mounted to the big Mercedes engine a push.

Nothing.

Manfred gestured with his finger in a circle, a sign for them to do it again.

Still nothing.

He circled his fingers one more time, with the Albatros firing up. Manfred looked around as all the planes in Jasta 11, his old squad that was now part of his new command Jagdeschwader 1, a newly created battle airplane wing of the German Air Force. Everyone was leaving their individual hangar tents and starting to taxi to the adjacent runway that was little more than a grass field. Manfred mused on about his red Albatros D. V, the *latest* offering from Albatros — if by latest, you meant not quite as good as everyone wanted. It was, after all, a sesquiplane, a biplane whose lower wings were shorter than the upper ones. Although a step in the right direction, this Albatros was not without its design problems. Even though it had a six-cylinder 180 horsepower Mercedes D.IIIaü engine and could reach an attitude of over 18,000 feet, it had structural weaknesses with its V-struts in its wing configuration. At speed in a dive, turning forces would crack the struts and shred the leading edge of the cloth on the wings.

As with all battle fliers, Manfred saw shortcomings in its maneuverability, its unneeded weight, and the list could go on if you were sipping tea or the occasional bottle of cognac back at the commandeered Schloss Markebeeke. The Germans called it a *Schloss*, but the countries of the Entente used the Belgian appellation and referred to it as *château*. But the airplane wasn't what he wanted. He thought it felt slower than its older sibling, the Albatros D.III. Nonetheless, with his fifty-seventh kill just a few days earlier, Manfred was ready to lead Jasta 11 into combat. The Albatros did have, after all, two Spandau LMG 08/15 machineguns, each of which fired over four hundred and fifty 7.9 x 52 mm Mauser rounds per minute.

Manfred actually had two more kills than the fifty-seven, but the central command of the German Air Force would not acknowledge those victories. They needed ironclad confirmation. Since no one else witnessed them, as far as the big shots in Berlin were concerned, those victories didn't count. Manfred was more than a little miffed. His word should have been good enough, he thought. He was, for certain, a Prussian aristocrat and fully in his family's military tradition. To lie would have been a mortal sin. But, it was to no avail. If he were a Prussian, the boys in Berlin were even more so, in an inflexible sort of way. Manfred's only solace was to frequently talk about the matter with his younger — by two years — brother Lothar, who had been with him since Manfred commanded the now famous squad, Jasta 11.

As he took off and started to climb with his wing mates to meet the British — and the French, and the Dutch and the Belgians — the problems with the design of the Albatros and the discrepancy in counting his number of victories were inconsequential to the overarching issue: the war had not gone as planned. Sure, he was miffed once again six months earlier when the General Staff delayed and delayed   in sending him his Blue Max, the *Ordre Pour le Mérite*, the highest military honor that Germany bestowed. It did eventually come. How many people could claim they had gotten a telegram that read: "To the brave battle flier Lieutenant Manfred von Richthofen, we have awarded the *Ordre Pour le Mérite* on today's date. Congratulations! Wilhelm, Rex." In the same immediate sequence of events, three days later, to be more precise, he was given command of Jasta 11. This was all welcome, but, as a man of action, Manfred hated waiting.

At times, as the war progressed, he wondered about the whole idea of creating *heroes*. Manfred eventually realized that his actual formal meeting of Kaiser Wilhelm II and Kaiserin Augusta Victoria, was simply a propaganda exercise. Now, her name was quite a name, he used to chuckle to himself. Although she was popularly known as Kaiserin Augusta Victoria of Schleswig-Holstein, her full name was more than a mouthful: Augusta Victoria Friederika Luise Feodora Jenny von Schleswig-Holstein-Sonderburg-Augustenburg. Anyway, Manfred flew to the Kaiser's new Headquarters in the spa town of Bad Kreuznach, southeast of Frankfurt. The town was recently famous for its new *radon inhalatorium*, with inhaled radon providing relief for those suffering from arthritis. Yes, the marvels of modern medicine. The next day was Manfred's birthday, when he met with Field Marshall Paul von Beneckendorf and Hindenburg. Not a bad birthday present! The day after that, he met with Kaiserin Augusta Victoria. It was no surprise, then, that the day after that, now May 4, the German press went with a story released by the Central Office for Foreign Services. It alleged that the British Royal Air force had created its very own Anti-Richthofen Brigade, that a reward was posted for anyone who shot Manfred down. This squadron was supposed to have its very own cameraman who was to photograph Manfred's demise. Manfred played the game here with a great sense of humor, writing a letter to the *Vossische Zeitung,* a liberal Berlin newspaper, in which he asked what would happen if he, Manfred von Richthofen, were to shoot down the cameraman?

As if that publicity wasn't enough, later that month, Manfred spent a week at home in Schweidnitz with his mother, youngest brother Bolko and sister Ilse. Although he wanted to be with his men back as Jasta 11, Manfred was ordered home, ostensibly, for a little bit of vacation time. But, while there, a German publisher sent a wonderful looking young woman there to take Manfred's autobiography in dictation, soon to be published as *The Red Battle Flier,* a book that was expected to be snapped up by the German people, even though there was a famine on and money was very tight.

All of this would bubble up from Manfred's subconscious to the point of near obsession. He kept trying to push back down into the dark, hidden and secretive recesses of his quick, agile mind. The pressure of the war — his command, his flying, worrying about his family, worrying about Germany, and now with his command of Jagdeschwader 1 all that paperwork — made his own feelings somewhat irrelevant in the grand scheme of things. No, there was no time for distractions. So, with his conscious mind, Manfred needed to be as sharp as could be. Innately and supremely confident, always intent on prevailing, Manfred knew that Jasta 11 and his larger Jagdeschwader 1 would dominate in the inevitable air battle that was just a few minutes away.

He was concerned, though. Things had not gone Germany's way in the war, even though the Germans and their Austro-Hungarian allies were only a relatively short distance from Paris. With a jewel like the French capitol nearly within grasp, many people couldn't imagine why the German war machine was stopped in its tracks for nearly three years now. The frustration was real, because, for instance, the air war was particularly well organized. The Germans had created their Flight Reporting Service. From a combination of observation balloons, spotters in church steeples and troops on the ground, information on approaching enemy airplanes was telephoned directly to the German squadrons, who would take to the air immediately to meet the enemy.

The war had lasted much longer than the experts on both sides had predicted. The German plan of attack, the Schlieffen Plan, looked fine on paper, which meant for many in Berlin that it would work on the battlefield. The idea was for Germany's army to sweep in a big line that began vertically at the German border and then to curve its direction with the shape of northern Europe in a circle down to the south. It looked as some sort of geometric abstraction guided by a compass on the map. According to Germany's finest military minds, it was a plan that would crush the enemy in a show of German military dominance. The only thing, a rather important one, was that reality got in the way. Someone forgot to tell the Dutch, Belgians, French, British and now, it was beginning to appear, the Americans, that the Schlieffen Plan was supposed to result in certain German victory. All along the way, on the ground, in the air and at sea, opposition to German might was fierce. For both sides, the fighting was difficult, with inhumanity commonplace and millions now dead. The official German response was to retitle the Schlieffen Plan as the Hindenburg Line in an attempt to add a heroic tint to their now stained strategy of holding their position along No Man's Land.

Manfred reflected back to a conversation he had with his mother, "It's good to be home, Mamma."

"It's your birthday. Number twenty-three," Kunigunde pushed a cup of hot chocolate across the tea table to her son.

"May 2. We are almost a year into the war," Manfred pointed out.

"I'm sorry, no whipped cream," Kunigunde apologized.

"Yes, the rationing. Whipped cream is against the law, isn't it?" Manfred had a comical look on his face.

"I believe so," Kunigunde returned her son's sly smile.

"We could be law breakers. Criminals, you know, if we could get some cream from a farmer and whip it into a froth," Manfred chuckled.

"Prison for the whole family," Kunigunde laughed at her son's usual irreverence.

Manfred became serious after he took a sip of the chocolate, "The deprivation is much worse than anyone imagined, isn't it?"

"Yes, but the Kaiser says victory is possible. I see we're having a good number of victories on all fronts," Kunigunde responded, looking her son in the eye. "The newspapers are optimistic."

"I know, I read them too," Manfred took a long drink of his chocolate.

"We've lost a few relatives, so the reality of the war has hit home — I think, though, not just for us, but for every family," Kunigunde was now serious.

"I think we will lose the war," Manfred dropped this artillery shell in the middle of afternoon tea just ten months into the war in 1915.

"But we're winning a good many battles," Kunigunde offered up.

"I know, but the opposition is fierce. Strong resistance. Look at the Somme. Ridiculous casualties and no progress," Manfred forehead was furrowed.

Kunigunde was stunned, but kept her composure, "I see. I never thought about this before."

"An optimistic note, Momma," Manfred smiled again.

"What is that?"

"I'm leaving the infantry," Manfred looked his mother in the eye.

"Really?" Kunigunde was very surprised.

"I'm going over to the fliers," Manfred said with anticipation in his voice.

Not only had Manfred joined, he was musing in his head as he looked at the ground far below his Albatros, he had done quite well at this new style of warfare.

Manfred and his new wing, Jageschwader 1, had been moved to Markebeeke near Ypres in Belgium at the end of June. Ypres had, for the Germans, proved to be a major stumbling block in carrying out the Schlieffen Plan. At this point in 1917, the Germans suspected that the Entente was going to start another push in the area fairly soon, especially given that the Germans had perceived enemy activity in the area. So far, the battle here had taken shape in two major parts. The first took place in the latter part of 1914 where the Germans lost the town to the Entente. The second part of the battle went through May of 1915. The town itself had been bombarded into oblivion by both sides. Casualties from both sides totaled well over 300,000. Adding to the inhumanity, it was in the second part of the battle that poison gases were first used in combat.

Manfred and Lothar's father, Albrecht, Baron von Richthofen, had talked to his sons just a few weeks earlier about the nature of fighting in war. The *Baron*, a major, was reactivated for the war and placed in command of the occupied Belgian city of Harlebeke.

"It is paramount to be a warrior and not be consumed with killing to the point that you become a butcher," the elder von Richthofen explained to his sons.

Manfred, who as eldest could also claim the title *Baron*, understood this distinction. Even though he was a captain with his own command, Manfred welcomed the confirmation his father was now providing to the way he approached air battle. Manfred also knew that Lothar, slightly more irascible, would find this difficult to do because he became emotionally engaged. Lothar became angry as he fought.

Manfred's approach worked well for him, too. He thought about his success, which was no minor detail in the development of this new art of war, that of the *battle flier*. If there was a stalemate in the general progress of the war — the Hindenburg Line and all that — Manfred had proved himself and those under his command as outright winners. He was quite the shooter. From the time of his first air rifle when he was nine, Manfred went out into the countryside surrounding his home in Schweidnitz to plink at small animals, rocks, branches and blossoms. As he grew, his uncle Alexander, who had hunted throughout Europe, Africa and Asia, taught Manfred how to shoot and hunt.

"Practice your hold, with the sight picture, eye on the front post. Always the front post," Uncle Alexander would say.

"Yes, sir," Manfred would then hold, relax, and then hold again. After a while, he became rock steady, even in the standing off-hand position.

"And squeeze the trigger. Always squeeze. Never pull or jerk," Uncle Alexander would remind him.

"So, I should briefly hold my breath, too?" Manfred asked, although he already knew the answer.

"Yes, pause your breath at the end of the exhale.   Relax your body, while firm and still with it."

Manfred recalled that he fired his first grownup gun years ago, a Mauser 71, a black powder, needle pin rifle with an 11 x 60 mm round. Even at that time, that Mauser 71 was already antiquated. He imagined his father and uncle wanted him to see the progress Germany had made in firearm design, so they let him shoot the rifle for a week or so. Then, they quickly relegated it to the status of a collection gun in the family's arsenal.

"Old stuff, certainly, in the face of German progress," his Father chuckled.

After letting him try that old 71, the von Richthofens were doing what every other aristocratic hunting family was doing. They had moved on to hunting versions of the Mauser K98, known for its technological   innovations with its new receiver, faultless bolt action, inventive stripper fed magazine and powerful yet accurate 7.92 x 57 mm cartridge. A great invention by Paul Mauser, an archetype of German origin, it inspired emulation by the Americans in the form of the American M1903 Springfield and the British with their Lee-Enfield, each great rifles in themselves.

As Manfred was nearly at the top of his and Jasta 11's climb, he thought of his favorite rifle, the 1903 Mannlicher-Schönauer hunting carbine. Yes, this was the epitome of rifles with its light recoil, buttery bolt action and iron sights. He also shot at game with a modern scope made by M. Hensoldt and Söhne in Wetzlar. This pancreatic "Solar" model scope had an adjustable magnification that he could look through quite easily because his Mannlicher had an adjustable cheek piece that he could elevate to make his eye level with the longitudinal axis of the scope. Although it was a technological marvel, Manfred preferred iron sights, when possible, as they demanded a mastery of the technical aspects of shooting. Manfred had met and exceeded that demand by taking much game with its 6.5 × 54 mm smokeless cartridge. He held, in that bridge between the subconscious and conscious self: a memory of spotting a wild boar, raising his Mannlicher-Schönauer, sighting the target picture with rear "V" sight and front post. He focused on the front post as the boar went blurry just behind it. Manfred squeezed the trigger. The boar went down.

"You do well, Manfred," his uncle commented.
"You should. You're the older brother," Lothar teased.

"You should grow up, Lothar," Manfred shot back.

"You make it look easy," Uncle Alexander concluded.

It had not been so easy sixteen months earlier up here in the air, or as people down there called it, *up there*, as though it were some mystical feat to fly. Perhaps it was, but it was not at all romantic, as the papers on both sides of the war had characterized it. No, it wasn't as though *medieval knights* were fighting in a fair manner for truth, justice and honor, maybe even in the spirit of sport. It was not easy for either side, but especially for one if they had grieving family members and forlorn comrades who felt the losses.

No, it was not easy.

Hawker, the British ace Lance Hawke, took some real work. He was a flier you had to respect, Manfred used to tell his men in Jasta 11 well before he engaged him *up there*.

"Hawker knows what he's doing. He is the consummate warrior," Manfred would tell his men.

"Yes, Sir. We'll be wary of him," invariably one of them would reply.

The British knew and respected Manfred, as well. They also wanted him dead—yesterday, if possible. They had put a bounty on Manfred's head. This became general knowledge within the German military, so much so that his father, a major, was upset enough to telephone Manfred at the front to tell him, "Be focused. They want to get you."

"I know, Papa," Manfred would laugh.
"It's not funny."

"I know what I'm doing."

"I imagine so," his father would admit. "But, they do want to get you, to kill you."

So much did the British want to get him that one night, having reconnaissance where Jasta 11 was camping, they came after Manfred in an improvised bombing run just as everyone in Jasta 11 was falling to sleep.

Menzke yelled, "The British planes!"

Everyone grabbed a Mauser as they headed to a makeshift underground shelter. Bombs were crashing, men were firing in the air at the sound of the British planes and chaos reigned for a few minutes. However, Manfred and his men were unscathed, thanks to an inability of human beings to see well after the sun went down.

"At least they can't see in the dark," Manfred observed.

"The things one puts up with being your brother," Lothar cracked after it was clear the British were leaving.

"It's a small price to pay, little brother," Manfred smiled back as he put his arm around his brother's shoulder.

Hawker, though, was tough.   The top British ace—really, the British Boelcke—knew his way around a dogfight. Boelcke, the late German ace, wrote the book on aerial dogfighting, to be certain. He was, rightfully, everyone's idol and his *Dicta Boelcke* was the bible that people flew by if they wanted to prevail in aerial combat. Now, Hawker earned the respect of battle-fliers on both sides of no-man's land. And, that damn Airco DH 2, that *pusher* with the propeller just behind the shortened fuselage, was more agile than his old Albatros D.II. The fight between them went on for a long time, with both ascents and descents, twists and turns. Manfred felt the compression as he was pushed down into his seat as he pulled out of a dive. Hawker did several somersault rolls, as did Manfred in the wicked dance they were improvising. Each had tried a zoom climb, where they used the kinetic energy, the inertia of their dive to try to gain an advantage in climbing at the end of it.

When Hawker tried to break it off to get back over his own territory, he was vulnerable for a moment. Manfred, in dogged pursuit with nothing elegant about this brawl, pounced. He followed his own rule as Hawker was late in timing his "break," a maneuver successful battle fliers could execute almost on instinct, a sharp turn to evade an enemy's trained machine gun burst at close range. Manfred's rule was, much like Manfred himself, simple and direct: shoot at the man, not the plane. Manfred fired. Hawker, then, took a bullet, Manfred's bullet, to the heart. Once again, the Red Baron, the man the British derogatorily named *le petit rouge*, the little red one, was successful in dropping down behind his enemy — this time, Hawker — much like a hawk chasing its prey.

The newspaper wrote of this new art of war, this battle-flying, when they described Manfred's *falcon tactics*, his practice of dropping down on an enemy pilot from above, sighting in immediately and shooting to kill. It was a quick, no nonsense approach that minimized the attacker's exposure, and hence, vulnerability, in battle flying. Like perfecting his hold with Mannlicher-Schönauer, he could sight in on an enemy plane at close range with regularity and precision.

"Forget elegant flying, forget the medieval knights, the quicker you can get it done, the better," Manfred would instruct his men.

Hawker, though, was Number Eleven, forty-six kills ago. Nonetheless, Manfred was confident that today would be *at least* Number Fifty-Eight, if not more. It was early July just two days after those apparently meddlesome Yankees were celebrating their Independence Day. He was not happy they were going to enter the war on the other side, but he respected the Americans, as they were gadget people, similar to the Germans. If it needed engineering, workmanship, manufacturing and tinkering, the Americans were as formidable as his Germans. It was several decades earlier that Field Marshall Helmut von Moltke the Elder had Prussian officers travel to American to learn the speedy techniques American circuses used to load and unload their trains from town to town. In fact, Manfred mused, once they formed Jageschwader 1, they used those very techniques to move the entire unit by train from point to point for quick deployment. Manfred smiled. That was how they came up with their nickname that June, *The Flying Circus*. And, Manfred had what — at least for him — was the ultimate appraisal of America: he fired a Springfield rifle before the war and concluded it was a fine piece of hunting equipment.

Manfred began his work as a commander when he assumed command of Jasta 11 in January earlier that year in 1917. He developed the relatively small unit into a fine squad of battle fliers. By the end of April, though, everyone would know about Jasta 11 and its ace, Manfred von Richthofen. The British were angry enough to start calling him "*le petit rouge*," much in the way one might characterize a hurricane as "a bit of a tempest" in an attempt to wish away the storms severity. The British began April with an offensive at the Battle of Arras. By the end of the month, they would term it *Bloody April* because of the losses the British Royal Flying Corp sustained.   Two hundred and ninety-eight losses, with Jasta 11 accounting for 89 kills.

Manfred Richthofen had 21, Kurt Wolff 22, Karl Schäfer 15, Manfred's brother Lothar 15 and Sebastian Festner 10.

Once again, with success, came a balance from the other side, ever the aggressor. Even though the British RFC suffered heavy losses, they were able to accomplish their mission. They provided the army with fresh aerial photos, garnered relevant reconnaissance, especially for British artillery, and engaged in successful bombing raids.

Leading up to this very July day, Manfred had lost three close comrades from his old Jasta 11 squad. He wept for each one. The first to fall, Sebastian Festner, was an NCO who began his military career as a mechanic. He was shot down Flying Albatros D.III during the Battle of Arras on April 25 while near Oppy in Pas-de-Calais, northern France The next, Karl Schäfer, flew a red and black Albatros D. III. He was killed at Becelaere-Zandvoorde in Belgium. Cosmopolitan, he spoke fluent French and English. Studying engineering and quite refined in the art of drawing, Karl found himself in Paris at the start of the war. He took command of Jasta 28 at the end of April and managed to write an autobiography, *From Soldier to Pilot*, before his end. Yet one more, Karl Allmenröder, was a medical student at Marburg before all the action began. He earned the Blue Max on June 14, just thirteen days before he was killed while flying his deep red Albatros D.III that he had cheerfully highlighted with a white nose and white elevators.

In war, Manfred observed, good and bad seem to come as a symmetrical pair. Manfred was confident in himself and in his fliers in both Jasta 11 and his new unit Jagdeschwader 1. But, *again,* he knew in his heart that things had not gone as planned for Germany.

As he now reached cruising altitude and Jasta 11 was assembling itself into an echelon, he understood the British Royal Navy was an effective instrument of war. Beginning two years earlier in 1915, they had effectively blockaded Germany. Interdicting shipping on the high seas, throughout the Baltic Sea, Britain was starving Germany. The Germans complained of a violation of the rules of war as its people began to feel the pinch of a food shortage. By 1916, German civilians were in the early stages of a famine. In fact, as early as June of the previous year, the government had begun to ration bread, which should have been a warning that things were only going to get worse. By now, the bread was dark, not white, the sausage meager, with no fat, and the butter scarce. Families were down to three pounds of potatoes a week. Manfred and Lothar could eat that in one sitting at their mother's table.

Women had protested the lack of food with gatherings outside shops. It might have been funny, these so-called *Butter Riots*, but tuberculosis had spread throughout the country, with children suffering most, including rickets and that horrible abdominal swelling with   edema. There was not much to laugh about. As a counter measure, the Germans unleashed their U-boats to start sinking ships indiscriminately. The Allies would retort that they began the blockade and its subsequent famine in order to simply try and stop the brutish *Huns* who were using captured French citizens as forced labor.

Manfred admitted to himself, and talked about this with his mother Kunigunde, that he had seen this very forced labor, *slave labor*. French teenagers, emaciated, underdressed in winter, were working on the very railroad lines that they used to shuttle Jasta 11's and now Jagdeschwader 1's aircraft from here to there, and back again, as the *Flying Circus*.

That very morning Manfred spoke with his mother over the phone. He was concerned, as he had heard through his older sister Ilse that Mamma had struggled under the stress of it all. She was better now, but had become jaundiced and required morphine to cope with the pain she was feeling from the malnutrition. That morning his mother let slip her dissatisfaction with the general state of affairs.

"Butter is now twice what it was before the war, if you can find any," Kunigunde complained.

"I see," Manfred tried to downplay it.

"And rice is five times what it used to be," she went on.

"I plan to be home in a few weeks, maybe some hunting," Manfred tried to change the subject.

But, all this was in his subconscious mind, just under the surface of his finely focused warrior skills that were now at the fore of his consciousness.

Manfred looked ahead.

Partway toward the eastern horizon, the landscape over West Flanders was torn in two. At a distance, it appeared a thick grey line — maybe a few hundred meters wide — that ran north and south between the two sides. An unsightly man-made mass of overturned earth lined with barbed wire and punctuated with thousands of holes made by a bombardment that had been going on for a long time. As you neared it in the air, the grey turned into a brown mess of soil and misery. Men on both sides were gaunt and ex-hausted. Disease was just an hour away, with cleanliness difficult in the rain and snow, and, now in the July heat, nearly impossible.

By contrast, the further you came away from the front, the beauty of West Flanders reminded him of the landscape that surrounded his hometown of Schweidnitz in Prussia. The greenery was a welcome relief in these times. A closer comparison of the two pastoral realms reminded him that his home countryside had more soft rolling hills that made a day's hunt both picturesque and a nice stretch of the legs. Times with his uncle Alex-ander were now a memory. The same for times with his father and Lothar.

Papa, Lothar and he would go out to take boar and roebuck for feasting back home with Mamma, Ilse and little brother Bolko. He loved the feel of his rifle, the Mannlicher-Schönauer, whether in a sling over his shoulder or raised into a hold as he aimed at prey. Hunting satisfied his warrior spirit. There was something meditative, too, in the quiet stalking of game. He missed the easy camaraderie he had built up with father and brother. Quiet, he would gesture to them to be still and silent. Then, rifle up, he would take aim with iron sights — rear v-groove, front post, quarry, then front post on the blurred quarry. He still practiced his hold every day so that he could focus in quickly, quietly and seamlessly. A local gunsmith had slightly lightened his trigger, so that the pull was never disturbing to his aim. Then and always, the quarry would drop.

But, *up here*, Manfred gestured a signal to his men. They signaled back in their biplanes. Everyone knew they would be into it in another few minutes.

If hunting was meditative and reached deep into his soul, horse riding satisfied his need for speed. The terrain around Schweidnitz gave Manfred tremendous possibilities. Although his mother would always complain that he rode recklessly, Papa would remain silent and only ask if he enjoyed himself. As far as riding was concerned, there was nothing like mixing in dodges through the woods, ducking under tree branches, letting loose with open gallops in lush fields and jumping over fences and boulders. His horse, Santuzza, was strong and relished the challenging rides as much as Manfred did. Besides, it was good practice for the competitions he enjoyed. Admittedly, sometimes he pushed it too hard. He was one to take measured chances and, as such, he did fall, bruise himself and make his sister laugh at him. Although it wasn't such a bad thing, either, since Ilse's girlfriends never seemed to mind helping him feel better later in the evenings.

These days, however, Ilse's friends and the bounty from mother earth were a thing of the recent past. The famine meant that the woods and forests were nearly hunted out. German agriculture had proven inadequate for the population it was supposed to feed. There was less and less to eat. Many were living on one thousand calories a day. People needed quality protein and they weren't getting it. Germany was now in the middle of a famine with no easy way out. It made The Blue Max, the *Ordre Pour le Mérite*, he had earned in January earlier that year pale in comparison to the lean, strained faces he saw when he flew over the trenches. The Max was just some ribbon and metal, while people were starving in Germany. Once again, he recalled that on his way to receive the medal, those emaciated young French teenagers were little more than boys and girls. Their tattered clothes could not have kept them warm that January day. Their blank faces were nothing that either side should have been fighting for.

Manfred, though, would hunt today *up here* in the sky.

He thought about his Papa, Albrecht, who had been attempting to rescue some troops in an engagement well before the war. As his men crossed a river, the elder von Richthofen saved a young soldier, but he was left permanently deaf in one ear when an explosion went off right next to him. He and his soldiers saved their river-soaked comrades, but the trauma left him dazed for longer than he would admit.

But, that was then. Indeed, now, this war had become a difficult affair, unforeseen by the experts.

Chapter Two

Manfred was almost at altitude. He turned and dipped to one side in order to see a large part of Jagdeschwader 1 climbing to meet Jasta 11. It was a clear day, perfect for early July. The small dots that were in the distance were now coming into a more recognizable series of shapes. If this holds for the next few minutes, the battle would be enjoined with Jasta 11 tackling a group of British F.E. 2d planes who were attempting to make it back to the British side after each dropped its six 20 pound bombs on German targets. Manfred was looking forward to shooting down more than one of these *Big Vickers*, as he nicknamed them.

The F.E. 2 d, with the F.E. standing for Farman Experimental, was functioning quite well as a bomber for the dogged British. Carrying two people, the F.E. 2d was a model of progress. There was an observer in front who could fire a free rotating Lewis machine that faced forward or a rear facing Lewis gun that required him to stand up and face backwards. This still left the plane vulnerable from the rear and below, but Manfred could begin to see that these six planes were taking care of that with a new strategy that protected each pilot's vulnerable parts. The pilots sat up and above the observer and could fire two fixed forward facing Lewis guns with their strong .303 British cartridge. As a pusher, many felt this plane was an outmoded design, but its Rolls-Royce Eagle engine could put out 250 horsepower, so it could lug the four machine guns, bombs and two man crew on par with the German Albatros design.

"John Bull, we are ready," Manfred said out   loud to himself in the cockpit of his Albatros.

Oh, yes, he was ready for a head-on onslaught. That was fine with him. He automatically recalled the *Dicta Boelcke*, the rules of aerial fighting developed by his mentor, the late Oswald Boelcke.

Everyone recognized that Oswald Boelcke was the father of this new art of war, the art of the battle flier. A year earlier, Boelcke formed Jasta 2, or, as it became known, Jasta Boelcke. Among his handpicked members, was Manfred, who was just so very surprised and flattered that the famous Boelcke would travel all the way to the Russian front to ask Manfred to join his new Jasta.

Manfred briefly recalled the highlight of his sojourn in Russia. He was navigating for Count Holck in a two seat Albatros C1 on a reconnaissance mission. Manfred liked Holck, who insisted that they work as friends, not under the military and social formalities of *Count* and Manfred's title, *Baron*. This suited Manfred just fine and the two became friends. As they were flying, Holck swooped the Albatros around to get a better view of things below. Right in front of them was a huge plume of thick, black smoke. They had little choice, but to fly into it. It was really quite noxious, causing both of them to cough. Even worse, though, was the smoke's effect on the engine, which began to sputter and spurt. As Holck and Manfred looked down, they saw nothing but an immense fire. This was rather unsettling, as the Albatros, with its sudden loss of power, had suddenly dropped from 6000 to 1500 feet. With both their hearts pounding, the two of them were running out of options. It was a stroke of luck, then, that, as suddenly as they entered the cloud of smoke, they flew out of it, with their engine again running normally. A minute later, though, the engine decided to go on vacation. The

Mercedes simply stopped. Without power, they dropped down further and both wondered if they would clear the edge of a forest they were getting dangerously close to. They cleared the last trees, with Holck being masterful in guiding the plane to a safe landing in the adjacent field.

Out of their plane, each grabbed his luger, with Holck observing, "These may be necessary, Manfred."

"I agree. Better we meet some Slavic girls and not Russian soldiers," Manfred smiled.

"Let's be practical," Holck smiled back.

"Practical? Maybe best to head west," Manfred suggested .

"A good idea," Holck replied as they took off on a dead run.

After a few minutes, a soldier came into sight. Holck and Manfred automatically dropped to one knee to take aim with their lugers. They were relieved to see that the young man was a Prussian Grenadier.

"We've broken the enemy lines," the young man shouted as he and several comrades ran past them.

If that event ended on a light note, Manfred remembered one of the most foolhardy and terrifying things he ever did in a plane. While near the western front, just after Manfred took off, he found himself in the rain over the Moselle Mountains. It came down so heavily, he had to take off his goggles in order to see. In another minute, the sky turned so dark that he tried to dive below the clouds. The wind grew stronger, the rain thicker and the sky darker that he was practically flying blind. He couldn't see. His plane was thrown all over the place, while thunder and lightning crashed all around him. He got so low that he had to whip his Albatros over trees, houses and church steeples. Finally, though, this trial by nature's ordeal stopped as he flew toward the light, which appeared as some sort of miracle, out of nowhere. Manfred was out of the storm!

When he landed near Verdun, his best friend George Zeumer ran out to greet him, "We got a call saying they thought you'd be killed in the storm."

"It was an ordeal, George," Manfred smiled quietly.

"Stupid, Manfred. Just stupid. You should have waited," Zeumer admonished him.

"Maybe time for a little cognac to calm your nerves, old boy," Manfred quipped.

The dots in the distance were even larger now. Head on. That was fine. The Dicta Boelcke advised differently. Keep the sun behind you to obscure your opponents view. Once you attack, follow through. Only fire at close range. Never take your eye off your opponent. In the best of circumstances, it is highly advisable to attack from the rear. However, today, since they were being attacked from the front, meet the attacker head. If you're over enemy territory, keep your line of retreat fresh in your mind. Finally, attack in groups, with each one of you picking your own opponent. Manfred added one that he tried to observe religiously. It was a simple rule. One should know the difference between energy and idiocy. In other words, as he would tell his men, "Never let your confidence turn to recklessness."

Manfred was used to head on combat, in a manner of speaking. Quite often, he would charge head on towards his pet Great Dane, Moritz, as they fought for control of a stick, ball or knotted rags. Moritz, always the character, would exhaust Manfred alternately wrestling with the object of contention, teasing Manfred to chase him or chasing Manfred. More often than not, the two of them would end up lying on the ground, winded but smiling, after an hour of non-stop play.

Manfred recalled an early experience right after he got Moritz as a very young puppy because it contrasted sharply from where he now was and what he was about to do. Early in the war, Manfred was at a hotel on the ocean in Ostend, Belgium. It was a warm day, there was a gentle breeze and everyone had champagne. He was with comrades, most important among them, longtime friend George Zeumer. This was very different from duty on the Russian front. Zeumer and Manfred each just bought new Great Dane puppies.

"Much better here on the Western front," Manfred took a sip of champagne.

"Definitely. This is how war should be fought," Zeumer smiled.

"The wonders of the Schlieffen Plan," Manfred replied.

"So, you had an adventure with Holck, I understand," Zeumer changed the subject.

Manfred didn't respond, but leaned over to pet Moritz. After a few seconds of silence, Manfred offered up, "The newspapers make this out to be a game. We're in the Middle Ages and we're on white steeds."

"Rubbish," Zeumer said tartly.

"No doubt they have to sell newspapers," Manfred observed.

"And fill in the propaganda gaps," Zeumer went on.

Manfred nodded in agreement.

"Did you and Holck feel particularly medieval after making that emergency landing behind enemy lines?" Zeumer chuckled.

"No real time to think back then. Much better to be here in Belgium. I will say …," Manfred was cut off in mid thought by droning in the sky behind them.

Everyone turned to see a squadron of planes. After a few moments, they realized the planes were British—and, they were diving towards them in a strafing run. They grabbed the puppies and ran under the deck, with bullets just missing them as they covered the puppies. The planes only made one run and then flew over the train station on the harbor where they dropped bombs.

The reality of war was on the Western front, as well.

With the dots in the distance now appearing quite clearly as a squadron of six Rolls-Royce powered 250 horsepower F.E. 2d bombers, each with an observer-gunner in front with the pilot above and behind, Manfred recalled the time that Boelcke died. If one thing haunted Manfred, it was the loss of Boelcke, which seemed to indicate that fate could unsettle human reality in a moment's notice.

Sitting in their command post, Manfred was watching Erwin Böhme begin a chess match with Boelcke. As usual with the war, it seemed just a few moments later that they were in the air engaging the British. But, before that, they engaged in their usual pranks.

"Oswald, Menzke said there is a message for you outside," Manfred looked seriously at his commander.

"Sure, I'll get it. Just wait a minute. I'll be back," Oswald went out to see what Menzke had for him.

In the brief moment that Oswald was gone, Manfred swiped one of his knights and tossed it to Hans Reimann, who palmed in in his free hand as he lay on a cot with his head propped up with the other hand.

Boelcke returned, "Menzke wasn't there."

"Maybe he was called away," Böhme said nonchalantly as he focused his eyes on the board.

"Wait a minute. Just wait a minute!" Boelcke exclaimed as he looked around the tent. "Someone took my knight."

The men looked at each other, with Manfred replying first, "Erwin is an honest player."

"It's not him I'm worried about," Boelcke said emphatically.

Just then, Menzke stuck his head in the tent, "Commander, please. Can you come here?"

Boelcke went over to Menzke, "Could you please sign this form?"

Aa Oswald signed the form, Reimann tossed the knight back to Manfred, who gingerly placed it back in its spot on the board.

Boelcke came back and immediately noticed, "Hey, wait another minute! You fellows — what gives?"

Before anyone could respond, the bell rang with the men standing up to dash to their planes. Manfred whispered into Boelcke's ear.

"Yes, Lieutenant von Richthofen wanted me to remind you that we occupy the eastern side of No Man's Land," Boelcke shouted to the guffaws of his men.

Boelcke was in the lead on this cloudy and very windy day. Manfred focused in on one Brit who was eager to take on *le petit rouge*. Böhme and Boelcke fixed their sights on another Brit. Given the weather, with the clouds and the sharp gusts of wind, and the resolute nature of British pilots, the whole engagement was dodgy, with each side only able to fire short bursts with their machine guns. As Manfred forced his opponent to evade sharply, the Brit flew into the paths of Böhme and Boelcke. Although they each took evasive action, they collided. It was a glancing blow, with Böhme sustaining a tear in the bottom of his fuselage. But, it was worse for Boelcke, who lost the functional part of his outer left wing. Being the master, Manfred remembered, Boelcke seemed to have it under control as he glided down towards German territory. As he passed through a cloud, though, the sharp wind took his plane into a steeper dive, with Boelcke forced to land in No Man's Land, an uneven piece of earth filled with craters. He ran into a field battery and was killed instantly.

After that moment, the elation of victory in aerial combat was always bittersweet for Manfred. From that time on, he began to see that the German preparations for war were good and bad. His father helped him clarify the issue in his mind one evening at the dinner table when, on one of those rare occasions, the family came together for an entire weekend.

"The General Staff sees this entire process as a long term business investment," Albrecht began.

"How so?" Ilse wondered.

"From Bismarck on, the State has invested heavily in certain private industries—electrical companies, engineering corporations and communications with radio and telephones," Albrecht began.

"Sure, sometimes we can call home from our aerodromes," Lothar added.

"This is a nice thing," Kunigunde chimed in.

"Yes, communications and transport, all centered through Berlin, a mix of private enterprise and state planning," Albrecht went on.

"It's an efficient machine," Manfred smiled. "Very efficient."

"It has its drawbacks," Albrecht observed.

"How so?" Manfred asked.

"Ask your sister about the medical side of the war. She and I have been talking about this earlier today," Albrecht looked at each Manfred and Lothar.

Ilse thought for a moment before speaking. She wanted to be a good German and didn't like criticizing the war effort.

"So?" Lothar prodded her.

"Oh, well … see, it is like this," Ilse began. "Not enough ambulances to get people to the hospitals. Many are wounded at the front, but have no ambulances to get them to a hospital. They suffer and then die at the front."

"We can get ammunition to the front immediately, but cannot get the wounded back to the hospitals," Albrecht finished Ilse's thought for her.

"Not enough space in the hospitals," Ilse continued. "Two or three nurses are tending between one hundred and one hundred-and-fifty wounded at a time. It's endless.

"Maybe we need more nurses and more hospitals," Manfred suggested.

"Yes, but even now, not enough beds," Ilse was serious and everyone could tell she took her work as a nurse, as a humanitarian, very dutifully.

"I'll be honest," Lothar replied. "I hadn't thought of this side of the war."

"That's what I mean," Albrecht looked at his two sons.

"We also need more medicine and more doctors. More clean bandages," Ilse explained.

"So, they only planned for fighting war, not dealing with its consequences," Manfred concluded.

"I have helped debride hundreds of wounds. The stench is amazing," Ilse's face was fixed and unemotional.

"I see the men when I fly over their trenches. They are hard pressed just to live where they are, let alone fight," Manfred looked at Ilse.

Lothar took her hand, "We appreciate the job you do."

"I've changed thousands of bandages and heard so many cries of pain," Ilse's face became ashen. Then, she steeled herself, managed a little smile, "It is amazing that the whole country is pulling together."

"Yes, but a hungry country with this famine," Kunigunde said. "We do have a surprise. I found eight nice apples in the cold storage, so we have strudel."

"Well, let's end this depressing subject with dessert wine and Mamma's strudel on the patio," Albrecht made everyone laugh.

A British plane was flying right at Manfred. Manfred could tell that this one British plane was going to take him on. He was ready.

Once things got beyond the initial shock wall, aerial fights took on their own organization, each one unique. This required fliers to adapt and improvise. Ideally, if two battle fliers could work together, they would single out an opponent so they might force him down, which would give one of them the chance to drop down behind him, the best possible way to shoot him down.

Two to one was not always possible. Then, if you didn't have the advantage of altitude and the sun so you could drop down on your blinded opponent and fire from either above or behind, then it was a dog fight, with twists, turns, descents, ascents and even flying upside down. Max Immelmann perfected a half-roll ascent so you could get behind an enemy pilot if he were above you and flying in the opposite direction. Even this fancy maneuver was not applicable all the time, as everyone had taken to using sharp angles of attack, which made it difficult to follow someone, to get on his tail. Manfred knew that when someone used this tactic right from the start of an engagement, he was dealing with an experienced pilot who deserved respect and every consideration as an opposing warrior.

Of course, up here, up in the air, not everything was between airplanes. The Germans had the Zeppelins that they used to some minor advantage in flying over Britain for bombing runs. The Germans even sent their Gotha bombers across the Channel, but even this was only partly successful. The Zeppelins and Gotha bombers had trouble with the head winds, often had their squadrons scattered with only a few of the original party making it across. And once there — well — it was easy to get lost, miss the target and the have to try to fly back home. The Zeppelins could fly high enough to be out of reach of the British planes, but they still tried to do most of their missions in the winter under the cover of the darkness on those long winter nights.

As Manfred refocused, he could see that the British bombers were flying in a classic defensive Lufbery Circle. A defensive maneuver used often by slower flying planes, the Lufbery Circle was just that, a group of planes flying in a circle that moved slowly in one direction or another with the advantage that each plane's most vulnerable part, the rear, was covered by another plane following it in the circle. Planes were vulnerable from above and below, but not directly from the rear. Manfred could see that this was going to get even more interesting as the British had sent up a squadron of four Sopwith Triplanes, that single seater fighter with the nine cylinder 130 horsepower Clerget 9B rotary engine whose propeller was synchronized with a single Vickers machine gun firing that .303 British round.

All this aside, the British would soon be at a disadvantage. They were over German territory and Manfred's much larger unit, Jagdeschwader 1, would soon be arriving to reinforce Jasta 11 with another forty planes.

Chapter Three

It was strange.

Strange in that at this point in the war, with each side having learned so much about battle flying, that one of the British planes was coming directly at Manfred with its forward Lewis gun blazing away. Manfred knew that this pilot and gunner had singled him out with his easily recognizable red Albatros. That they seemed intent on coming after Manfred in their F.E. 2d was odd because those guns were several hundreds of yards away, well out of range.

"So be it," Manfred said aloud. "If this fellow wants to get shot down, that's his choice."

It would, he thought, have to wait another few seconds or so, since Manfred judged that it was now about four hundred yards away, still out of range. He smiled as he could see the Brit's machine guns continuing to fire.

Manfred reflected back to one of his young fliers that he brought up very literally through the ranks. He used to talk strategy and tactics with Sebastian Festner.

"It's better being a battle flier than a mechanic, eh, Sebastian?" Manfred used to smile at his young protégé.

"Certainly, sir. Although an appreciation of mechanics applies to military planning," Sebastian interjected.

"Well, I'll admit to that. You know, the German aerodrome is a marvel of both simplicity and completeness," Manfred replied.

"I agree. The simple tents we use to house our airplanes function in all sorts of conditions," Sebastian explained.

"They do, indeed. We can put them up to take care of as many or as few airplanes as we have," Manfred smiled .

"Simple and efficient, Sebastian smiled .

As he came back to flying in the moment, Manfred lamented that Sebastian was shot down and killed at the end of *Bloody April*. Manfred was about to reach up and take off the safety on his machine guns as he thought to himself, "A beginner or some ultra-patriot. No matter. This Farman Experimental 2d would be Number Five-Eight."

The pain was instant and sharp. It felt like his head with cleaved in two from the top down through its core. He had felt pain in the past when he had fallen off his horse while jumping. But those falls were relatively easily to shake off and never involved his head. This was different. This pain took over his entire consciousness while deadening his body.

Suddenly, everything was different. The war, the land locked military stalemate over No-Man's-Land, Britain's naval blockade, the famine in Germany, the Zeppelin strikes over England, German submarine warfare, the filth and disease of the trenches and the millions dead — all of these lost their import in a flash, because, for Manfred, everything went dark.

This was not right.

Darkness and almost no sound. Manfred could hear, but it was as though he heard everything through a long tunnel. He did not know what had happened. He did not know what was going on. Was he flying or was he just waking from a nightmare?

Always lively and blessed with eternal energy, Manfred loved his vibrant perception of reality. It made him enjoy his shooting, hunting, riding and flying. For him, everything seemed alive — and, he was a part of it. He could become one with his rifle, his horse, his prey — be it an animal or opposing battle flier. Once while a teenage cadet at the military school at Wahlstatt, he took a dare from classmates, climbed the roof of the local Benedictine abbey, St. Hedwig, in order to tie a handkerchief to the lightening rod on the steeple. That was an early triumph and a sign of greater things to come in the world of the warrior.

Now, all was dark, almost deaf and a strange combination of numbness and excruciating pain on top of his skull. He could not move and didn't know what was going on. After a few seconds, Manfred realized that   he was awake, but blind. He could barely hear the din of his Mercedes engine, but realized that he had been flying, with a sensation that his Albatros was now in free fall. His legs had gone limp and his arms were at his side. He had to get them working again if he were to save his Albatros and save himself.

His instinct kept trying to move his arms to grab the control stick. But, what the instincts wanted, the body did not seem ready to give. These past few seconds seemed like forever. Shouldn't he have hit the ground by now? Maybe he already had and this is what is was like to be dead. Good Lord, who would give Moritz dinner tonight?

As suddenly as his legs and arms went numb and limp, he could now feel them a little. Partial life was a start, he thought. Let's see if we can do more even though the pain was shocking and all encompassing.

By contrast, if Manfred was somewhere between unconsciousness and consciousness, somewhere between death and life, his comrades were fully awake and now realizing that something was wrong, that their leader might be dead in a plane that was plummeting to earth in a death spiral. The red Albatros continued down. Everyone knew, at this point, that their leader had been hit. Thoughts raced through their minds as they engaged the British. Was Manfred killed? Had he been wounded so badly he was unable to fly? Was he just unconscious? Would he wake in time to pull out? Indeed, they wondered, they feared, they held their breath — all at once as the red Albatros seemed to pick up speed on its way down, a speed hastened by the symbiotic acceleration of the Mercedes engine and gravity.

It turned out that the British pilot and his gunner were not out of range. A machine gun bullet, a .303 British round from a Lewis Gun, parted Manfred's hair under his helmet. Well into his scalp, having run a several inch furrow into both the   outer and inner tables   of his skull, the British round left a host of bone fragments in Manfred's brain. Reeling from the hydraulic reaction of the pressure wave the bullet launched through his brain, upper spine and lungs — it had a muzzle velocity of 2,440 feet per second — Manfred was numb, in shocking pain and now realizing that he was lucky to be alive.

Although Manfred could not see and his own engine seemed distant, he knew he was in his Albatros and not on the ground listening to planes in the distance. The searing pain in his head, down through his neck, shoulders, spine and torso, was sharp and throbbing. His nervous system was on overload. He thought, this cannot be happening. This cannot be my own body. It had to belong to someone else. This entire experience was beyond his understanding.

In that instant, Manfred could feel more in his arms. He instinctively got them up and then put his hand on the control stick. His vision had come back and the noise of the engine was no longer coming from the other end of long tunnel. Although he could not see beyond a blur, he could see enough to know that he was diving straight down to an earth that was patiently waiting to claim another fallen battle flier. The sensation of free fall, of the death spiral of his Albatros, told him he had to pull out of the dive.

He struggled to control the spin. He pulled back on the control stick with both hands. Strength returned to his hands and arms so that he could pull consistently.

In what seemed like ages, the Albatros finally responded. Manfred felt the deep, strong and most welcome compression as his dive bottomed out at five hundred feet. Unknown to him, two comrades — Otto Brauneck and Alfred Niederhoff — followed him down to protect his rear if he did manage to save things. He leveled the plane off and was able to recognize which direction to turn towards in order to land in German territory.

Manfred's vision went dark again. He put his hand up to his face and tried to wipe his eyes with his gloved hand. As he looked at the glove, he realized he was bleeding, with blood dripping down from the top and back of his skull. The Blue Max was insignificant as it hung around his neck. Yes, everything was different now.

Although he did not know it, Manfred was near Wervicq in Belgium. It was a lovely day. Away from No-Man's-Land, Flanders' fields were beautiful, although he didn't notice. It was enough to deliberately draw one breath after the other. It was enough to try and focus his eyes on the landscape below in order to find a place to land. When he had just begun to fly, Manfred had a terrible time learning to land. Most battle fliers did, too, but, given his high standards and his demanding personal style, being like the others didn't matter. He had crashed upon landing more than once. He remembered thinking that they ought to design the landing wheels and struts a little better. And, the fields they used as runways could have been graded a little more level, as well.

As Manfred cleared a wood, he instinctively lowered his Albatros to the ground. Far from elegant, this touching down was rough and bouncy, with his plane crashing into a thicket. He did not recall how, but he next found himself in the company of thistles, his helmet next to him. Unable to look around, his head in searing pain, his fingers felt a wet warmth as he grabbed for his helmet and pulled it off. He looked down and could see it filled with blood. Was it July or was it winter? He felt cold, with a chill on.

He felt the top of his head, then the back, where he found a wound. He now knew for sure that he had been shot.

Chapter Four

The take on events from the ground was no better than the   one on events *up there* .

At least, that's what Lieutenant Schröder at Flight Headquarters at La Mortaigne thought. Watching the clash through a telescope, Schröder was horrified when he saw von Richthofen plummet toward the earth. The red Albatros went down just a mile or so from where Schröder was standing. He grabbed a corporal and the two of them ran to see if they could help Manfred.

When they arrived, they found Manfred lying on the ground next to his wrecked Albatros. As they approached, they feared the worst, as he was lying there all still.

"Oh, Lieutenant, this is awful. Just awful," the corporal gasped out of breath and now his stomach turning slightly nauseous as he saw what might be a dead body on the ground just ahead of him. The boy was inexperienced in the field, with his duties usually keeping him at headquarters as a runner.

"Steady on, corporal," Lieutenant Schröder held up his had as if to calm his corporal's nerves. "Steady on. We have business that has to be done."

"Yes, Sir, Lieutenant," the corporal replied as he attempted to steel himself for the worst.

The two of them walked over to Manfred, with Lieutenant Schröder kneeling down next to the fallen hero's chest, "He's breathing, corporal. Give me a hand."

The two of them looked Manfred over. Each saw his helmet and, though not surprised, they were still sickened by it all filled with blood. They also saw that there was a large hole through it.

"He's got a bad one, Sir," the corporal remarked as he took a field bandage out of his pack.

"Yes, the wound goes from one side of the top of the back of his skull to the other side," Lieutenant Schröder was trying to sound conversational to allay his young charges near panic.

"I'm okay, Sir. Poor Captain von Richthofen is in a bad way. We need to help him," the corporal found some nerves by focusing on the task at hand.

"I don't think we can clean this properly, but we can dress the wound and bandage his head," Lieutenant Schröder was finding his resolve, as well.

"Yes, Sir."

"Listen. You run back, telephone and get an ambulance sent out here. Not a horse drawn one, a motorized one, you hear me? Tell them, under my orders, to spare nothing, that Captain Manfred von Richthofen has been shot and has a severe head wound. Unconscious. Heavy loss of blood."

"Of course," the corporal saluted as he ran back to Headquarters.

After about ten minutes, Manfred awoke.

"I am Lieutenant Schröder…from Headquarters, Sir. You've been shot down and wounded. Please be still. We've bandaged your head."

"Where am I?" Manfred appeared to be a bit feverish.

"Next to Wervicq. I ran from La Mortaigne, Sir," the lieutenant replied.

Manfred nodded. Then, he appeared to be in great distress, "It is too hot. I am boiling."

"You may have a fever, Sir. The wound is long. Across the back of your head. Please be still!"

Manfred started to roll from side to side, "Ah, my head! It's exploding."

"An ambulance is coming."

"I'm roasting," Manfred was tugging at his heavy jacket.

"Time to be still. You're bleeding," Lieutenant Schröder put his hands on Manfred's shoulders to hold him still. Their eyes met and Manfred was able to focus on Schröder's eyes.

"I don't remember."

"You took a bullet. Lucky it didn't tumble into your skull," Lieutenant Schröder tried to sound calm, but was getting upset as Manfred, who, beyond the obvious pain from his wound, was on the verge of irrationality and seemingly close to some sort of physical seizure.

All of a sudden, Manfred seemed to pass out.

Lieutenant Schröder had no medical training. He really didn't know what to do. The bandage he and the corporal wrapped around Manfred's head worked in slowing down the bleeding, but Manfred was in a perilous state. As Manfred lay there and Lieutenant Schröder sat on the ground cross-legged next to Manfred's head, Manfred started to shiver.

"I'm cold. Blanket. Blanket."

Lieutenant Schröder put his hands on Manfred's shoulder, again, "It's fine. It's fine."

Lieutenant Schröder turned as he heard a vehicle pulling up right behind him. He looked up at the sky and wondered why he was in the middle of such a mess on such a beautiful day in such a beautiful place. His momentary reverie was ended.

"We're here for Captain von Richthofen," shouted a voice belonging to a young man stepping out of the passenger side of the ambulance truck.

"Yes, his wound needs a better bandage. He's lost a lot of blood," Lieutenant Schröder stood up as a medic came out of the back of the ambulance.

"We're not that far from Menen," the driver observed as he walked around the front of the vehicle. "We'll get him on the stretcher and then over to the aid station in Menen."

The medic and his assistant were busy re-bandaging Manfred's head. The driver picked up his helmet.

"Bloody."

"Yes, but we've seen worse," the medic commented almost conversationally.

"True," the driver smiled. "It's not that far to Menen, anyway."

"We're just 8 kilometers or so from better than we can do here," the medic observed. As he counted, they lifted Manfred onto the stretcher.

"Be careful getting him in the back here," the medic's assistant said. For all their matter-of-factness, the three of them looked as if they had done this hundreds of times before.

"Get in," the driver smiled to Lieutenant Schröder. "We'll pass by Headquarters on our way into Wervicq."

"Sure, let me get in the back," Lieutenant Schröder looked down at Manfred as he situated himself in the back of the ambulance. "We're getting you to Menen, Captain."

Manfred opened his eyes and in a semi-lucid state insisted, "No. Courtrai. I want the German field hospital in Courtrai."

"We'll get you where you need to go, Sir," the medic calmed Manfred. "Do not worry, Captain."

In less than two minutes, they dropped Lieutenant Schröder off at the edge of Headquarters and proceeded apace through the town of Wervicq.

"Best to you all," Lieutenant Schröder saluted them as he stepped away from the vehicle.

"And to you, Lieutenant," the driver   saluted back as he let out the clutch and moved onto the main road into Wervicq.

After they pulled into town, they passed a column of troops headed out of town toward the front.

"Glad we're headed in the other direction," the medic's assistant commented. The medic nodded in agreement as he looked at their clean uniforms and relatively normal state while contrasting it with Manfred's flying outfit in disarray, covered in blood and dirt.

The driver looked up and thought, briefly, of his home and family in Mittenwald. His father, an assistant to a violin maker, used to tell him to notice each town, notice the history of Germany, of Europe, as a wonder.

"Not Menen, Courtrai," the driver heard Manfred shout. "I'm hot—open the windows!"

They passed St. Medard Church, a Gothic structure with a tall bell tower in the center of its façade. Unusual, the driver thought. The bell tower in the center. It would look more normal, better, that is, if it were on the side and flanked on the other side with a similar one. As they were leaving the town, they passed the Wervicq Mill, an old windmill that was quite picturesque.

"It's a beautiful day," the driver shouted to his comrades in the back.

"Yes, lovely," one of them replied, not at all sarcastically, as they were so used to each other now that they had bonded almost as brothers. The two in the back of the ambulance expected these types of *obiter dicta* from their driver, whose opinion on architecture they learned to respect.

"I'm not an expert, you know," he shouted back at them.

"We know, Cicerone" one of them laughed. "But, well, it's okay, you know."

"Yes, we are getting there. We'll get our fellow here to the aid station at Menen!"

"No. Not Menen! The field hospital at Courtrai! Courtrai!" Manfred shouted in a delirium.

The three of them ignored him as the driver pressed on. For some reason, Manfred's shouting made the trip seem a little more urgent and the driver unconsciously accelerated a little more than he should have. The ambulance bounced quite a bit on the dirt roads.

"Slow down," came the request from the back of the ambulance.

"Yes, of course!" The driver shouted back. "We'll be to Menen soon. Just a few more kilometers."

"I need blankets. I'm freezing … freezing … freezing!" Manfred was in shock. First he was roasting, now he was hot. "Not Menen! Not Menen!"

As they neared Menen, the belfry of the seventeenth century city hall rose out of the clump of buildings that made up the town. Heavy and ponderous, it seemed more of a functional building than an aesthetic one, at that moment, much like the war itself.

"We'll be to the aid station in another few minutes," the driver turned and tried to communicate this bit of news to his two comrades in the back without Manfred hearing the word Menen. They nodded in agreement.

They pulled into the aid station, where one of the doctors, a major, came out with orderlies and two nurses to meet them. The doctor and his crew made their way through a few horse drawn ambulances that were also unloading wounded men. One of the wounded was missing his lower leg, another's face was bleeding through the bandages that covered his face, still yet, another was able to walk with a crutch, but had his arm in a splint. As they opened the back of the ambulance, Manfred was lucid enough to pull back the blanket they had covered him with. He pointed to the Blue Max, "Courtrai, not Menen. I insist."

The doctor looked at Manfred writhe in pain trying to clutch his head. Then, he looked at the ambulance crew and his own staff. He paused in brief thought and was about to speak when Manfred again said, "Courtrai. Please, Courtrai."

The doctor, who was already convinced to let the ambulance drive on to Courtrai before Manfred interrupted him, agreed with the captain whom he outranked. He thought to himself: the wound appears severe, but better to let the national hero go to where he wants, as Courtrai had a real field hospital and was only seven or eight kilometers away. His experience had already taught him that sort of a head wound was, if the patient lived, life altering physiologically and also, as this new science of behavior was called, psychologically.

As the driver pressed on, Manfred went into delirium, again, "Courtrai! Open a window! I am roasting. Don't you get it?"

"Yes, we are helping!" They shouted in unison.

Manfred started to rock from side to side, so they struggled to hold him still. The medic said, "We could use morphine."

"We could use a good meal, too," his assistant   quipped. Before the medic could censure him, he replied, "I know. I understand. Just a lot of blood, you know."

"Um, yes," the medic decided to put another bandage over the blood-soaked one on Manfred's head. The two of them worked in tandem, as they had thousands of times before, and seemed to have put enough new pressure on Manfred's head to slow the bleeding to almost a stop.

"Courtrai?" the medic shouted.

The driver was looking ahead as there were more troops ahead marching toward the front. He shouted to the back of the ambulance, "A few more minutes."

He thought to himself as he was passing the troops: Courtrai was, given the circumstances, not a bad place to be. It certainly was no Mittenwald, with its sublime mountain vistas, but it had St. Martin's Church, a fifteenth century Gothic structure. Now, St. Martin's lacked the fancy flying buttresses that the French had, but its bell tower was something to see, over two hundred and seventy feet tall. By the time he stopped day dreaming, the ambulance was pulling up to the entrance of German field hospital on Voorstraat. Actually, it was a girls' school that the Germans converted to a field hospital in 1915. A doctor, a nurse and three orderlies were waiting as the driver maneuvered his way through the horse drawn and motorized ambulances that were arriving and leaving.

"Yes, we received a call from the aid station in Menen. Captain von Richthofen will undergo immediate examination and then, most probably, surgery," Major General Professor Doctor Paul Kraske knew that Manfred was up against it. Even though he as a doctor was exhausted, he was going to do his best to help this young man survive.

Chapter Five

Willi Sanke in Berlin and his band of photographers had taken hundreds of photographs of Germany's battle flyers. They turned these into postcards, which happened to be very popular throughout the country. Several of the Sanke Cards immortalized the individual men of Jasta 11 and other Jastas as a group of brothers. Of course, the most popular of the cards were of Manfred von Richthofen. Collecting these let the average person have contact—albeit a distant contact—with Germany's famous war heroes. So thought Professor Doctor Kraske who was preparing to diagnose and begin treatment for Manfred's head wound. His grandsons had collected several of these cards and had even done a series of drawings of Manfred's red Albatros. What had always struck the doctor about these postcards was Manfred's handsome face, commanding manner—a man born to rule—and those piercing eyes. This was the stuff that heroes were made of, Dr. Kraske thought.

Although his medical training taught him to be objective when dealing with patients' illnesses, injuries and wounds, army field and hospital medicine required even more of an attitude of detachment. He was devoted to humanitarian service, but he had steeled his character to view things at a distance, almost as if he were writing a medical article or textbook. It had to be this way. The injuries were horrific: soldiers missing feet, legs, hands and arms; young men with neither eyes nor ears; boys just turned men with burns over vast areas of their bodies; bodies with internal organs ripped apart from the infamous tumbling of the British .303 ball cartridge; skeletal structures with broken and shattered bones beyond repair and needing amputation; and, lungs crippled by nerve gas. Couple this with ongoing epidemics of dysentery, pneumonia, trench foot, frostbite, lice, scabies, dehydration and general infections, and the army medical personnel were taxed beyond their limits. Not that they weren't organized, but so were both the relentless enemy in their capacity to inflict injury and the biology of the soldiers crowded, filthy and stressed living conditions.

All of his objectivity could not save him from reacting with pathos from deep within when he saw Manfred's current state. He had envisioned Manfred as a young, active, athletic outdoor sportsman. Everyone in Germany knew that he loved to hunt, ride and hike. By contrast with that ideal image of the consummate sportsman was the reality of Manfred's current condition: Germany's war hero, flying outfit soaked in blood, hair soaked in blood, ashen face marked with blood as if it were made up for the theater with deep rouge to accent his incoherency.

"I am roasting. Open the windows."

"Yes, you are in Courtrai, the field hospital, Captain von Richthofen," Doctor Kraske smiled as he nodded to the nurse, who prepared the anesthetic.

Anesthetic was both a blessing and a curse. Progress with procaine, morphine, ether and chloroform made it possible to perform emergency surgery with patients by rendering them unconscious for long procedures that would have been impossible prior to these modern inventions. The problem with rendering patients unconscious with ether, chloroform or a combination of the two was maintaining the patient's breathing. It seemed that as many fell victim to anesthetic induced respiratory failure as to their battlefield wounds.

The doctor judged that the procaine, which was a local anesthetic, might interfere with the functioning of his brain, since it was known to affect human neurology. That was too risky. But, he had to sedate Manfred so as to shave his head and diagnose his head wound.

"Are you prepared?" he asked the nurse, who nodded in the affirmative.

They administered the chlorethyl anesthetic. Within a few moments, his unsettled body relaxed. Dr. Kraske looked at his staff, "Ah, this is better. Let us proceed."

Doctor Kraske and his team proceeded to shave Manfred's head. They did their best to use an antiseptic to clean the wound area. This was a delicate process, as the wound went down into his skull. The doctor used a set of calipers to take a measurement.

"Yes, approximately ten centimeters across the back of his head. Angled … maybe thirty degree upwards from left to right, fom one side to the other," Doctor Kraske observed. "Scalpel."

The nurse handed Doctor Kraske the scalpel, which he used to incise the skin so as to reveal more of the underlying skull.

"The wound is, more or less, along the lambdoid suture, which concerns me because there may be bone fragments into the brain."

Consulting surgeon Professor Doctor Lävin spoke for the first time, "I concur that further will be known after x-ray."

"Yes, the incision from the bullet is to the bone — and the bone exhibits a rough surface," Doctor Kraske continued.

"The x-ray will tell us about the inner table of the cranium, Sir," Doctor Lävin peered into the wound.

He went on, "Trauma, no doubt. But, the outer and inner tables of the skull with intervening diploë, the cranium is not too disturbed. "

Dr. Kraske looked more closely, "I suspect possible bone fragments inside."

Doctors Kraske and Lävin knew that Manfred's brain had already had enough damage, both directly from the bullet and the shockwave it produced. There was no need to provide any more disturbance with any invasive surgery. Besides, an x-ray was needed before a thorough diagnosis could be made. The skull was intact, but the skin and some underlying tissue was altered. The goal, for the moment, was to keep this procedure as atraumatic as possible. Each doctor suspected, though, that later surgical interventions and a debridement would be needed to clear what the x-ray might show.

"We do not have enough skin to close this completely, but I will use catgut to suture the galea best we can over the cranium," Doctor Kraske sutured the galea, the tough connective tissue that protected the cranium under the skin and over the bone.

The surgical team watched Doctor Kraske's experienced hands tie the suture off.

"I'd like silk to suture the skin, please."

Doctor Kraske was suturing the skin when he spoke to Doctor Lävin, "What do you think about the location of this wound?"

"I do not know the details, but it may be friendly fire, given its location and orientation," Doctor Lävin surmised.

"Yes, that is possible. We are going to have an opening to the skull here. Not enough skin left to suture this wound completely closed — approximately two centimeters by three centimeters in size."

When Doctor Kraske finished the sutures, he looked at his surgical team, "There is to be no mention of this to anyone — family, friends, casual conversation. Captain von Richthofen is to be accorded the decency of privacy.

Of course, everyone also knew that the Government would want to deal with this issue in its own way in its own time.

Chapter Six

Field Hospital 76, formerly a girls' school, was, from the point of view of the German command structure, a decent place. Much better than an aid station, which in turn, was better than field medicine right at the front because it had real doctors performing real medicine. Indicative of field medicine, the typical medical field kit included special forceps, saws and suture gear for on-the-spot amputations.

As such, medicine in wartime is not a pretty affair. Casualties are traumatic from rifle fired ball ammunition that could penetrate two, three or four bodies with a single shot. Artillery shells exploded, with the force of the blast and its accompanying shrapnel, providing a destructive force that the human body was no match for. Even the new weapon, aerial warfare, had its bombers that dropped bombs, which, when on target, were as deadly as artillery blasts.

In a way, the unseen and often unconsidered enemy of filth in the tranches — seasonal precipitation and dirt equaled eternally present mud dotted with puddles of stagnant water, which meant germs, infections of all sorts and an inability to get rid of human waste — took an equal toll on the troops at the front. Indeed, the stench from the mud, human waste and unwashed clothes was an experience to remember.

By comparison, a field hospital was almost paradisiacal. A stone or wood floor, solid walls with real glass windows and a roof over one's head was a luxury when compared to life in the trenches. Fresh running water, sanitation facilities and electrical lighting brought it up another notch. Add in real doctors, nurses, orderlies, medical supplies and operating theaters and you have something approaching the expectations of modern medicine in this modern and progressive age of 1917.

Manfred was not particularly aware of all this at this time.

He remembered a mask with a screen covered with cotton going over his face. He smelled something medicinal. Next, he was in a large dark cavern riding on his back down a circular slide that was dotted with foggy lights. He remembered taking his last inhalation and   relaxing into sleep. Now, he was in a well-lit place with the evening sun coming nearly horizontal through the windows. His head ached, his body felt stiff to the point of being immobile and he tried to breathe in and out as best he could.

Manfred moved his head side-to-side just a little. He could have fallen into a deep sleep, but he wanted to know where he was and what was going on. As he turned his head away from the wall, he blinked his eyes several times in order to bring them into focus. Things were still a blur and he really wasn't fully awake. Yet, he was confused, as he saw a grown man walking in what seemed a large baby's diaper. Naked, other than the diaper, this fellow's body was contorted. Instead of the normal linear posture of a regular person, he was chimerical, with his rear sticking way back and over to one side. His feet were angled weirdly with the toes pointing way inside their normal gait. With his head cocked to one side and his shoulder distorted because of the twist in his spine, he could not walk straight. He seemed to pirouette awkwardly one moment, then jerk from side to side as he walked between the beds of the men, some of who moaned in pain, others who were unconscious, perhaps a blessing.

Manfred, himself in pain and his thoughts half-formed as the anesthetic was lingering, was shocked to see this figure. Were he conscious and able to move about normally, he might attack this character as some sort of demon. Perhaps he was a phantom who had come to prey upon his mother and sister in his absence. Maybe he was sent to play tricks on his mind, to dissuade him from his efforts to fight the good fight in this long war.

Behind this herky-jerky figure, Manfred saw two orderlies bend over a bed in the large ward. Together, as though they had done this hundreds of times before, they picked up a figure. Momentarily Manfred could see its silhouette contrasting with the sunlight that seemed about to disappear as evening turned to night. It was a torso, with a limp head, with only one leg and one arm. Lifeless, this body — or what was left of a body — had blood stained bandages on its stumps. As the orderlies quickly wrapped it in a sheet and placed it on a cart, Manfred rolled his head back into his pillow.

Exhausted, nauseous and unable to sit up, he let his eyes close. He let go as he no longer had the strength to resist. His mind drifted, with consciousness gone and Manfred now standing in a foggy dark wood with a crescent moon overhead. His headache now somewhat subdued, he could move his legs as he felt his feet standing on the ground. His Mannlicher-Schönauer's sling over his shoulder, Manfred felt the weight of his rifle on his backside as he peered out of the brush he found himself in. He noticed he could see his breath in the air before his face and with what little moonlight there was, he could see a white frost on the leaves and branches.

Manfred took his rifle off his shoulder, checked to make sure the safety was on and moved a branch out his face with his right hand as he stepped onto a path between the trees and bushes. He felt a poke in his ribs. He turned to see that his brother Lothar was with him. Lothar put his finger up to his lips to reinforce that they had to proceed quietly. Manfred nodded in return. The two of them stepped forward, stealthily, with Manfred in the lead.

After they had walked for a few minutes, they crested a little rise in the trail. Lothar grabbed Manfred and pulled his ear to Lothar's mouth, so he could whisper, "Kurt Wolff has the right flank, Werner Voss the left."

Manfred nodded to his younger brother. They continued to move forward. Manfred held up his right hand as a switched off the safety of his rifle with his left. There was a stirring in the woods about a hundred feet ahead. Manfred took his rifle in both hands, ready to shoulder it, aim and take whatever foe was ahead. He looked to his right where he could see Kurt Wolff's rifle glisten out of a clump of brush. To his left, he saw Voss's silhouette, with the master marksman ready and able.

Manfred moved forward, one step every ten seconds or so. It was slow going, dead quiet and the moonlight brighter than before. The bushes stirred up the trail in front of Manfred. He sighted his rifle on the rustling brush ahead. He heard a snort and more rustling.

All of a sudden, he heard a boar shriek ahead and one from the rear. He looked to the right. No Kurt Wolff. To the left, no Voss. He turned his head quickly to the rear and there was no Lothar to be seen. Alone, Manfred could see a boar charging from the front and as he turned his head again to sight in on the animalistic battle cry from the rear, he could see another giant boar coming full blast towards him.

Manfred turned to the front to sight   on that board, since it seemed closer. He went to fire, but his trigger wouldn't move, even though he had ticked off his safety minutes before. The shriek of the boar from the rear sounded like a British Sopwith, as he turned to see the boar, gigantic, unreal in its size, upon him with teeth bared and tusks ready to tear into his flesh.

Manfred woke up with a nurse gently stilling his rocking shoulders with her soft hands, "It is all right, Captain Baron von Richthofen. A bad dream from the anesthetic. That is all."

Manfred, a national hero, had just met his private nurse, Käte Otersdorf.

Chapter Seven

It may be that women suffer most in war as their men kill each other off. But, among the women, mothers suffer the worst as the deepest of primal bonds make these losses the most dear. Kunigunde was talking with friends when she heard of Manfred's head wound. She did her best to bear up, but was shaken to her core.

"Oh, dear. We always thought Manfred was invincible. Now I have two sons who have been shot," as Kunigunde reflected back on the events of the year, her friends excused themselves and left her alone with Ilse.

Earlier in the year, May 13, to be exact, Lothar had led a squad of five Albatros against a larger squadron of British B.E.2s. Although he shot down his twenty-fourth enemy plane, Lothar himself was shot in the hip by ground fire. Nearly blacked out from the shock of his injury, he struggled to bring his plane down in German held territory. He was lucky enough to be taken to a field hospital in Douai, where he was operated on by Professor Doctor Burkhard, one of Germany's finest surgeons. The bullet had gone clean though his hip bone, leaving a hole that forced the doctors to leave the exit wound open until the bone would heal itself through. As Lothar described in a letter to his mother, he was recuperating, but had to lay still in bed. This made sleeping the night through close to impossible. Lothar pointed out that receiving the *Ordre Pour le Mérite* the very day after he was shot was a good thing, but that it was easier to sleep the night through on morphine. Kunigunde felt for her son's suffering. She also imagined the bigger picture, which was painted by her daughter Ilse, a nurse, that this was a common desire of many wounded, morphine.

Kunigunde took a moment and decided to cheer herself. She knew, after all, that Manfred was strong physically and possessed a steadfast character. She smiled reminding herself that the French had nicknamed him *le diable rouge*. Ah, she thought, the French! Her Gallic neighbors had even gone so far as to cheer themselves by fostering a rumor that Manfred was a woman battle flier, a Teutonic Jeanne d'Arc. Oh, well—so goes the dark and defiant humor of war to help people to make themselves feel better about things. All this aside, when Kunigunde got word from Headquarters that Manfred was seriously wounded in the head, everything was overturned. Kunigunde wrote in her diary that night that all hope was thrown overboard.

Everyone, especially Kunigunde, had deluded themselves into thinking of Manfred as invincible. Kunigunde had, from a very early age, seen her son as a young Siegfried.

"Do you remember the story Menzke told us about Manfred hunting in the moonlight?" Ilse asked.

"Yes, the two of them were in enemy territory trying to find a boar for some good meat for the men," Kunigunde cleared her memory.

"Yes, Mamma. Menzke explained that they were sitting there, on a knoll, when Manfred heard a rustling in the bushes far ahead," Ilse started to recount Menzke's anecdote.

"And Manfred saw a rustling of the branches, took aim and fired," Kunigunde continued the story.

"Yes, one shot. He killed the boar," Ilse finished the story. "Such a man is above the rest of us. Have faith, Mamma. I know our Manfred. He is exceptional and strong."

"My little Siegfried…," Kunigunde's voice trailed off.

The two of them sat there for a few minutes and Kunigunde began with her daughter, "I've always seen Manfred as Siegfried, you know."

"It's hard not to, but as my younger brother, he's got the element of a real pain in the ass, too."

Kunigunde chuckled.

"Even more than Lothar. Of course, Bolko is always a little darling to me," Ilse tried to keep thing light, as Mamma had been through a lot. In particular, the famine had taken a toll on her nervous and digestive systems, with Kunigunde unable to sleep the night through. Ilse watched as Kunigunde put her head forward with her arms on the chair rest as though she were Rodin's *Le Penseur*, deep in thought. In these moments, her mother looked all the much older, her face ashen, haggard, even ill with some longstanding disease that eats away at both body and soul.

But, suddenly, Kunigunde's face lightened, "He's taken his duty to lead Jasta 11 and now Jagdeschwader 1 very seriously. I know that Lothar wants to get back to active duty, but Manfred has always been able to steel himself for difficult competitive situations."

"True. The steeplechase, football, hunting alone in the rain and always coming back with game," Ilse observed.

"I don't like how the British have characterized him as some sort of killer, an evil Hun," Kunigunde went on. She took a sip of tea and then poured some more into her cup from the pot, "It's a little cold. Can I freshen yours?"

"No, Mamma — I am fine.   You know, he is as Siegfried, slaying the dragon — only for him it is day after day," Ilse was proud of the oldest of her three younger brothers.

"Well, the British think they own the world," Kunigunde began what was a constant topic of observations on the contemporary state of affairs.

"We committed atrocities in Belgium early on, but they've attempted to starve all of us to death in Germany with the blockade," Ilse was focused and firm.

"Papa told me they've killed our sailors after sinking our ships. Yes, right in the water as they struggled to stay afloat. Or they took them on board and killed them after what they call a trial," Kunigunde got up and walked to the window.

"Manfred is aware of this. I'm sure this is part of his motivation to continue on," Ilse added.

"I worry about the government using him. He's a man, not a machine," Kunigunde thought of her last few conversations with Manfred. She reflected on what he told her about his beloved Jasta 11 sitting for portrait drawings by Professor Arnold Busch beginning in June and carrying into July.

"The portrait drawings by Professor Busch were—so Manfred told me—both an honor and an inconvenience."

"I can imagine both," Ilse was thinking about this very thing.

In fact, Professor Arnold Busch was a member of the Artists Group Schlesien in Breslau. His work at that moment would turn out to be a group portrait of Jasta 11, with each flier's head as an individual portrait bust, with the most finished figure being Manfred in full flying garb in the middle of the large drawing. In addition, Professor Busch told Manfred that the War Ministry has asked him to do an individual portrait drawing of Manfred alone. All of this was, of course, pure propaganda. Arnold Busch was a second level artist at best, but he was part of what the German establishment viewed as a safe artist. None of this Expressionism, nor any of that abstract art. No *die Brücke* or *der Blaue Reiter*. And certainly none of this new *Dada* art movement. After all, French ex-pat Marcel Duchamp tried to enter a urinal entitled *Fountain* in an art show in New York City earlier in spring this year.

The *Dadas*, overwhelmed by the horrors of the war, were questioning the validity of civilization itself. Their art of nonsense, shock effect, obscenity, the *non sequitur* and mockery was to be pushed as far under the rug of society as far as possible. No, these were times that called for some good common sense. In art, the General Staff wanted straight, simple and unadorned realism. To make it even better, Professor Busch would note that Manfred's portrait would be annotated "in the field" so as to emphasize that he was doing his duty for Germany and the war effort by being at the front while he sat for his portrait, not enjoying café life in Berlin.

Chapter Eight

The night in the field hospital was restive.

The British sent bombers to nearby targets, which they missed because it was dark and the Germans threw up enough anti-aircraft fire to dissuade them from flying too low and looking too closely for whatever it was they had been assigned to bomb. Several patients woke up in pain, their morphine having passed through their systems. A few screamed when they came out of their stupor, while others simply moaned and called, "Nurse!"

Sometime just before the early Belgian July sun crested the horizon, Manfred stirred, but did not wake. His mind began to turn on again as he found himself staring into a wide open field. The sun was bright, the grasses ankle height and the breeze sweet. He heard a grunt and feared the boars were near. He turned around and noticed he was naked. There were no boars behind him, but, instead, a sandy beach that began where the field left off. The ocean was gentle, with gulls overhead cawing as they wafted on the thermals over the beach and the field.

Manfred wasn't alone. There were other naked men, a few in the field, a few on the beach.

"Hey, hello!" Manfred shouted and waved as he stepped towards one of the fellow near him. The young man was standing right on the edge of the beach looking out over the ocean. As Manfred took a few steps, his legs felt heavy and he had a limp. He looked down to steady his slow gait and when he looked up, the young man was gone.

"Hey, fellow, where did you go?"

Manfred turned around and realized he was alone. The field and the beach were empty. He saw no one.

"Hey, hey, where did everyone go?" Manfred asked as he stepped onto the beach and struggled to walk.

"Hey, hey," Manfred continued to walk—or more rightly, limped along slowly, turning his head best he could to see if he could spot anyone else.

A few feet ahead, he spied what looked like some dark green canvas, partly covered with sand and muddied, with frayed edges and almost worn through in spots from what apparently been a lot of use. Suddenly, the canvas was thrown to the side as a man sat up and swept the canvas to the side of a perfectly dug rectangular ditch about one foot deep with a theatrical gesture with his arm. There were two other naked men in the ditch with him, one on each side, each covered with a well-worn threadbare piece of canvas.

The naked fellow who sat up, had long hair and a full beard. He resembled the characters Manfred had seen in some illustrations of the Norse myths, only his face wasn't idealized and full. Rather, it was gaunt, with sunken eye sockets with huge circles not simply under his eyes, but deeply wrinkled in their blackness all around each eye. His lips were deep red, but that was underneath an irregular pattern of dry, cracked dead white skin.

"You are disturbing us," the man looked deeply at Manfred.

"I … uh … what?"

"We are trying to sleep," he cut Manfred off as he grabbed the canvas, snapped it in the air and lay down, with the canvas floating down to perfectly cover their shallow grave. The grave should have been deeper and filled with only one of the fallen, but, as was the case in wartime, you had to make do with what was there, with meagerness itself.

Manfred awoke from his nightmare and was still very much very much in a fog.

His had a deep feeling of regret, that he committed some unforgivable sin—a feeling that resonated somewhere from deep within his being, a feeling of fear and dread.

His head ached like never before. The pain radiated down his spine into the rest of body, which because of the lingering morphine and surgical anesthetic, was slow to respond to any commands from his brain. He struggled to make his limbs move, but everything felt heavy, as if his body itself were a foreign object that had imposed its weight and will on his very personage. He vaguely remembered a litheness of physical being, an athlete capable of moving without physical limitations. Now, he was struggling simply to stir a slight motion in his limbs.

Manfred wondered: was he crippled? Perhaps paralyzed from whatever had happened to him *up there*?

His head racked with pain, Manfred tried to wiggle his toes and move his fingers beyond the sort of lifeless weight that they projected back to his brain.

"Well," he thought, "Pain is the price a warrior pays for doing his duty."

Nonetheless, it was more, as he realized his abdomen was beginning to convulse in a contraction that made him sit partway up.

"Yes, the doctor warned us about this Captain," nurse Käte Otersdorf said with a practiced calm as she gently held his shoulders while another nurse held a bedpan under Manfred's chin as he vomited.

Nurse Käte was a well put together woman. Beautiful, for certain. A very nice figure, possessing feminine delicacy, yet strong, with good muscle tone. A beautiful face, chiseled while rounded delicately in the right spots.

Manfred felt like vomiting again, but had nothing left, as the bile, sputum and saliva were ejected from his stomach a few moments earlier. He could not yet talk, but moaned in a few short grunts of pain.

"There, there, Captain. All will pass and you will be walking in a day or so," Nurse Käte smiled. She could see that Manfred was lean, athletic and quite handsome. In fact, she had a small collection of Sanke Cards, bought one at a time over the past two years. A few were of Jasta 11 and two of them were of Manfred himself.

She wiped his face with a damp towel, making sure to clean his chin and lips, as they were covered in a thin residue of vomit, "We will try to keep up and get you feeling better, Captain."

"Ah, good," was all that Manfred could manage in a whisper as the other nurse left to clean the bedpan.

Professor Doctor Kraske, who was going to entrust Manfred's initial post-operative care to Doctor Lävin, had drafted a medical report, with recommendations about Manfred. He diagnosed, "there is no doubt that Captain von Richthofen's brain suffered a serious concussion. It is also probable that he has had a cerebral hemorrhage." Doctor Kraske's prognosis was going to be one that Manfred would neither want to hear, nor adhere to, because he wrote, "Due of these injuries, sudden changes in air pressure while in flight may cause problems with his consciousness".

Nurse Käte was happy to have been assigned the role of Manfred's private nurse, a rare blessing in this time of medical scarcity on the German side of the front. Vomiting was certainly easier to deal with than men shrieking in pain from blown off limbs, eviscerated torsos and horrific burns. Having your hands on a young human being who was going to die in the next minute had put a permanent wrinkle in Käte's brow, never before seen crow's feet at the outside corner of each eye and a new habit of a slight, stiff downturn of her mouth. It wasn't really a frown, but part of her overall mien of coping in very disagreeable situations. As if to speak, she also found herself pursing her lips while in deep concentration as she tried to focus on her nursing duties while dissociating herself from her human emotions. Only, she never spoke. She remained silent, bearing up against the load that was thrust upon her. She was no different, as all the other nurses did much the same, each in her own way, as the casualties kept coming.

Often, as she lay awake in bed while her body was racked with complete exhaustion, she realized that this divorce of human feeling from nursing duties was never going to happen. She was young and very much herself inside. This was fine with her. By contrast, according to what the newspapers were saying about the war and *psychology*, she and others like her were simply too soft. She knew different. Ha! Anything but soft!

"They should try my job," Käte would murmur out loud as she was about to drift off.

Still, deep inside, she knew she was young and that her life was ahead of her. But, she had to admit, these days she felt heavy and much older as things dragged on with the war. So, for her, Manfred was a welcome respite, an escape from much of the daily horror she was never quite used to dealing with. And he was handsome!

Manfred was trying to remember: was he injured while hunting those wild boars?

He looked over to nurse Käte, but was unable to speak.
"How are you feeling this morning?" Käte asked him with a well-practiced smile.

Manfred couldn't speak, with his throat so dry, so he nodded to her.

"And your head, Captain? How is it?" Käte asked.

Manfred realized that he had one roiling headache. It radiated from the upper section of the back of head throughout his entire body. He moved his head slightly from side to side to say "No." Finally, though, he managed to speak in a raspy whisper.

"Am I paralyzed?"

"No," Manfred heard a deeper voice answer his question. He moved his eyes down toward the foot of his bed where he saw Doctor Lävin.

"A bullet grazed the back of your skull. You're lucky this British .303 round didn't catch a millimeter deeper or it would've tumbled through your skull and Germany would be mourning you today, Captain," Doctor Lävin began to explain.

Manfred looked at Doctor Lävin, "Not paralyzed?"

"Not paralyzed, Captain, but a significant head wound," Doctor Lävin explained. "Concussion and most probably a cerebral hemorrhage."

"So, uh … I …. wonder if …."

"You are going to have a strong headache for a while, along with some nausea," Doctor Lävin went on gently, while he nodded to nurse Käte, who pulled up the sleeve of his hospital suit and wiped his arm with an alcohol swab.

"Captain, it is time for some sleep," Doctor Lävin nodded to another nurse, who gave Manfred a shot of morphine.

Manfred saw the ceiling become wavy, felt a release of all the tension he had built up as he struggled to move and speak, and closed his eyes.

Chapter Nine

Manfred felt a deep pain as he moved forward. He moved his head from side-to-side as he had trouble focusing his eyes. But, he knew he had to hurry. He was late. He couldn't remember for what, but he just knew he had to hurry. The pain radiating from the back of his head down through his spine and the rest of his body didn't help matters. It made moving his head quite difficult, but he just had to make his eyes focus better.

If he were late, he knew he'd catch the dickens from his mother. Such a lovely woman, but one you just didn't trifle with in these delicate social matters — if he could only remember what even he was rushing to! His eyes started to focus so that he could see a group of people standing with their backs to him. Manfred finally managed to break into a jog, with the sound of his footsteps causing the stones on the road to crunch into each other. One of the people ahead of him turned, with the others following suit.

"You know, young man, if you are going to get shot, you should at least wear clothes," Kaiser Wilhelm said sternly to Manfred as his mother, who stood arm-in-arm with Kaiserin Augusta Victoria wagged their heads reprovingly in unison.

Manfred looked down to see that he was, indeed, naked. Panicked, he tried to look around for his clothes, but as he looked around his feet to find some clothes on the ground, he felt a warmth start to drip down his fore-head, around his ears and down the back of his neck and shoulder. Manfred could no longer move, but was only able to see drops of blood land on his feet and the stones on the road.

"Did you know, Captain, that it is Saturday?"

Manfred coughed as he came out of his nightmare. He opened his eyes, only to squint in the late day sun that was raking across his bedding at a low angle making his window appear as if a bright orange bonfire was just outside. Manfred blinked several times in trying to clear his eyes and get them to focus. Ah, his head hurt! After a minute of struggle, he was able to see nurse Käte holding a glass of water.

"Oh, water."

"Yes, glad to see you among us, Captain," she said as she went to the door and motioned.

Two orderlies came in to gently lift his upper body to put a few pillows under his upper back and head.

Manfred lifted his arms toward the glass and whispered, "Water … nice."

He took a sip, but almost dropped the glass. Nurse Käte steadied his hands and wiped the spilled water off of his sheets with a practiced simul-taneity that was impressive.

"Easy, Captain. Easy. Just a little," Käte smiled. "You were sick earlier. A reaction to the anesthetic."

"Ah, I don't recall."

'How are you feeling?"

"Well, I remember an ambulance, a boar, a stone road," Manfred tried to remember.

"Ah, hallucinations!" Doctor Lävin was standing at the door. He came in all energetic, as if it were early morning and he had just taken a brisk walk across a frosted field.

Manfred looked at Doctor Lävin as he strode to his bedside. He said under his breath, "Nothing like a German doctor."

Käte heard this and smiled, while Doctor Lävin missed Manfred's soft, raspy voice, "What was   that, Captain? Good to see   you with us here in Courtrai."

"Ah, I see … Courtrai," Manfred responded. "My stomach is empty."

"Well, you've got a concussion. We talked before about this, Captain," Doctor Lävin smiled. He paused for a moment, took Manfred's pulse, muttered something, wrote on a chart and smiled, "Sir, you are going to be fine. Do you understand?"

"Yes, I understand," Manfred thought of his academy days and the literal nature of military questions. So, medicine is not so different.

"I can see the wheels turn," Doctor Lävin made gestures with his hands like circles around each side of his head. "The old machine is working again, young man."

Manfred felt exhausted, all of a sudden, "Sir, some food."

"We can arrange some tea, broth, perhaps bread to get you started … slowly, Captain. Slowly."

"We want the food to stay down," Käte explained, as she nodded to the one remaining orderly, who left to get some food.

"I want to fly. Do you understand? Jageschwader 1," Manfred raised his voice, but it was still comparatively soft.

"All things are possible," Doctor Lävin began. "All things are possible, young man. But, remember that all things are not probable."

The orderly returned with a tray with tea, a cup of broth and some bread. Manfred took a sip of tea and took a bite of the bread. His mouth was more than dry, so he lifted to cup of warm broth and took a sip to help him break the bread and swallow it.

"This is most welcome," Manfred took another sip of tea. His stomach was settling down and he thought he could finish the bread on his tray and, maybe, the broth and tea. He took another bite of bread and started to chew.

"We're going to get you up and going again, Captain. Slowly, but you will be up and around in a few days," Doctor Lävin explained as Manfred ate. "Now, you see. The boar. Well, the boar is something you will have to bear up under, Captain."

"What do you know about the boar?" Manfred asked.

"The orderlies heard you saying that word in your anesthetic sleep," Dr. Lävin said as he jotted down one more note.

"All right," Manfred said as he finished swallowing another bite of bread.

"Can you promise me that you will try your best, Captain?" Doctor Lävin looked Manfred directly in the eye while holding up one finger so as to reinforce his point.

Taken aback at his directness, Manfred met the good doctor's gaze, "Sir, I will be ready."

"Excellent. I will check in on you in a few hours, Captain. Be prepared for some more discussion. Do not forget the boar," Doctor Lävin spun around on his heel to be gone before Manfred could muster a response.

As Manfred finished his first piece of bread, he thought of his mother. How she was bearing up through all this? Was she able to sleep? Was she taking the god-awful morphine? Was Lothar any better, was Bolko good and was Papa well?

"Your father will be here tomorrow, Captain," Käte said as if she could read his mind. "I did hear that your brother Lothar is doing well."

Manfred took a double bite of the next piece of bread and washed it down with the rest of the broth. He took a deep breath. His stomach was relaxing more, while he was able to stretch his legs out a little as he lifted and relaxed his shoulders.

"You can sleep a little, but the Doctor will be back in an hour or two," Käte explained.

"Why is this? I'd like to sleep the night through," Manfred was well enough now to begin to complain. His strength was returning as his body absorbed the energy from the tea, broth and bread.

"Some people get concussion, fall asleep and never wake up. A coma, Captain, is not what you need," Käte removed his tray, went to the door, waited and then handed it to an orderly. She turned around and went back to his side. She took the extra pillows out from under his shoulders.

"I feel much better," Manfred said as he drifted off,

*   *   *

"Yes, I fell off my horse when I was home on vacation from medical school," Doctor Lävin gently rocked Manfred's shoulders around midnight. Manfred stirred, then woke up much more easily than the last time. His head ached, but the nausea was gone. As an outdoorsman, he was no stranger to pain—especially just one pain, something he practiced at surmounting. He looked to the corner of his room, where an orderly, now dozing, had replaced Nurse Käte.

"You know, Captain, the British did an aerial bombardment of one of our hospitals a few weeks ago," Doctor Lävin changed the subject to see if Manfred could follow.

"Yes, I know. The boar follows us, Doctor, doesn't it?" Manfred was able to meet his gaze in the darkened room just fine.

"This is good. Nice connection, Captain. See you in a few hours," Doctor Lävin was up and almost out the door when he turned, "We have too many other patients here, Captain. We are all too busy."

Manfred would have agreed, but he fell asleep alongside his orderly in the corner.

*   *   *

Around five in the morning, Manfred felt a soft cool cloth bathe his forehead and cheeks, "We let you sleep a little extra, Captain. You are doing well."

Manfred opened his eyes and saw his nurse seated on a chair next to his bed, with the welcome coolness of the damp soft cloth making him feel more and more a part of the world he was trying to get back to.

A naked figure, walking awkwardly and gesticulating, paused on the doorway, only to let out some sort of animal sound, unintelligible, with sadness in his eyes.

"Argh."

Two orderlies motioned for him to leave and tried to lead him away. Manfred realized that things could have turned out much worse for him.

"How many?" Manfred asked.

"How many what?" Käte was curious and more than a little startled as to Manfred's lucidity.

"How many are like him?" Manfred wondered.

"Ah, I see, Captain," Käte thought about an answer, but as she counted in her head, she gave up as the number got higher and higher. "This is difficult to say."

"You sound like a diplomat, nurse," Manfred sounded acerbic, a tone that even surprised him. The Kaiser, let alone his mother, certainly wouldn't approve.

"The doctors know it comes from the loud concussive forces from bombs and shells going off," Käte got to the point. She could see that Manfred was a very direct man

"I fly over the trenches. Our men wave from the filth. Heroes, all of them, if you ask me," Manfred was serious.

Käte took a good look at him. She thought of her Sanke Cards. In fact, there was one, Number 511, she had just bought a few weeks earlier. The one with Manfred and Jasta 11. They looked so confident. All of Germany knew they were good warriors. Standing there in their black leather coats, smiling, a sense that they had always been together, always friends, always comrades in arms—a group that was, indeed, formidable.

Now, though, Manfred had sunken eyes that indicated so much had happened in the past two days. Käte concluded, though, that Manfred's medical case was better than many. To say that the hospital was full or morose patients completely ignored the reality of death mayhem and chaos that most of its inhabitants had known.

"Yes, the trenches. We are in this together, you know, Captain," Käte continued to bathe his face. I was going to say that ..."

"I need to get back to Jageschwader 1," Manfred interrupted her. "Do you understand?"

"This is admirable, Captain ..."

"You don't know what's going on," Manfred sounded angry as he grabbed her arm, squeezing so tightly that he left bruises.

"Captain Manfred, Baron von Richthofen," Käte slapped Manfred hand and twisted her arm away. "Get control of yourself," she raised her voice as she rubbed her arm where he had hurt her.

An orderly came into the room, "Should I get a doctor, Ma'am?"

"No, things are under control now. Thank you, but we'll be fine. The Captain is … well, enthusiastic — actually, a very good sign," Käte reassured the orderly.

"Very well. I'm just in the big ward, if you need me," the orderly assured Käte.

Outside some of the outer rooms in the hospital was a large ward with beds stacked next to each other like some sort of military barracks. The men there were in a variety of states, from amputations to dysentery, from severe burns to the complications from that wickedly tumbling British .303 projectile. The most baffling for the doctors and nurses — and especially the orderlies who had to chase them down — were the men with shell shock, a disorder that proved difficult to treat medically as it presented with no obvious physical wounds, though the doctors knew that severe trauma had taken place in the brain itself.

"Captain, we are getting you out of bed after some breakfast. First, you will use a wheelchair, maybe some fresh air on the porch," Käte explained as she stood up, placed the cloth in the small basin and headed out the door. She needed a break. It was clear the Captain was an intense man, but, as she had seen with so many victims with head wounds, not himself, not able to interact within normal expectations. But, as a soldier, Manfred was no different than the other casualties who came through the field hospital bound by their duties. These men wanted to get back to the front as soon as possible, a fixation that enabled them to either ignore or remain ignorant of their wounds in the first place.

As if to reinforce what Käte had learned by experience, Manfred propped himself up onto one elbow and followed her lovely figure out the door. As she turned around the door's edge, he saw into the ward as the early July morning sun was waking the wounded. Manfred saw the same gesticulating man ambulating in the nude, his face contorted, while order-lies were lifting other men off their bedpans, since they were amputees who had yet to learn how to do so themselves.

Chapter Ten

Manfred had nodded off after a light breakfast of some bread, broth, tea and porridge. His stomach was slightly upset, especially after he moved his head around as he tried to stir himself back to normal by moving all the parts of his body. He thought: if I can only wake myself up, all will be back to normal.

As he lay somewhere between consciousness and sleep, he felt he was torn between two places at once. From one side, he saw a darkness, out of which came a series of older authoritative voices yelling at him to do things the right way. On the other side, he saw a thick forest, filled with impenetrable brush all darkened by a tall canopy of trees, thick with leaves that blackened the peaty floor below. Manfred was, at once, trying to cope with the corrections the voices were yelling at him and mindful of the forest. He was concerned that the boar might reappear at any moment. All of this while he was consumed by some unknown but overpowering guilt. No! He had done something terribly wrong.

As he lay there, he moaned quietly as his stomach turned. He convulsed upwards, vomiting to the side.

"Yes, a nightmare, Captain. All is good. We are here," Käte caught his vomit with a small pan. "Most of your breakfast passed through your stomach, which is a good sign."

"Ah, this is awful," Manfred managed. "My head aches and my stomach …. Well, better now that I've vomited," Manfred sat up on his own and looked around the room.

"You were having another nightmare," Käte explained.

"Oh, believe me, I was. I know," Manfred turned his body and dropped his legs off the side of the bed. "I need to get the hell up, nurse."

"Käte. My name is Käte," she smiled at him.

Manfred stood up, slightly bent over as he steadied himself with one arm on the side of the bed.

"Excellent work, Captain!" Doctor Lävin beamed as he stood in the doorway.

"Very well, Käte. I apologize for my earlier … abruptness. I am better now," Manfred steadied himself and fell back on his bottom on the edge of the bed.

"You have progressed, maybe a little too quickly, Captain," Doctor Lävin smiled. "We do have a wheelchair for you. Time to get on the porch for some fresh air."

An orderly pushed a wheelchair into the room. Käte took it, moved it next to where Manfred was sitting and smiled at him.

"Let me get into this thing," Manfred began to say as he stood up, took a few small steps to position himself properly and   then sat down in the chair. "That was easy. Yes, fresh air will be nice. It is … what day?"

"Sunday morning, Captain," Doctor Lävin answered as he looked at Käte with both of them understanding that an inability to independently comprehend time was a sign of impaired brain function.

Arriving at the east porch of the porches of the hospital, Manfred covered his eyes, "The damn sun is so bright!"

Manfred realized that his head was bandaged — in fact, that they had shaved his head. He felt all around his crown,   "This is different, Käte. I guess I am injured. What do you think?"

"The wound is along the place where the back plate of your skull meets the top plate. You are lucky the bullet did not enter and tumble. They may do another surgery to clean out some bone fragments," Käte paused the wheelchair and looked into a stand of trees at the edge of the hospital property.

"Can I stand?"

"I think standing is fine," she answered.

Manfred bent forward to place the bulk of his mass over his feet. He felt the back of his head throb as he tipped it forward, but was glad that he could feel his balance under his torso down through his legs to the stone porch that chilled his bare feet. He rocked slightly forward and pushed up with his legs.

"Look at this, Käte. Standing up!" Manfred smiled and was buoyed by his success.

"Quite good, Captain."

"Please … Manfred. Call me Manfred," he said as he took a deeper breath than he'd had in days.

She leaned forward to say under her breath, "They want us to keep military formality."

"They want a lot from us. You call me Manfred," he was smiling for the first time. "Manfred."

"Maybe in a day or so you can take a walk. July is a beautiful month," Käte smiled.

"I think I'll sit down. Part of me has an urge to go to sleep," Manfred started to explain.

"I appreciate you confiding in me. This is the concussion talking. Better to stay awake," Käte's voice softened.

"I remember the ambulance people shouting at each other as they drove me here," Manfred was free associating, something that Käte had seen with dozens of severe head wounds.

"Do you know what day it is?"

Manfred was silent as he sat down, "I am tired and now I'd like to go in."

"The doctor would like you to be out here a little longer. By the way, I understand that your father is coming to visit tomorrow," Käte changed the subject.

"I hope to have my uniform. Do you know about that?"

"Yes, maybe even later today for that. The Blue Max is on your nightstand. Very nice looking, I'd say," Käte added.

"My brother Lothar earned his in mid-May this year."

"Ah, Lothar. Is he flying these days?" Käte was asked by the doctors to see how the conversation went. So, far, she judged, just a little bit of *non sequiturs*, but Manfred, she judged, was doing just fine, considering.

"No," Manfred was taken aback as he thought about his younger brother Lothar. "He's not flying. He was struck in the hip. The British .303 from ground fire. He's convalescing."

"He's in good spirits?" Käte smiled.

"He's written to Mamma. She's responded for all of us. Yes, he's got his sense of humor back. Can't sleep. The wound is kept open to drain and heal, you know."

"He'll be fine, I'm sure. If he's gotten this far without an infection, it means he has a good constitution. A family trait, I bet," Käte pushed Manfred next to a chair and sat down to look into his face. It was a beautiful day, she thought. He'd be fun on a picnic.

"Lothar and I hunted, you know. All the time, but my best time has been hunting on my own. Shooting, you know," Manfred just started to talk.

"Interesting."

"Lothar is quite the flier. Now, we both got our Great Danes together, he and I. Yes, good old Georgie. Zeumer the Great. He was my best friend, Georg Zeumer—helped teach me how to fly. My Danish hound is Moritz. He's a big fellow, he is. Georg's dog is Max. Poor old boy, lost in an accident with a vehicle, you know," Manfred was rambling.

"Georg was lost?" Käte looked him in the eye.

"Oh, no! Not then. Max was killed. George was injured—shot while in combat—on the way to hospital—ambulance overturned—Georg, a broken leg. Permanent limp, poor fellow. We nicknamed him *Black Cat*, you know. Never walked like a cat again. Just that limp," Manfred got serious.

"What about Max?" Käte pressed on.

"Ah, poor Maxie was run over by a truck or something. But Georg died on June 17. Moritz is fine, though. Almost lost his head to a propeller. One ear is much shorter, but, I like to think my dog has real character," Manfred sounded definitive, but was rambling.

"I can't imagine your dog not having character," Käte smiled. I bet he loves to be outside with you."

"On a day like today. It's beautiful, isn't it? Well—any day. He's no shrinking violet when it comes to weather," Manfred was starting to really start moving with the conversation, if in a convoluted way.

Käte saw that they were bringing tea out. "We're getting some tea here."

Manfred went on, ignoring the tea, "Now Holck, he used to fly with his little dog."

"Holck?"

"Yes, shot down in action, too," Manfred's mood changed from all smiles to a somber, reflective demeanor, now picking his words much more slowly.

"Tell me about your best friend, Georg, Manfred. Please," Käte tried to get Manfred back on subject.

"What's not to like. He's a small man. You have to admire his tenacity, his courage," Manfred finally took his tea cup and had a sip.

"I see. Interesting man, then?" Käte was making mental notes about what to tell the doctors.

"He visited us just a while ago. Brought a bottle of cognac. Limping, but always smiling."

Manfred put the cup down and tried to   stand. He wavered a little, stepped to the side and bent over involuntarily. He vomited.

"Maybe this is my fault, Captain ... uh ... Manfred," Käte waved for two orderlies to come over to help Manfred get back in the wheelchair.

"No, this just sort of happened, Käte. We'll be fine," Manfred sat back as one of the orderlies helped him by wiping his mouth.

"We'll get you back inside. You are making progress, dear boy — yes, you are," Käte started to push Manfred back to his room.

"I have better control of my stomach ... really, I do," Manfred started to explain.

"You are much better today than yesterday, Manfred," Käte continued to move the wheelchair forward.

As they entered the hospital, Manfred could, after being in the fresh air, smell the unsettling mixture of antiseptic, bedpans needing to be changed and wounds that were festering.

"Not the best for the appetite," Manfred tried to look back at Käte as he finished this quip, but his injury limited the range of motion in his neck.

"Your movement will come back. This is only the third day after your injury," Käte assured him.

"You have to wonder who shot me. I was flying right at the British in front of me, but was hit in the back of the head," Manfred felt that his brain was returning. He was starting to put things together.

"Georg, you know, he died in combat up there on a Sunday. It was June 17," Manfred felt he was lucid. He was also beginning to see the depths of what he hadn't talked about for the past several months as he had pressed forward to shoot down enemy planes while leading his men in Jasta 11 and now Jageschwader 1. Part of him was afraid to go to sleep for fear of what he would meet in his dreams.

"I want to get back to my Schwader, Käte," Manfred insisted.   "I'm close to being better."

Käte would have a much different view that she would present to the doctors.

Chapter Eleven

"If the two of you could be still for a moment, that would be excellent," the photographer smiled as Manfred, uniform on and head bandaged, sat next to his father, Albrecht.

Manfred, ever the eagle-eye, looked at the lens, "I see a Dagor lens on your Goerz-Anschütz."

"Yes, I have several cameras, as you can imagine," the photographer mentioned in passing.

"We have a Kodak Brownie, but cannot send it to Rochester, New York for processing. Alone it sits on a shelf in my study," Albrecht laughed.

"Clever man that George Eastman. You know, I have a Swedish Hasselblad. It takes Kodak film."

"No Zeiss?" Manfred asked.

"Well, I have a Kodak Junior Number 1," the photographer started to talk as he walked over to a large satchel and took out this camera that he proceeded to open up. He walked over to Manfred and Albrecht.

"See. Kodak Junior Number 1. Very nice. It takes 116 film."

The two of them looked at it for a moment.

"It is very technological," Albrecht observed.

The photographer murmured something.
"Compact and easy to carry," Manfred piped in.

"Yes. My brother found it at the front," the photographer explained. "I like this a good deal, but we need the medium format for clarity."

"We understand," Manfred was staring at the Kodak Junior. "At the front. That would explain its olive color."

'I have a Zeiss with a Planar lens, as well," the photographer was surprised his two subjects knew anything about cameras.

"We use the Zeiss binoculars for surveillance, the   D.F. model, I believe," Manfred observed.

"Do you like the Zeiss?" Albrecht asked.

"Certainly, but, for today, we have Goerz-Anschütz," he smiled, much happier that he could work with people who knew what he was doing.

"You are doing well, Manfred," Albrecht observed towards his son.

"Just hold," the photographer said as he took a picture. "Just a few more."

"The bandage—does it add anything?" Manfred tried to put a good face on things.

"No talking, please," the photographer insisted. He took several more photographs.

Then, Käte showed up.

"We want one with you and Nurse Käte Otersdorf," the photographer explained as he shuffled plates in the out of the camera.

Manfred was not pleased. He could see where this was going. More propaganda for the newspapers, which were starting, day-by-day, to show select images of the war.

"Is this really necessary?" Manfred asked. Käte looked sheepish as she stood next to Manfred.

Manfred stepped away, as if to offer up a momentary protest. Käte tried to put a good face on all this. She really didn't want all of Germany looking at her, especially with her in her nurse's uniform. How unflattering, she thought.

"You ride horses, don't you, Captain?" the photographer asked.

"Yes."

"It's like riding when you pose for the camera. It's easy and will not hurt," the photographer finished setting up the Goerz-Anschütz.

"A little surprised, Käte?" Manfred looked her in the eye.

"Yes, quite a bit, actually," Käte forced a smile.

"You know, my brother is also a photographer," the photographer tried to take the edge off of things.

"Really? For the military?" Albrecht asked.

"No, for his own studio in Dresden. He uses a Thowe — a large format camera.

Before Manfred could respond, he snapped one picture after the other, pulling plates and all the rest. Manfred was calmed down by now.

"You look fine, Käte," Manfred reassured her.

"Thanks, Manfred," she looked at him a moment, then walked away.

Albrecht was a little surprised at their informal form of address, but had been advised that Manfred might have a short fuse. Such behavior was, well — not typical for his oldest son, who was usually calm, collected and socially smooth.

"The artist fellow, Busch, if I remember, did sketches of us beginning last month up until a few days ago," Manfred began.

"Yes, well, the General Staff wants to put a good face on things," Albrecht tried to console his son.

"I need to sit down," Manfred sat in his wheelchair. "I'm tired, Papa."

As an orderly started to push Manfred back into the hospital, Manfred closed his eyes. He tried to take a deep breath, but, with his headache getting worse, flaring into one of what he was beginning to understand was a recurring moment, he had trouble letting go with his body. After a few more breaths, with his eyes closed, the rhythm of the wheels with the bumps on the pavement and their regular squeaks let Manfred nod off into a faraway place.

Manfred was at a stable and there was his first real horse, a petite mare he had named Santuzza. Although slightly stocky and small in stature, Manfred felt a deep pride about everything she stood for. As he swung his right leg over the saddle he realized how much he had taken a liking to Santuzza. Not a thoroughbred by any stretch, but more of a general warm-blood, Manfred had convinced himself she had a bit of the Brandenburger in her.

Manfred smiled to himself as he pressured the reins lightly while he just pressing a bit with his ankles to get Santuzza to turn and move toward the open field. By now very much like hand-in-glove, Santuzza responded to Manfred's almost psychic urging by galloping. He urged her to the left, which cut the field off so that they were heading under the trees. Santuzza might have bolted in another direction because the branches were fairly low, but Manfred held her on course. She also had developed a faith in her rider through the countless hours they had spent galloping to and fro. As Manfred leaned his body the front of his saddle, he ducked his head forward to clear the low branches.

"This is wonderful, Santuzza," he praised his horse as they kept the pace up while he weaved her around the widely spaced tress with their low lying branches. Santuzza responded in kind, bowing her neck back   with power in her gallop as if she were some powerful spring bounding across the landscape.

They came to a stream, where Manfred slowed and then stopped, taking his reins in hand as he walked Santuzza forward for a drink. Just turning seventeen, Manfred had convinced himself that he was going to make a name for himself as a rider. As Santuzza drank, Manfred chafed in the summer heat with his woolen riding pants. He thought of American Indians from one of the magazines his mother would get. Minimal leather clothing, possibly some war paint and even a bow and arrow. Now, that was riding, he thought as he mounted back up. He was thinking about joining the local Indian club, something he would have done a while ago if he hadn't been so bogged down with his schooling at the academy. His father had pressed him to join one of the Roman clubs where members attempted to recreate a functioning Roman legion from the time the Romans had colonized what is now southern Germany nearly two millennia ago.

Manfred, who loved the outdoors and the speed that came with horseback riding, opted instead for being alone with Santuzza on the open rolling meadows of his native Silesia. There he was—he felt this reminiscence deeply—stepping out of the water and remounting Santuzza. In the blink of an eye, he was in the middle of a meadow taking Santuzza on a walk around a fallen log that was simply lying in the middle of this large open field. With no other trees around it and no sign of its roots, Manfred wondered what it was doing there—but he didn't waste too much time trying to figure that out. No, for certain, he was glad it was there because it was the perfect size for practicing jumps.

Manfred cantered away from the log, paused for a moment after turning and proceeded to canter towards the log. As they neared, almost on top of it, Santuzza, who was proving herself the natural jumper, adjusted the length of her stride in the approach and then took off with an assuredness that came from her natural jumping ability. Even though horse and rider were airborne for only a moment, Manfred found this part of the jump exhilarating. The arc of Santuzza's trajectory in the jump was usually symmetrical, as she lifted her forelegs as her shoulders first cleared the jump, with her hind legs keeping in rhythm by extending as her hips followed the path of the arc. The two of them would land with grace as Santuzza stretched her forelegs to the ground and flexed them in absorbing the landing. The two of them would recover together, canter away from the log only to do it again and again.

The threshold of his hospital room was raised, so when they went over it, the accompanying jarring motion woke Manfred out of his pleasant reverie, the first one he'd had since he was injured.

"You with us again, Manfred?" his father asked.

"Ah, my head is back to reality," Manfred tried to make light of things, but was again being overcome with nausea, as he turned to the side and vomited on the floor in his room.

Chapter Twelve

Manfred woke up at daybreak on Wednesday. His head hurt, but by now he was accepting that as part of his normal routine. Doctor Lävin, who was working alone since Dr. Kraske had been called to another field hospital, had decided to do another procedure on Manfred's wound. He had explained that further x-rays reveals a few bone splinters that might cause trouble down the road, so Manfred underwent surgery two days earlier. He spent most of the next trying to get the anesthetic out of his system — and, as such, he wasn't sure what Käte had tried to explain to him after he started to wake out of his anesthetic stupor the past two days.

"I thought you might have died and I would have a single room."

"Really?" Manfred retorted to a familiar voice. "Are you alive or a spirit?"

"I'm not sure," the voice replied to Manfred.
"You're alive. Spirits, I think, know most things," Manfred chuckled, now recognizing the voice he heard across his room.

"So, they had to shave your head?"

Manfred smiled. He knew who this was. He forced himself to sit up and look at the bed across the room.

"I had no choice in the matter," Manfred smiled as he looked at Kurt Wolff, fellow pilot from Jasta 11.

"Well, you know, I was after one of those Sopwith Camels when I took one through the shoulder and, maybe the same bullet, in the hand," Kurt was his usual smiling self.

"Better that than one in the head," Manfred was now sitting up with his feet on the floor.

"These things are never easy, I think," Kurt started to explain.

Kurt was very thin and as tall as Manfred. He had delicate features, to the point of looking effeminate. Yet, he was anything but *soft*. He was awarded the *Ordre Pour le Mérite* in early May that year, having finished *Bloody April* with twenty-two victories in that month alone. Although he was nicknamed "The Delicate Little Flower" for his thin physique and girlish facial features, Kurt had learned well from Manfred as he was now a fearsome warrior of the sky. Two days after earning The Blue Max, he was given his own command, Jasta 29. Then, after Karl Allmenröder was killed while commanding Jasta 11, Kurt was shifted back to his old unit as its commander.

Manfred, who was now injured nearly a full week, was glad to see *Blümelein*, for he felt a certain permanent moroseness starting to settle deep within his person, "I am struggling with this damn thing."

Kurt's shoulder and hand hurt, but he was able to get out bed at the same moment that Manfred sat back down on his bed's edge. He walked over to Manfred and put his right hand on Manfred's shoulder.

"Steady on, *Old Man*," Kurt used the nickname the slightly younger fliers had given to Manfred.

"Ah!" Manfred let out a sound of frustration as he felt his head throb as he lay back on his pillow in order to try and recapture his balance.

Kurt went to the door and nearly bumped into Käte who was coming with a tray with a steeping tea pot and two cups with saucers, spoons and sugar.

"Yes, he's having some trouble," Kurt managed to blurt out.

"It's to be expected, Lieutenant," Käte said matter-of-factly. She set the tray on the nightstand and then leaned over Manfred.

"So, tell me: what is going on?" She asked.

"Ah, well … just a little loss of balance," Manfred said with his voice sounding weaker than normal.

Kurt looked deeply at Manfred. This was not the man he expected to meet in the hospital when they told him he was going to the same field hospital as Manfred. No, somehow in his mind, Kurt had convinced himself that being in the same place with Manfred for convalescence was going to be something of a vacation. Manfred was a dynamic leader. He filled his men with the measured confidence of good hunters: from where to attack; when and how to fire—always short bursts, you know; when to pursue and when to break off; mental attitude, especially the idea of concentration within the bounds of good judgment; and, defending your comrades. Yes, all this was instilled in the men, first   in Jasta 11 — and now, in the much larger Jageschwader 1. Then, there had been nights with shared cognac, the occasional roast boar that Manfred would hunt in the moonlight and laughter as the men in Jasta 11 swapped stories about women who couldn't help themselves with fliers. Through all of that, Manfred had been steady, demanding yet tolerant, and a bearer of an inner optimism. When he laughed with them, his men felt as if they were, indeed, brothers capable of surmounting anything.

Now, Kurt realized that Manfred was struggling, perhaps even, faltering.

"You know, Kurt, I'm getting there. I really am," Manfred forced a chuckle as he tried to convince himself that he was going to heal and become the Manfred of old.

"Well, maybe some tea for the both of you," Käte smiled as she poured each of them a cup. "You have to get up, Manfred. Perhaps sit over across the room. The doctor wants you up and active. Enough of this inactivity."

Manfred sat up, steeled himself to stand and managed to walk across the room.

"I'd advise you to sit slowly," Käte said as she put a filled cup and saucer on the nightstand next to the chair.

"I'll try some of that tea. Any chance we have some cookies to make this more of a formal tea? Kurt asked.

"I'll see what I can find," Käte smiled as she walked out the door.

"Not too shabby, Manfred. Make any progress with her?" Kurt chuckled.

"Ah, well, that's not really been on my mind," Manfred sounded apologetic.

"I can see it's been rough in here," Kurt took a sip of his tea.

"I suppose. But, you know, walk around here and you'll see that we've been pretty lucky," Manfred started to explain.

"How so?"

"It's part of the war we don't see when we're *up there*," Manfred went on.

"The trenches look pretty bad — we've all agreed about that," Kurt put his cup down and walked over to the window. "Maybe we can get out for some fresh air."

"After I get something in my stomach," Manfred was glad to see Käte come back with bread, butter and a few cookies.

"No real breakfast," Kurt wondered.

"This is it, for right now," Käte smiled. "Trust me, gentlemen — butter is rare these days."

Manfred actually felt his appetite come back for the first time since his injury and Kurt hadn't eaten in two days, since he was mostly comatose the day before.

"This is quite good," Kurt smiled as he spread some butter on another piece of bread.

"Maybe we get outside after breakfast?" Manfred asked with his mouth full of tea and a cookie.

"I'll be back in a few minutes," Käte smiled as she left their room.

The sun was now above the horizon with the dew disappearing in what was going to be a very hot July day. Manfred sat on his bedside as he put his uniform on.

"You're going to have trouble with your hat with all those bandages," Kurt observed as he took in the top half of Manfred's head that was bandaged around and around as if he were wearing the beginning layers of a turban.

"We both need this humor. I miss the Schwader, but even more, I miss the old days of Jasta 11," Manfred was opening up to Kurt, something he had never really done before, even though he considered all of his comrades from Jasta 11 to be his brothers.

"The war is different now," Kurt sounded bitter.

"That's for sure, my friend," Manfred finished buttoning his jacket.

"The Tommies and the Parlewuhs—they're getting the Americans soon," Kurt finished his food and stood up.

"Let's see if the two of us can walk out to the porch. Maybe sit on the steps for some fresh air," Manfred focused and started to walk very deliberately in order to keep his balance.

Käte was waiting for the two of them at the threshold of their door, "This is encouraging. Do you need help?'

"I think we are fine," Manfred forced a smile, but Käte looked at his sunken eyes and drawn complexion, wondering if she'd ever see the von Richthofen of her Sanke cards.

"I am supposed to follow you out, but I'll give the two of you a little space," Käte smiled. "You seem to have a lot to say to each other."

"So, the American Expeditionary Force has started to land," Kurt began to talk.

"We need to hit La Pallice and Saint-Nazaire—bombing, for sure," Manfred finished Kurt's thought.

"Don't forget Brest, too."

Each of them managed to sit on a step to take in the fresh morning air.

"You are getting around well with that shoulder," Manfred mentioned as they were getting comfortable.

"Yes, well—my shoulder is tolerable, but the wrist has a hole in it," Kurt smiled.

"We need to get back. Things are going to heat up once the Americans throw their weight behind the Entente," Manfred seemed on task for the first time since his injury.

"If my wrist heals miraculously …"
"The Russians—what have you heard about the Eastern Front?" Manfred changed the subject.

"Trying to push forward—but, we are going to smash them—I'm certain," Kurt smiled.

"The West side of this war will determine the outcome," Manfred was thinking strategically.

Kurt stood up, "Do you think you can make it out to that tree at the edge of the lawn?"

"Let's try," as Manfred stood up so that the two of them could amble across the grass.

He was about to speak, but Kurt interrupted his very thought, "Festner. Zeumer. Allmenröder — fine comrades — under the turf now."

Manfred paused before he spoke. He looked down at the grass, then lifted his eyes skyward. He turned to Kurt, put his hands on his hips and spoke with a little smile, "I can see Georg have a whiff for the nose and then a sip of fine cognac as he floats on the clouds."

"I was impressed with both of them, but Georg — very strong to continue with that damaged leg."

Manfred nodded in agreement, "He was a fine man. Courageous. Shot down attacking an R.E. 8 — one of their bombers."

"Vickers in the front and …"

"… Lewis in the rear," Manfred finished Kurt's sentence for him.

"Yes, that damned .303," Kurt said as he rubbed his wrist as if he were trying to make it heal more quickly.

"What got you?" Manfred wondered as they sat on the grass, which was still damp from the morning dew.

"One of the new Sopwith   Camels. The Tommie Triplane," Kurt explained. "Impressive piece of machinery."

"I wonder how the new Fokker will do for us? I've been talking with them over in Schwerin," Manfred began with some enthusiasm.

"What's going on?" Kurt was genuinely curious.

"Back in April, some of our planes failed for no apparent reason. I wrote an angry letter to Berlin."

"How did that go over?" Kurt wondered.

"The called Anthony Fokker," Manfred went on.
"Yes, now I remember this fellow who was out talking to you," Kurt recalled.

"Yes. Anthony was very interested in what was going on. He observed our planes in battle — talked with me a good deal," Manfred continued.

"He wanted to know what we needed," Kurt concluded.

"He was impressive. I can say that," Manfred said.

"So, they — the big boys in Berlin--they listened to you." Kurt concluded.

"Feed back. A new idea. Anthony called it *feed back*. He wanted to go back and forth between us and them to make the design better," Manfred said.

"I like this," Kurt rubbed his wrist again.

"Anthony says it is the future of the industry," Manfred was talking with even more enthusiasm.

"We need better planes and don't have a lot of time," Kurt sounded concerned.

"Time, time, time. We can get there, little Kurt," Manfred sounded confident. "Fokker is working on a new plane. Have faith."

'Let's hope for all our sakes."

"You may be *up there* before I am," Manfred pointed up in the sky as some robins flew overhead.

"Robins! Tiny birds. What I wouldn't give for some   roast goose tonight," Kurt said.

"I'm not sure how my head will do if I fire a rifle … or a shotgun," Manfred half-joked.

"Getting back to the Camel," Kurt changed the subject back. "I'd love to give it a go again now that I see how the Camel maneuvers."

"Tight turns?" Manfred wondered.

"Have to drop down on them with our unfair *falcon tactics*," Kurt laughed.

"It's never hurts, does it?

"Never."

Chapter Thirteen

Manfred stared into the steam that rose out of the teapot as he moved the tea ball around to hasten the brewing process. He liked strong tea. The steam wafted up, mesmerizing his eyes. It was late in a day that he spent trying to appear as normal as he possibly could. And he succeeded, what with walking everywhere, talking and conversing with focus, and simply showing that he could get around on his own. In a moment, though, his exhaustion came through. He lost his focus and his consciousness was taken away … walking through a brush filled wood in the landscape outside his native Schweidnitz, alone, his rifle slung over his shoulder, the dew fresh from a chilly night with a cold breeze out   of the East. The sun   had just crested the horizon, a cool scent of spore turned his head to the left and his ear heard a gentle rustle ahead off to the right.

As he pressed forward, quiet and slightly crouched, Manfred unshouldered his Mannlicher-Schönauer in one smooth motion as he undid the safety, put his left arm through the sling and loosely held the butt against his right arm pit. He was alert and ready as he stepped forward, instinctively moving the downward pointed barrel of his gun around branches as he continued to press forward. A twig cracked behind him. Unexpected, he turned his head to see, when a loud shriek came from thirty meters in front of him. Manfred snapped his head forward, aimed his Mannlicher-

Schönauer, but had no target to fix on. Instead, the creature was off to his right, now only ten meters away. His rifle barrel got caught on a branch. He froze with the boar only two meters away.

Manfred gasped audibly as he jerked his head back as if he were run over by that giant boar. Some tea spilled out of the top of the pot as he unconsciously slapped it while in his head he was still trying to aim his rifle.

"Are you alright?" Kurt asked.

Manfred's head hurt—this time throbbing with his elevated pulse--and he was becoming nauseous like he had right after his injury. He took a shallow breath, moved his head from side to side and looked at the wall above and behind Kurt. As he brought his eyes to focus on his comrade, Manfred, said, "I'm back. I'm back. All is in place, my friend."

"Well, for a moment there you were somewhere else."

"Yes. I realize this looks bad," Manfred was honest with his friend.

"But we won't say anything to anyone," Kurt smiled as he poured some tea for the two of them.

Despite his recurring nausea and regular headaches, both of which he took to lying about to the medical staff, Manfred felt he was making real progress. He was getting around now, fully ambulatory. Kurt, who was, more or less, up and around a few days after his surgery, was good for Manfred. The two of them engaged in badinage, trading quips all day long. More and more Manfred came back to being partly impish, partly imperious—very much like his old self. Although he was never a loud man, his friends knew him to be good humored and well intentioned.

"Are you going to eat all your bread?" Manfred asked as Kurt took a sip of tea.

"Yes, they gave it to me for a reason," Kurt smiled. "Besides, you'll probably waste it by vomiting it all over the place."

"Well, I haven't vomited in a few days, so maybe you should share," Manfred shot back.

Käte walked out with some fresh fruit, "Share what?"

"Manfred would steal bread from the poor, so watch yourself," Kurt smiled.

"Ah, well … very good—humor—I see," Käte said, with her mind elsewhere. She stood next to the table.

"You have something there?" Manfred asked.

"I managed to get you each an apple and a few fresh plums."

"This is welcome, Käte. Very nice," Manfred looked her in the eye.

"It's Monday the 23rd. We are going to the Schwader on Wednesday," Käte offered up.

"I know I am ready to go back," Manfred said deliberately, perhaps in too focused a manner, which, for all Käte could judge, meant he really wasn't ready to go back.

"Yes, well, Manfred, a change of scenery will do us both some good," Käte let down her guard and looked softly in his eyes.

"The men will have no sympathy for you with that bandage on your head," Kurt smiled as he ate the last of his bread. "They will either be jealous or wary of your leadership since you have a full-time beautiful nurse."

That momentary softness disappeared in a flash as Käte looked sharply at Kurt, "The two of you are getting better, but I am still in charge."

"Ah, well, our quarters at Schloss Markebeeke will be welcome. You know, with the Czar having abdicated in March, he's probably worked his way West, don't you think, Kurt," Manfred was playing the imp.

"Most certainly. I can't see him going East to the Japanese," Kurt played along.

"He's probably close enough now that we could invite him to stay a few days with us," Manfred went on.

"Maybe if we call it Château de Markebeeke—you know, the French name for the place—the Czar would show up!" Kurt waved his right arm in the air, as his left was still bandaged.

"Joking aside, you know that I will be there providing some care," Käte started to explain.

"This will be good for you, Manfred," Kurt had a sly look in his eye.

"If either of you want to eat anything at all for the next two days, I'd advise you to keep your decorum while I am here," Käte admonished.

Manfred and Kurt smiled at each other, but silently decided to mind their manners instead of carrying on like a couple of school boys.

"I appreciate all you do for us, Käte," Manfred started to explain as Doctor Lävin walked into the room.

"Good evening, Doctor," Manfred put on a good face sine he wanted to get the hell out of the field hospital.

"Good evening, Captain, and Lieutenant. I see our appetites are normal," Doctor Lävin began.

"He's trying to steal my bread," Kurt began.

"This is excellent. Is he succeeding?" Doctor Lävin joked, but his eyes were penetrating, with Käte knowing that he was in the process of possibly clearing Manfred for a return to his squadron.

"I'm feeling well," Kurt went on. "My shoulder is sore, but the throbbing pain stopped a few days ago."

"And your wrist?" Doctor Lävin asked.

"It's best we keep it immobilized," Kurt admitted.

Doctor Lävin took Kurt's hand and moved his arm just a little, "Pain?"

"Yes," Kurt winced.

"How much?"

"Better than last week," Kurt took a deep breath.

"This is good. You are healing. I'm happy to say no infection—for which you should be grateful," Doctor Lävin concluded with Kurt as he turned to Manfred.

"Tell me, Captain. How is the boar?"
"Ready to be shot," Manfred lied.

The Doctor looked at him with a penetrating gaze. Then, in a measured tone, he spoke, "You've come a long way. I see you walking the grounds that past few days."

"I'd like to get back. I'm feeling confined," Manfred opened up about how hospital life was feeling for him.

"You're lucky you can walk … and talk, Captain," Doctor Lävin explained. "The two of you have looked around the ward, haven't you?" He gestured with his arms to outside the door.

"Yes," they both replied.

"We have men here who show no obvious sign of injury, but who are totally incapacitated. They are not the same as they once were," the doctor shook his head.

"I thought I was having a nightmare the first night I was here and saw these poor fellows," Manfred admitted.

"It was no nightmare, Captain," Doctor Lävin went on. "For them yes—it is a total nightmare. But for you back then, no—you were just observing what was in front of your eyes. We have no medical study of this condition, yet. I believe it has to do with shock waves from explosions affecting the physical nature of the brain. But …"

Manfred nodded as he thought about that first night. Kurt watched his face and could see that, for a brief moment, Manfred's eyes looked deeply sunken, his face ashen and his head bent forward like an old man. It was just a momentary thing, but, nonetheless, Kurt knew that Manfred was different. Manfred, as if he knew what Kurt was thinking, took a deep breath, puffed his chest out with his shoulders back and stood up.

"My balance is fine, you know, Doctor," Manfred walked a bit.

"Well, Captain, you will be going back to Schloss Markebeeke in two days," Doctor Lävin made a few notes on his chart. "As for you, Lieutenant Wolff—your shoulder and wrist are doing better than expected."

"This is good news, Doctor," Kurt winked at Manfred.

"He needs a new … psychological examination—that's the new word, isn't it? Psychological?" Manfred joked.

"Yes. Yes, it is," Doctor Lävin chuckled. "Psychological. Psychology. The new science of the mind."

Manfred and Kurt looked at each other and smiled as Doctor Lävin walked away.

"Oh, I almost forgot," Käte said, more to herself, as she ran out of the room to return thirty seconds later with a package. "This was delivered today, Manfred."

Manfred knew what it was as he took the small package with a jeweler's return address in Berlin, Wagner & Son.

"Something from an admirer?" Käte wondered as Manfred wanted to unwrap the package, but he needed to cut the string.

Käte left, but was back in an instant with a pair of scissors.

"These help," Manfred cut the string and unwrapped the brown paper. He took the lid off and removed the packing paper. Inside was a tiny object wrapped in a piece of soft cloth. Manfred took it out, carefully removed the swaddling and held it up for Käte and Kurt to see.

Manfred had a small silver cup in his hand.

"A schnapps cup?" Käte asked.

"Ah, one of your Hero Cups," Kurt answered as he took the cup from Manfred's hand.

He handed it to Käte. She turned it around in her hands. The cup was only a few centimeters tall, burnished in a soft glow with a number and an unknown inscription on it: 57 and R.E. 8.

"So, what it the 57?"

"My fifty-seventh victory," Manfred explained. "I shot down a British R.E. 8, which stands for Reconnaissance Experimental, Number 8 model. It was the second of July. Just after 10am. I dropped down on them from behind. Their observer began firing his Lewis gun like mad. I focused in quickly, fired and was down out of range of the Lewis gun — all in a few seconds."

Chapter Fourteen

There was a sense of permanency about the Schloss Markebeeke—at least, that's what Manfred thought. Perhaps it was the fact that it was built by Belgian supporters of Napoleon in 1802. Maybe it was simply its Neo-classicism, with two stories separated by a simple entablature with the lower story having rusticated stone broken by windows with arches, while the second story was a smooth surface punctuated by classical rectangular windows—all surmounted by simple attic windows, three to a bay unified by Doric pilasters. Anyway, the stairway, grey stone, made a statement without being obvious. And, it was flanked, as it were, by two pedestals, each crowned with a seated roaring lion bearing someone's coat of arms.

It might simply be good at the Schloss Markebeeke for the more obvious. Manfred was out of that damned field hospital   with its horrifically wounded soldiers, men incoherent and errantly wandering with battle fatigue, and that smell that permeated his entire experience there--festering wounds, blood-soaked bandages and bedpans needing changing. All this, of course, underscored by an unsettling but almost musical cacophony of men moaning for more morphine.

Yes, it was good to be back both to command Jageschwader 1 and to see his men in Jasta 11. There were no jokes about Manfred's head bandage and, much more importantly, nothing over the top about Nurse Käte Oters-dorf. Manfred had grown fond of Käte, but not for the reason that was im-plied in the German press and — Manfred was sure about this — surmised in every German household. No, Käte was not a romantic interest, even though she was beautiful and quite intelligent. She was definitely her own woman with her own will and her own thoughts. This made her very at-tractive, but Manfred and Käte were anything but romantically involved. Manfred liked Käte simply because they had come to know and understand each other. Manfred was also grateful that she had taken such good care of him, because, deep down inside, he thought his best outcome was going to be that of a surviving wartime cripple, damaged both physically and, as they now say, psychologically. With all his nausea, the vomiting and the erratic but often disabling headaches, romance was the furthest thing from Manfred's mind. So, he simply liked Käte. And, he liked to think that she liked him.

All that decided in his mind, Manfred wanted to be back with both Jasta 11 and Jageschwader 1. He was angry about the progress of the war, especially given that the German command knew that bearing up in what was clearly a war of attrition was going to be difficult now that the Ameri-cans were disembarking in Belgium and France. All the while, the British naval blockade was unintentionally making sure that the next generation of Germans would suffer such deprivation that they would hate the outside world with a vengeance.

Manfred was also angry over the fact that he'd been shot down and nearly crippled or killed, depending on how you look at it. He was still con-fused about who actually shot him. It might have been an errant shot from one of his own or some sort of lucky extremely long range shot from the British. Regardless, his native confidence was in no way dampened. Rather, he was confused and, perhaps, even a bit suspicious about how things work out when you think you are holding all the cards. More than anything, he wanted to get back into action, prove to himself he was, as the French had nicknamed him, *le diable rouge*, the red devil.

Well, if the public let loose with its imagination regarding a Manfred and Käte romance, they would have to face the fact that Manfred still had his head bandaged while he sat with ten of his men from Jageschwader 1 for an informal group portrait on the steps of the Schloss Markebeeke. To make sure the message got across, those from the Central Office for Foreign Services placed a propeller — rather large, in fact — from a British R.E. 8 as a sort of battle trophy on the left side of the steps.

"Let's all find a spot around the Captain, gentlemen," the photographer kept saying.

Reserve Lieutenant Reserve Konstantin Krefft was milling on Manfred's right, while he was flanked on the other side by Lieutenant Eberhard Mohnike.

"Like I said, let's get seated, the Czar is my next customer. He hates waiting," quipped the photographer, much to the delight of the men.

Manfred was standing on the second step, when the photographer said to him, "Captain, maybe sitting on the fourth step?"

Krefft, somewhat new to Manfred, seemed like a happy fellow, smiling and laughing. Mohnike was not far behind with his slightly quieter mirth. The photographer was clearly experienced at this sort of thing since he was practiced at making sure his subjects were in a jocular mood, smiling and laughing.

All joking aside — and with Lieutenant Carl August von Schönebeck, First Lieutenant Karl Scheffer, Lieutenant Wilhelm Bockelmann, First Lieutenant Hans-Helmuth von Boddien and Reserve Lieutenant Alfred Niederhoff, all from Jasta 11 on the top row, there was more than enough joking to go around — Manfred was tired, trying to hold it together physically as his nausea was kicking up, and finding that the usual humor was distracting him from some rather deep thoughts that he couldn't quite shake.

Ilse had spoken to him by telephone earlier that morning, "It's been difficult for Mamma."

"Tell me what is happening," Manfred was more than concerned.

"It's the famine, the deprivation," Ilse began.

"They spoiled me at the hospital. I had enough bread and some fruit, along with meat and poultry," Manfred began to feel guilty about how well he and Kurt Wolff were treated during their convalescence. They were even allowed out for walks in Courtrai's *Parc du Peuple* and *Le Cercle Musical,* simply wonderful public parks.

"Ah, well …. She needed new shoes, so she traded an old pair in for a coupon," Ilse went on.

"Yes,"

"Then, she shopped all day long in town trying to find a pair of new ones. Many shops were close to empty. She ended up spending a small fortune for a pair she really hates," Ilse was distressed.

"It would be funny, if there weren't a war on," Manfred tried to smile.

"Mamma took them to a cobbler and had extra leather sewn on the heels so they would last longer. She's worried that nothing will last, you know."

"Papa and I talked about the bigger view here," Manfred countered.

"What do the two of you think?" Ilse was curious.

"The famine, it's made worse by the Hindenburg Program that General von Ludendorff began last year when he took over a million men from the fields and even more from the front lines," Manfred began to explain.

Ilse realized that her brother, the young smart-aleck, was different. He was more mature. Usually, he was making jokes, poking fun at the nurses she worked with and, generally, much more of a light-hearted fellow, Now, Manfred seemed more reflective, much more the thinker.

Ilse hated to bring this into the conversation, since her work was, to be quite blunt, dirty, bloody and unsettling, "Yes."

"I saw people in the hospital. Soldiers, you know," Manfred started to open up.

"Go on."

"Some men had no outward wounds, but were — as if they were broken," Manfred was pained to think about this.

"Oh, I know, Manfred. I do know. The doctors think the brain no longer functions like a well-timed watch," Ilse explained.

"I've seen this. It's frightening," Manfred admitted how he felt.

"And you, Manfred? How are you," Ilse was asking as she had been scared to death that her once jubilant brother would end up like one of these brain damaged victims.

"As I wrote to Mamma, we Richthofens have hard heads," Manfred joked.

"Yes, I saw the letter," Ilse responded. "She was relieved that you could be so cavalier at such a serious moment — reminds me of ..."

"My old self!" Manfred interrupted.

"Exactly," Ilse smiled.

"I'm working on it."

"Captain, take a seat," the photographer snapped Manfred back to his current reality.

Manfred sat on the fourth step, flanked by men on either side, with another row of battle fliers standing and seated a few steps above them. He had on that damned bandage, which the doctors insist he wear since his wound was open to the bone. Would his scalp ever grow back? It seemed as if nothing was working out well.

"It's an honor to have you back, sir," Reserve Lieutenant Krefft sat next to Manfred.

"A good nurse can do many things for a wounded man," Reserve Lieutenant Niederhoff leaned forward and cracked as the men were settling in.

The men chuckled as the photographer said, "Good," over and over as he snapped pictures and pulled plates out of his large format camera, a Fotografiska AB from Sweden. The photographer was very pleased as he took several images, with the men talking and joking the entire time. There was sense in this portrait of ease, of speaking likenesses of the men, both individually and as a group. Yes, that ease they projected masked the serious thoughts that Manfred had bubbling up from his subconscious. Contrary to anything serious, this light mood was just what the Central Office for Foreign Services was looking for. Despite the fact that the General Staff knew the war was not going well, that Germany could no longer win the war, the photos — and the drawings done by Alfred Busch a month earlier — would send a message to the public. It was pure propaganda that there was no sense of worry whatsoever, even though Manfred was sitting there with his shaved head covered with a bandage like a bright white winter cap. That Germany's ultimate hero suffered severe headaches and nausea, despite his loyal character and strong will, was nowhere in any of these photographs.

Above all, Manfred wanted to get back *up there*, to rejoin the action.

Chapter Fifteen

"I've heard that Lothar will be out at least one more month," Manfred said to Menzke, his orderly.

"Yes, sir," Menzke was happy that his Captain was back.

"I spoke with the proper people. He's coming along, but can't fly for a while longer," Manfred explained. He walked over to the French doors of his quarters at the Schloss Markebeeke to look out over the large lawn.

"I'm sorry to hear that, sir," Menzke replied.

"Well. It is what it is. Damn ground fire plays hell with us when we are in the middle of things *up there*," Manfred chuckled as if to make light of the seriousness of air battle.

"Yes, sir."

"By the way, I appreciate you traveling to Schweidnitz to   get some things for me," Manfred changed the subject as he walked back to his desk to sign some papers.

"Yes. Your Mother was most kind. She insisted we have tea and wondered all about you," Menzke explained.

"Well, I wrote her a letter the first week I was in the hospital. And I managed to telephone her later," Manfred smiled as he was signing some things.

"She mentioned that, sir. She was glad you still have your sense of humor, you know," Menzke stood there in a soft attention posture, which went with his entire demeanor, a rather rumpled old sweater type of look, even in full uniform. He and his Captain had been orderly and captain now for long enough that they went together like hand and glove. There was, indeed, a comfort about their relationship.

"Did she look well?" Manfred was concerned, especially given that the famine had started to take a toll on her much earlier in the year.

"She looked—like you told me over the telephone—a little tired," Menzke was trying to sound diplomatic.

Manfred put his pen down, set the papers in order on the corner of his desk and looked Menzke in the eye, "Hell, Menzke, don't talk like one of those people at the General Staff in Berlin."

"Well, sir, she looked thin and slightly weak," Menzke was more open about his impression of Manfred's mother .

"Hmm…I appreciate you going. I regard this as a personal favor," Manfred looked at Menzke.

"My pleasure, sir."

"Now, listen. Send these papers to the General Staff—it's important," Manfred pointed to the papers he had signed.

"I can get these off now, sir."

"Go, then. Don't miss the courier flight," Manfred's face became serious as Menzke showed some speed leaving his quarters, practically running to his motorcycle.

The weight of command was something Manfred had been looking forward to. He wanted to prove to himself that he could still do it. The images of the over-gesticulating injured soldiers in the field hospital came to the surface of his mind with disturbing regularity. He was dead set on not being one of them, although Käte had clarified what Doctor Lävin told him before he left the hospital. She told him he was not to fly — that he had to promise not to fly — until he felt better. They made him promise, but, promises are often in the eye of the promiser. Manfred wanted to prove to himself that he was as good as his old self, so he kept telling himself that he felt better.

Out of nowhere, Manfred went from feeling fine to being in the grip of that raucous nausea that was dogging him like some forest predator. He doubled over and almost heaved. He took several awkward steps finally getting to the edge of his bed, where he sat holding his head in his hands. No longer able to stand it, he fell onto his side, curled up with his knees raised.

Käte, who was folding some towels just outside Manfred's room, stepped quickly into the room to guide his shoulders as he wrenched himself up from the fetal position. He was hunched over, feet on the floor, head between his knees. He began to wretch in a pan that she held just under his chin.

"That's better, Manfred."

"It came on quickly. I was doing …."

"… very well today — until now," Käte interrupted.

Manfred tried to stand up, but struggled with both his strength and balance.

"Maybe in a few minutes, Manfred. There is no shame in putting your head down. I'll close the door, so no one will know — just for a few minutes," Käte watched Manfred lean sideways and collapse on his bunk as she walked to the door, stepped outside and pulled it close.

Manfred was a hard-driving personality, but the hard-driving was more on himself than on his men. He thought that you didn't have to lean on your men if you picked the right ones to start with. The men Manfred had in Jasta 11 loved to fly and they loved Manfred, who had their welfare in mind as he commanded. Besides, his men looked forward to going up on patrol or to get a phone call from one of the spotters, take off, climb and then engage the enemy with a calculated fierceness.

Manfred wanted to get back to this more than anything else. But, he realized that he had to prove himself — again, as he had when he began over a year earlier under Boelcke's command. This time, though, it was not about a young battle flier earning his place. No, this time Manfred realized — especially after he repeatedly saw those men at the field hospital who were crippled with battle stress — that he had to demonstrate psychologically that he was mentally competent.

For him, this demonstration was a multi-pronged effort.

First, there was the day-to-day running of the Schwader, a much larger command than his former command of Jasta 11. The Schwader consisted of four units, Jastas 4, 6, 10 and 11. Manfred knew the strategy behind forming this new larger unit was the simple fact that the Entente was massing larger numbers of airplanes to try to overwhelm and swarm the German Air Force. This was especially true because Germany was in the middle of shortages of food, weapons and supplies. She could ill afford the war of attrition that the Entente had settled on, especially now that the Americans were officially entering the war with troops and materiel.

Next, Manfred wanted to show he grasped the larger picture of command at the strategic level. That was why he had been on the telephone with the General Staff and had Menzke send along all the requisite paperwork. Manfred was bringing Werner Voss into the Schwader as the new commander of Jasta 10.

Five years younger than Manfred, Werner Voss was, in a way, cut from the same cloth. He was adventurous and charmingly flippant. Werner and some of the men referred to Manfred, three, four or five years their senior at the ripe old age of twenty-five, as *The Old Man*. Flippancy aside, they had other things in common. Each liked the outdoors and the adventures it could present. They both loved to hunt. Werner, like Manfred, was a crack shot. It's not surprising, then, that each was drawn to battle flying, with its speed, danger, shooting and new type of physical experience *up there*.

Precision at speed was natural to each of them. If Manfred loved horseback riding, Werner loved motorcycling. In fact, Werner would leave his staff car parked in order to make his command rounds on his motorcycle. He often tinkered on his motorcycle in the hangar alongside the mechanics. On a first name basis with them — itself highly unusual for an officer — Werner would be completely at home covered in oil, grease and grime. He had a high-minded side, though. He took his patriotism seriously. He got around the age limit to join the German army when he was just seventeen. Coupled with his boyish looks, these may have inspired his nickname *Bubi*, or Little Boy.

For their similarities, there were differences. Manfred and Werner knew and used Hochdeutsche, the Standard German, the formal language used by all Germans, but each spoke their own regional dialect. Voss spoke Krefelder Low German, while Manfred grew up with Low Prussian. Werner's father, who owned and operated a dye factory, was successful upper bourgeoisie, while Manfred's family was grounded in the Prussian aristocracy. This never interfered with their friendship. Each visited the other's family, with Werner's father, Maxmilian, giving Manfred an open invitation to the Voss family hunting lodge.

It was no surprise that Werner was awarded the *Ordre Pour le Mérite* in early April that year after he scored his twenty-fourth air battle victory. The Blue Max mandated a thirty day leave, so Werner missed out on the successful German air battles during *Bloody April*. If he had been allowed to fly during that time, he might have a victory total that would begin to rival Manfred's.

Menzke knocked at Manfred's door.

"Come in," Manfred raised his voice.

"The courier plane left a little while ago, Captain," Menzke reported to Manfred as he walked in, saluted and picked up the tea service that Manfred had used at mid-morning.

"I think I will try lunch," Manfred said as he walked over the French doors to the outside.

"I can bring it, sir," Menzke said .

"No, not necessary. I want to eat with the men," Manfred replied as he looked out over the lawn of the Schloss Markebeeke.

"The men are looking forward to lunch with you, sir," Menzke started to explain.

"That is fine, Menzke," Manfred said in a matter of fact manner as he was getting ready to walk to lunch.

Käte walked in and interrupted, "I forgot something. By the way, we can do your bandage now or after lunch. You need a clean one. You're a day old."

"Captain von Richthofen, allow me to present Lieutenant Wilhelm Reinhard," Menzke interrupted Käte. "Forgive me, but I forgot to mention this to the Captain this morning."

"Yes, pleased to renew our acquaintance, Lieutenant Reinhard," Manfred returned the lieutenant's salute. "At ease."

"I am glad to see you back, Captain," Reinhard began.

"It is good to be here. Thank you, Lieutenant," Manfred replied.

Wilhelm Reinhard was a new member of Jasta 11, having come in at the end of June after having attended one of the German Air Force's new Jasta Schools.

"I wanted to inquire, sir. Some of the fliers want to know about the rumors," Reinhard began.

"What rumors?"

"The new plane from Fokker, sir," Reinhard started to explain.

"Ah, yes. Well, lieutenant—we will have someone here in a few days who knows a good deal more about it than I do," Manfred smiled.

"I see, sir," Reinhard kept his formality, but was elated to hear that progress was being made on the new Fokker. Manfred could see that Reinhard was very happy to know that a new plane was in the works.

"I did speak with Anthony Fokker earlier this morning. By telephone." Manfred continued to smile. "He's had battle fliers testing prototypes and working on final plans to produce something."

"This is good news, sir," Reinhard could barely control his smile.

"Listen. I'll be over in a few minutes for lunch. We will have a lot to talk about," Manfred saluted Reinhard, who returned the salute and turned to walk through the door that Menzke was holding.

"By the way, lieutenant," Manfred interrupted Reinhard's walk to the door.

"Yes, sir."

"I understand you've been wounded twice," Manfred looked Reinhard in the eyes.

"Yes, sir. Once in fourteen, in the artillery. Then, a year later while flying. I came here after the Balkans, sir," Reinhard explained.

"I'm glad to see that you've been able to bear up under all this, lieutenant," Manfred saluted him again.

"Yes, sir," Reinhard returned the salute, turned and walked out the door.

"Käte," Manfred look at her. "This may be a long lunch. I have a lot of catching up to do. Let's do my bandage now."

Manfred sat down. Käte took out a pair of scissors.

"I could do this myself, by now. Did you know that Menzke?" Manfred smiled.

"No, sir. I did not," Menzke smiled at Käte, who had taken a pair of scissors out of her medical bag.

"Let's leave the medical work to professionals, Manfred," Käte smiled.

Manfred made a funny face, which made Menzke stifle a laugh.

Käte alternately cut and unwrapped Manfred's extensive bandage. When finished, she took out gauze and tape.

"It's itching, again," Manfred began his usually daily commentary on the state of his skull and scalp. "They say this is good, right? Itching means healing."

"Either that … or lice," Käte joked.

As soon as she said that, Manfred drifted away. He saw men in the trenches, dirty, diseased and suffering. In the middle of them, there he was: the man from his first night in the field hospital, wandering naked while the German infantry kept themselves   hunched in the trenches and foxholes. The naked gesticulating man, walking — better, yet, ambulating as if crippled and retarded, unaware that there was a war on with real shooting. Manfred kept flying very low in his Albatros, with British Sopwiths chasing him. He saw a forest ahead. If he could only make it there to hide in the trees. He pushed his throttle forward. The British were gaining on him.

"Manfred?" Käte gently jostled Manfred's shoulder. "Are you with us?"

Manfred shook himself back to his quarters at the Schloss Markebeeke, "Yes, Käte. I am here."

For the first time, Menzke saw what had happened to his Captain. Manfred's head was shaved. Menzke also saw Manfred's eyes for what they now were, deep dark sockets sucking his eyeballs into his skull. They were the eyes of an old man, tired and beaten.

Menzke also saw that the wound was still open, down to the bone of his skull. Just below this opening in his scalp, there was a long furrow, still covered in a scab. This is where a bullet had done its damage. Indeed, Menzke thought to himself: this is why my Captain has not been himself. And the wound—it looked much worse than he thought.

Chapter Sixteen

Manfred could see that as soon as Werner Voss arrived, he was bring-ing a much needed energy to Jageschwader 1.

"So, Bubi, did you notice that there is a war on?" Manfred quipped as he saw his friend.

"Oh, *that's* what all the fuss was over that way," Werner pointed to-ward the direction of the front at Ypres as they stood on the porch of the Schloss Markebeeke.

"Yes. Ruined my vacation a few years ago on the beach in Belgium," Manfred retorted.

"Well, it's only July 30th so there is plenty of summertime left for fun," Werner joked.

The two of them saluted, shook hand and embraced.

"The office is nice here, *Old Man*," Werner began by looking into Manfred's quarters on the right of the porch of the Schloss.

"Let's sit. I've got them bringing us tea," Manfred pointed out a small table with a few chairs on the other side of the porch. "What's that you've got in your hand?"

"The latest copy of Youth Magazine!" Werner smiled, holding up the cover to Manfred.

"I know him," Manfred joked back.

"Yes, dear *Old Man*, there is a painting of you on the cover, Blue Max and all," Werner was teasing.

"No wonder you have all this energy. You've come to destroy me!" Manfred feigned being wounded.

"There you are on the cover, a portrait by Karl Bauer. Nice work, but they left out the shaved head and bandage," Werner laughed.

The two of them walked over to the table. Käte came out to introduce herself to Werner as the two of them were sitting down. They immediately stood up.

"Kate Otersdorf, please let me introduce you to my rival, Werner Voss," Manfred was at his politest, but still able to make a smart remark.

Käte held out her hand, which Werner kissed, "It is my pleasure. Please call me Werner."

"Nice to meet you, Lieutenant Voss," Käte wanted to start out on the formal side, since, in her experience, fliers were notorious womanizers who take any sense of the casual as an invitation.

"Yes, well, I can see my good friend Manfred here is in good hands. I do want to thank you for taking care of him."

"Surprise of surprises, but he's been relatively subdued," Käte smiled.

"Did you see the latest *Youth Magazine*?" Werner held the cover up for her to see.

Käte giggled as she looked at the serious portrait of Manfred.

"Now, there is a poem by Lothar Ring called *The Flyer*. Yes, it concludes: *So near the sun I've been!*" Werner read the last line of the poem.

"Can it hurt to exaggerate?" Manfred asked.

"Maybe not. Next, there's an article on you by Franz Carl Enders. It concludes by wishing all of us to find our inner Richthofen, to work for the fatherland," Werner stopped teasing his friend at this point.

"Well, the two of you enjoy the summer day," Käte started to leave. "But, be careful. His head really is wounded, Lieutenant Voss."

"Oh, I thought that was some sort of white hat he had on," Werner smiled at her. "Let's see, Manfred. Were you wounded?"

Menzke came out with tea, "Sir, tea is ready."

"Thank you, Menzke," Manfred gestured for everyone to sit down.

"No, thank you. I've a report to write," Käte smiled and left as quickly as she had come by.

Manfred gestured for Werner to sit down, "I've set things up for you at Jasta 10."

"Tell me about it," Werner wanted to know the details.

"Well, I know how you enjoy the paperwork of command, so I've arranged for this fellow—First Lieutenant Ernst Weigand to take over all that stuff for you."

"Seriously?" Werner was incredulous, but happy, if this were true.

"Yes, I am serious. This detail stuff has always bothered me," Manfred opened up.

"Why are you doing it?" Werner asked rather naively.

Manfred looked him in the eyes, but kept quiet.
"Oh, yes, I see," Werner got it. "You have to convince them you're not crazy or something."

Manfred nodded his head yes while he took a sip of tea.

"What's with the tea and no cognac?" Werner then took a sip himself.

"Headaches," Manfred said just one word.

"I could imagine, with a bandage like that, you must have a wound for the ages," Werner looked Manfred up and down. He thought he looked a little thin—and those sunken eyes were not like the man he remembered.

"So, the men want to know all about the Fokker," Manfred changed the subject to something more his liking.

"They pulled me off combat in early July and sent me to Schwerin to be a test pilot for them," Werner began.

"Well, after July 6th, I was not much for anything," Manfred laughed.

"You're laughing, Manfred. This is a good thing," Werner got serious.

"I'm laughing and you're serious," Manfred laughed some more.

"Yes, well—you had a lot of people worried, *Old Boy*. A lot of people," Werner was still serious in voicing his concern for Manfred. "I want to pass your victory total, but only while you are alive."

"All well and good," Manfred waved his hands as if to brush these remarks off his Captain's jacket.

Manfred could see the enthusiasm in Werner's body posture and hear it in his voice.

"Tell me all about it!" Manfred wanted to know just as badly as everyone else. "I did speak with Anthony on the phone, but what can you get from that?"

"Well, let's see. It's small, has a tubular steel frame and a rotary engine," Werner began.

"Power?"

"Not as much as I'd like—as you'd like, either," Werner admitted one of the Fokker's weaknesses.

"What else?" Manfred wanted to know more.

"Cantilevered wings," Werner replied as he stood up to stretch out his back.

"So, not all those wires and struts," Manfred liked what he was hearing.

"Yes, very modern," Werner replied, sitting back down and taking another sip of tea. "Fokker is forward looking. I know he talked with you. *Feedback* and all that."

"I like this idea, you know. Designing, testing, talking with the pilots who have flown in air battles," Manfred was in rapt attention.

"So, this little Fokker, it has blue on its underside — like the sky.

"Harder to see from the ground," Manfred finished Werner's thought for him.

"And it has grey and olive, sort of, on top," Werner went on.

"The idea is to blend in from your point of view — on the ground or from above in another airplane," Manfred was getting excited about the prospect of a new and better plane.

"So, anything else?" Manfred nodded and gestured for Werner to keep going.

"It's small and light, so it climbs like a little demon. I imagine in battle, we can climb above to avoid fighting purely horizontal. Think of that," Werner tossed that out there for Manfred to muse over.

"I like that. Always having the high ground," Manfred nodded as he was thinking all of this over.

"It's unbalanced in its controls, so it maneuvers very well. Little thing is quite agile," Werner went on.

"More so than the Albatros?" Manfred wanted to hear "yes."

"No comparison. Much better in this regard than the Albatros. We'll be a match for the Camels, for certain, Manfred," Werner concluded.

"I heard that the Office of the Inspector for Flying Troops has ordered us some," Manfred added.

"I hope they arrive like they've promised — in a few weeks," Werner looked serious again.

"Other than a bit on the slow side, any other problems?" Manfred wondered.

"A tendency for ground looping," Werner started to explain.

"So, when you land, it wants to spin sideways in circles?" Manfred had real concern on his face.

"Yes, between you and me. They are working on this, so let's not alarm the men," Werner smiled.

Manfred laughed his old laugh, "This makes perfect sense. Let's let them find out when they land in heavy winds late this October here in northern Europe."

"Glad to see you laugh again, Manfred," Werner smiled at his friend.

"It is good to look forward. You've brought something   here, a new spirit," Manfred complimented his friend.

"One more thing," Werner said.

"What's that?" Manfred asked.

"Fokker mentioned that after we get the new planes, he will be here with some celebrities," Werner explained.

"Yes, the propaganda!" Manfred was derisive.

"Just like the magazine here, my friend," Werner waved the   Youth Magazine in the air.

"Yes, well I don't look like that at the moment, do I?" Manfred pointed to his bandage with both hands.

"No, but there is a certain *je ne sais quoi* about your new look," Werner smiled.

"Believe me: this has been no fun at all—and the field hospital!" Manfred remarked.

"So, Fokker mentioned that Crown Prince Wilhelm may be here," Werner said this with an almost undetectable sarcasm.

"Better they should focus on getting the country some food," Manfred said.

"Or even a Fokker with a little more power, which would make it invincible, I think," Werner looked Manfred in the eye and nodded to reinforce his point.

"By the way, a few days ago the Tommies made a run on this place," Manfred changed the subject.

"That's what I was given to understand," Werner smiled at his friend.

"Bombing and then ground strafing," Manfred observed.

Werner took this in to think about later.

"So, I'm back here two days and they come here for bombing practice," Manfred laughed.

"Your reputation gives Germany a huge propaganda advantage," Werner took the final sip of tea in his cup.

"If you pass me in victories, well—maybe they'll come after you," Manfred was simply happy that Werner Voss was here to help him get Jageschwader 1 ready to strike back at the British. "You know, something is up. They've been shelling us heavily at Ypres for over a week now. Nonstop. So, I imagine there is a new offensive in the works."

"More than Ypres, they want our U-boat base at Ostend," Werner looked serious.

Menzke came to the table, "Sir, a report came to you from the General Staff."

"Very good. Let me see," Manfred opened an envelope.

"Ah, it's just confirming what we've known for quite a while," Manfred looked the brief report over.

"What was that?" Werner asked.
"We should strive to conserve food. There is a famine," Manfred rolled his eyes. Then, he and Werner laughed.

Käte had been spying on them from inside the Schloss. She was happy to see Manfred smiling and laughing. She found his casual manner attractive and imagined that before his wound, he must have been a charming man to know.

Chapter Seventeen

Now that it was mid-August, Manfred was burning more and more to get back *up there* .

The trouble was his head wound was not cooperating. He was having these damn recurring headaches, fits of nausea and — as much as he tried to hide it — fits of general irritability that simply were not who he was. Manfred was under a lot of self-imposed pressure to help the cause, to get back *up there* to shoot down the enemy. He had been back to the field hospital in Courtrai twice to have Doctor Lävin remove more splinters. He still had that bandage on his head. His wound was still open to the bone. And, the boar would come in his nightmares, sometimes twice a night. Along with that, there were those yelling voices, too.

Mother Nature was not helping things, either. It had been raining now off and on for several weeks. No Man's Land was even more of a disaster than before. What had once been idyllic fields of grasses and flowers, and deep woods with verdant trees and mossy forest floors were now explosion scarred tracts of land with no flora and fauna, save for leeches, maggots and bacteria. The land was barren and misshapen with deep holes everywhere from where artillery shells had exploded. The   woods remained as some apocalyptic vision with mud, holes and broken trunks of trees in the place of much taller and flushed out foliage that invited you to enter for hiking, hunting and summer recreation. With the rain, the entire mess was a morass of mud and water.

Flying was difficult, as well. Thunder, rain and wind made it difficult. The British and French had re-armed their air power so they now outnumbered the German Air Force. It was clear that Germany was now locked into a permanent war of attrition that her leaders had hoped to avoid. Her forces were split between the East with fighting the Russians and the West where it was the other members of the Entente. The Americans were coming ashore, the Western Front looked more difficult each day and there was a rush to end the fighting in the East. Perhaps the Germans could get the inexperienced Bolsheviks to come to favorable terms so the Germans could move their Eastern troops to the Western Front.

Things were hot at Ypres. On July 31, the Entente started a major push on the ground, with accurate artillery fire from their intelligence from the Royal Flying Corps. They advanced some, but were pushed back. The weather coupled with the field conditions made the going difficult for each side. Men would advance on duckboards, because, if you tried walking in the mud, you sunk up to your knees. With the weight of a full pack, if someone fell off the duckboards into a hole filled with water, they would drown, as the holes were often deeper than the tallest soldier. By mid-August there were over 50,000 casualties, if you counted both sides together. It appeared that this was going to be another massive slaughter.

Not that the previous ones had gone unnoticed by the troops and the folks back home. French troops had gone on strike as a protest against futile and stupid battle plans. British troops protested, as well. There was general strife in Germany, with some people floating the idea of a national strike because of living and working conditions brought on by the famine and Germany's shortages of just about everything.

Leaders on both sides realized they were treading in delicate waters. Some advocated a violent put down of any protest, while others were more reasonable with wanting to listen and learn from the people they were supposed to lead. Manfred knew what things were like in Russia, with social chaos the order of the day with no one really governing as there was an exiting aristocracy and an incoming socialist cadre, neither of whom, quite possibly, knew what they were doing.

This very morning Jasta 11's quarters had been bombed at six am. Manfred decided it was time. The men wanted to hit back. Battle flying was no longer about simply meeting the enemy in the air. It had developed into much more complex attacks. A few weeks earlier, one British flier caught the Germans off guard. He had time to bomb several targets and then engaged in strafing runs on planes, hangars and men. For a few minutes, all was chaos on the ground. As such, the men had a much grittier attitude towards flying, attacking and carrying out their missions.

With all this new tension, Manfred felt relieved. It was now a Thursday, August 16. He was pulling his helmet over his bandage, climbing into his Albatros D.V, strapping in with the help of Menzke and firing up the Mercedes D.III engine. It was still early morning, just before seven am. The sun had already crested the horizon. Menzke gave Manfred the all clear sign as the rudder, ailerons and elevator were working just fine. Manfred looked around, made eye contact with his Jasta 11 members and then taxied to the runway. The wind was gentle out of the West, so Manfred taxied to the East end, worked his controls one more time and gave his Albatros full throttle. The plane accelerated, with the dirt runway choppy due to the exceptional rains they had been experiencing. Manfred's head bounced and he winced in pain as the plane left the ground.

The goal this early morning was to simply patrol as a squadron of five planes. The British had numerical superiority, but the General Staff was pleased with the tactic of putting several Jastas into a larger Jageschwader unit as a counterweight. In fact, Manfred knew that they would be officially forming a second Jageschwader, Jageschwader 2 the very next day August 17.

Within fifteen minutes, all of them were at fifteen thousand feet. Manfred was admitting to himself a mixed message. On the one hand, it was good to be flying again. On the other hand, as he got above four thousand feet, his head started to hurt and he was experiencing a constant nausea. There were bouts of dizziness, too. It was taking all of his self-control not to vomit or to feel as if he were spinning in his seat. Manfred, though, was determined to reassert himself as a battle flier and as a leader of his new and much larger unit. He took his role as military commander and national leader seriously. He felt that there was always room for chaos, especially in times like these, but that responsible and honorable leadership could avoid that.

As Manfred and his comrades were cruising, he spied a French Nieuport 23 with British marking. Manfred positioned himself out of the sun and then dropped down on the Nieuport.

The Nieuport was quite a plane. Designed by Gustave Delage, it was like the Albatros, a sesquiplane, with the lower wing of its biplane configuration smaller than the top one. It had 120 horsepower from its Le Rhône 9Jb, a 9 cylinder rotary engine. Firepower came from one forward firing fixed Vickers .303 machine gun mounted on its top wing.

Manfred was fixed on his target, but the British pilot was experienced. He led Manfred on a long chase. This was not an easy task, nor was it enjoyable for Manfred. Both diving and turning sharply to keep up with attempted breakaways really bothered Manfred's head. Yet, he had promised himself he would show that he was back, that he was the Manfred of old, that the British would have to take notice.

The fight, then, when he caught the Nieuport, was brief. He shot its fuel tank and engine. The Nieuport went into a spin. Manfred followed suit, pursuing his opponent down, drawing close and firing again, thinking to himself that he would hammer this British bastard into oblivion. The plane crashed into the ground, with Manfred pulling out of his dive to pass through the flames and noxious smoke from the Nieuport's gas tanks.

Happy that he had gotten Number Fifty-Eight, Manfred signaled to his men that he would return to their aerodrome. Actually, Manfred had no choice. By this time, he was lucky he could fly his plane with his headache, dizziness and nausea. The wound itself was throbbing, as well. Manfred pointed his Albatros home, looked over his shoulders on each side to make sure he wasn't being followed and cruised at five thousand feet. As he descended to one thousand feet, he saw the wind sock indicating the gentle wind was still out of the West. He circled one more time, aligned himself with the runway and dropped down to land. Manfred taxied back with Menzke jumping up and down, as an observer had called the base to let everyone know that Manfred had another victory. This would mean another silver cup, along with a toast of champagne later that day.

"You know, Menzke, this had been a lot of effort to get Number Fifty-Eight," Manfred forced himself to smile, but Menzke could see his face all lined and strained.

"Yes, sir. This is a good moment," Menzke smiled as he helped Manfred unstrap himself and get out of the cockpit.

"Who are those people standing over there?" Manfred wondered about a group of what looked like civilians off the edge of tents where they parked the planes.

"Civilians. Excited to see you back, I imagine," Menzke could see Manfred was in no mood for this sort of thing.

"Ah, slackers. Nobodies. They do no one any good," Manfred said tersely as he leaned over to then whisper in Menzke's ear. "Get the staff car and take me directly to the Schloss. I may get sick, but no one is to know."

Käte was gone. She was back at the field hospital. This was, at least today, a good thing, as Manfred locked himself in his quarters, vomited into a bedpan and lay on his cot curled up on his side for the rest of the day. Moritz was with him, on the floor at the side of cot.

Chapter Eighteen

Manfred realized, as he had been lying there before the sun came up, that in his effort to get back to where he had been before he'd been shot, he was in almost constant pain. Given all the rigor of his military education, the implicit call to duty in his aristocratic Prussian family and his own innate drive to excel, Manfred had unconsciously put that pain well into the background. It had been enough to deal with the expected symptoms of his skull wound — the headaches, dizziness and nausea. Yesterday was a bit of a respite, Sunday September 2, as Anthony Fokker had shown up to work with the men on the new Fokker Dr.Is. Anthony was happy, out-going and a bit of a devil. But, Manfred did not have time to enjoy those thoughts because Moritz was pacing impatiently around his shuttered room at the Schloss Markebeeke, tail wagging and needing to be let out after a night in. And, Manfred realized that his body ached from deep inside. He was tired. As he sat up on the side of his cot as he heard a knock at the door.

"Come in, Menzke," Manfred said as he pointed to the door, giving permission for Moritz to go outside to relieve himself.

"You know, Captain, this is going to be a boost. These new planes look so modern," Menzke began as he got Manfred's uniform out of the armoire.

"Yes, those three wings," Manfred replied.

"I noticed no wires," Menzke continued.

"Cantilevered wings. Very strong structure. They do have a couple of braces, but—what is the word?" Manfred was searching.

"I'm not sure," Menzke said.

"And, *streamlined*. I think that is the word: *streamlined*," Manfred smiled.

"I see," Menzke stopped for a moment and thought.

"Somewhat like a bird in a dive. Not as much wind resistance," Manfred explained. "Anthony and I talked about this last spring. After I wrote a letter complaining about some of the shortcomings of the Albatros."

"Well, this is above me, but I like what I see," Menzke beamed as he was helping his Captain.

"Something to look forward to, eh, Menzke?" Manfred walked across the hall to the privy.

He was back in a few minutes, having shaved and splashed cold water on his face.

"Anthony Fokker is going to continue his motion picture making today, I hope," Menzke began.

"Yes, spending time with us," Manfred was brightening. "I'm looking forward to the next few days."

"It must be a nice change of pace, sir. He is substantive," Menzke was clearly excited.

"Well, I will admit, August had come and gone before I knew it," Manfred was pulling on his pants.

"You had victory Fifty-Nine on the 26th. The SPAD VII with your Albatros. Two days ago, Saturday, an R.E.8 with the new Fokker," Menzke was chatty. "Which plane do you prefer?" Menzke asked.

"The R.E.8," Manfred joked. "When they saw the triplane configuration, they thought I was a Sopwith Camel, one of their own. I got real close before they realized what was happening. My easiest victory."

"Very well, sir," Menzke played along. "But, which of *our planes* do you prefer."

"I'll let you know in a week or so. But, I will say that the Fokker is maneuverable," Manfred smiled.

"I will hold you to that, sir. I'll ask again in a week," Menzke was humorously bold to his Captain.

Manfred stood up so that Menzke could help him with his jacket, "You do remember that not only is Fokker here, right?" Manfred smiled.

"Oh, yes, sir! The Kaiser will be here, too," Menzke smiled back. "Yes, the Kaiser."

"Good. Not a good thing to forget him."

"I agree, sir," Menzke smiled.

"I think we're done here. Go see what trouble Moritz has gotten into," Manfred wanted to be alone for a moment. Once, again, the dizziness, headache and nausea came on.

Manfred thought, though, maybe he was done with that damned bandage! The wound was still open to the bone, but this new contraption Doctor Lävin had Käte bring over was a welcome improvement. Two rubber bands attached to a small bandage. The rubber bands went under his chin and held the bandage over his open skull wound with no problem at all.

"He is happy, sir," Menzke was back at the threshold of Manfred's quarters with Moritz, who was wagging his tail and wanted to play. As the two of them came in, Moritz began to wander like a large errant child.

"He's happy, isn't he, Menzke?" Manfred commented and asked at the same time.

"He is, sir. I think these rubber bands under the chin and the small bandage to keep the wound clean will work just fine," Menzke changed the subject. He knew that Manfred had been struggling, which was difficult for him to watch. He was used to seeing his Captain sharp, insightful and ahead of the game.

"I think so," Manfred adjusted the rubber band one more time.

"This is much better, sir," Menzke helped Manfred adjust the covering so that his wound wasn't open.

"Thank you, Menzke," Manfred grabbed his jacket, which Menzke helped him put on.

"Indeed, August has flown by, sir. September will bring new things," Menzke smiled.

Manfred hoped the next few days would be enjoyable. He thought back for a moment. In addition to his chronic problems with his health, there had been some additionally stressful moments the past few weeks.

The worst day had been Sunday August 19. General Erich von Ludendorff had come to inspect Jageschwader 1. What made it perfect for the General was the fact that Jasta 11 had its two hundredth victory two days earlier. Lieutenant Hans-Georg von der Osten was the lucky fellow. And with Manfred's fifty-eighth victory the day before, it was an ideal moment for not only the General, but for the Central Office for Foreign Services' propaganda machine.

Earlier that year in early May, Manfred had met the rulers of Germany in Kreuznach. General Paul von Hindenburg was a warm fatherly figure. He made a point of telling Manfred that he had lived in the same room as Manfred at the Cadet Academy in Wahlstatt forty years earlier. At ease with Hindenburg, Manfred expected the same as he approached Ludendorff's office. General Erich von Ludendorff was unexpectedly terse. He didn't think highly of the air war. And, he peppered Manfred with questions as though this were a police interrogation. He wanted to know about their progress at the front and quickly became impatient when Manfred tried to be personable with explanations through anecdotes. That wouldn't do. Ludendorff, at his best, was blunt, cool and detached. Cut and dried, he wanted concise answers so his organizational mind could process the information efficiently. After Ludendorff, Manfred then met Kaiser Wilhelm II the next day, May 2, which, Manfred was happy to say, was his twenty-fifth birthday. Compared to Ludendorff, meeting the Kaiser was a walk in the park.

So, Manfred already had mixed feelings about these propaganda opportunities. The fact that he was meeting General von Ludendorff again was something he was not looking forward to. And it wasn't simply an inspection of the troops with salutes and handshakes. No. It was a staged photographic event. To be sure, as he approached the General that day on Sunday, August 19, Manfred noticed something he hadn't the first time that he met the General. His military decorations: Knight of the Military Order of Max Joseph; Grand Commander with Star of the House Order of Hohenzollern, Ordre Pour le Mérite; Grand Cross of the Iron Cross; Knight of the Military Order of St. Henry; Knight of the Military Merit Order; Knight Grand Cross of the House and Merit Order of Peter Frederick Louis with Swords and Laurel; plus, others he did not recognize.

At that moment on that Sunday, Manfred thought about a painting he had seen in a recent magazine. Noted artist Professor Hugo Vogel painting a dual portrait of Hindenburg and Ludendorff. In it, Hindenburg looks relaxed and almost casual seated before a table that Ludendorff is standing at, bent over as he studies field maps in order to plot strategy. That captured the differences between the two in one easily grasped picture. Manfred thought to himself: Ludendorff had served under Field Marshall Alfred, Count von Schlieffen, the very man who developed the Schlieffen Plan that Germany was now bogged down with. Earlier in his career, von Ludendorff was charged with researching the Schlieffen Plan. He was even sent to examine the fortifications around the Belgian city of Liège as part of the preplanning for an expectedly eventual use of the Plan. Yes, Ludendorff was a detail oriented German nationalist—he even wanted to annex Crimea as part of Germany.

"Sir, are you alright?" Menzke brought Manfred back to the present. Manfred cleared his mind. He wasn't sure which was worse, remembering his experience with von Ludendorff or having a recurring nightmare about the crazed boar that was trying to kill him in his dreams.

*   *   *

Anton "Anthony" Fokker arrived at the air tents as stylishly as one could imagine. In his racer-like Austro-Daimler Boat Tail automobile, he was all cheers and laughter as the men were getting ready to go up for a patrol. An accomplished pilot, airplane designer and more than a bit of a wheeler-dealer, Fokker was energetic as he greeted Manfred, Werner Voss, Konstantin Krefft, Wilhelm Reinhard, Gisbert-Wilhelm Groos, Karl Meyer, Eberhard Mohnicke and the others.

"Yes, boys, good to see everyone. We are going to learn   even more about my new Fokker Dr.Is and make a moving picture while you shoot down some of the enemy!"

"Hello, Anthony! How are you?" Manfred was hale and hearty, even though he was hiding his usual nausea and headache.

"Ah, Manfred—should I say, Captain?" Anthony joked.

"Sitting behind that curved windshield you can say whatever you want," Manfred said very loudly to make everyone laugh as a crowd of the men gathered around.

"As we discussed yesterday, you and Werner have had victories in the plane." Anthony got out of his car and stood next to Manfred with the men around them.

136

"Quite nice, Anthony," Werner lit a cigarette. He offered one to Anthony who took it, while all the other men lit up, as well. Given that several of them had the Blue Max, there was an aura of the elite sporting club, a certain casualness about the way they interacted.

"Yes, Anthony, let me tell you," Manfred said off-handedly.

"Go ahead, please," Anthony laughed. "I'd love to hear, *Old Man*. That's what someone told me they call you," Anthony winked at the men as they chuckled.

What came to pass in the next few minutes was strange.

"There we were—cavalry at the start of the war," Manfred unexpectedly began an anecdote about his early days in the cavalry. Usually, he talked about the plans for the morning mission.

"What is this about?" Werner Voss asked, unable to follow what Manfred started to talk about.

"Ah, well—good question. There we were. I was a new Lieutenant—relatively new—our charge was simple, but dangerous," Manfred tried to explain, but the men around him were a little bewildered by his *non-sequitur* .

"Yes, our goal was a simple one--get to the rear lines of the enemy, find important targets and then destroy them," Manfred was self-mesmerized, smiling, but appearing to ramble.

The men realized he was making a point. Perhaps he was, but they were trying not to look confused—or to embarrass their leader. Instead, they were intent on trying to focus and understand what he was talking about.

"I was at the head of my column of men, on horseback. It was midnight. We came to a bridge. I expected a battle, but we crossed unimpaired," Manfred went on.

"Where were you, sir?" Krefft asked.

"Poland, of course. Yes, Poland. Midnight," Manfred went on like everyone should understand.

Menzke saw this from a distance and shuddered. He had known that his Captain was out of it from time to time, but as far as he understood, this had never happened outside his quarters in view of a larger audience beyond him, Käte and Moritz.

"We came to a village — Kieltze."
"And then what?" Krefft asked.

"Getting there, Krefft. I see everyone has a lot of energy today," Manfred looked around at the group.

"Yes, sir," came the agreements from the men.

"Poland. I locked the local priest up in the bell tower. We thought, you know, he'd be trouble — you know, someone to inform against us," Manfred chortled as if he had said something funny.

The men looked at each other.

"Yes, we locked up *the Pope*." Manfred continued.

"Sir," Menzke saw what was going on and tried to intervene.

"Not now, Menzke. Anthony here wants to know what happened over there in Poland," Manfred was very focused, his brow furrowed and eyes fixed.

Anthony looked at Manfred and simply nodded, "Proceed."

"Sorry, sir," Menzke decides that it would be better the let this event pass as quickly as possible.

"Well, I had to send a dispatch out every day. After several days, I'd sent out people, but not everyone was sent back, so our numbers were low. I didn't have enough men by the fifth night! Then, a guard wakes me to tell me that there are Cossacks everywhere on the main street!" Manfred goes on.

"And then?" Anthony asked.

"It was pitch black out there and raining some. I went out to scout them. On the main street, there were a lot of them—more than we could have handled—maybe forty of them. They were loud. I know they didn't know we were there."

"What did you do?" Werner Voss asked.

"Do where?" Manfred, momentarily bewildered, seemed to forget where he was in his story.

"You know, Poland, the dark night? The rain?" Krefft tried to refresh Manfred's memory.

"Yes. I decided to keep us hidden until they left. It was a lot like cops and robbers when I was playing as a child," Manfred concluded his story.

The men all feel an embarrassed unease.

"This is interesting," Werner Voss tries to cover and give Manfred a graceful way out.

"But, with Anthony here today, we have enough men and now planes. We can attack the Cossacks," Manfred looked at everyone. "No one is gone and hasn't returned."

Perhaps he made a point, somewhat longwindedly, but he made a point, nonetheless. The men nodded carefully and then prepared to take off. Anthony took out his motion picture camera, got his tripod ready and was all cheers as they started their planes.

Chapter Nineteen

Manfred was on patrol with several fliers from Jasta 11. They were at
15,000 feet. As they had ascended, Manfred's headache worsened, which,
by now, was customary. Doctor Lävin had tried giving him aspirin a week
earlier, but Manfred told him that his pain was such that morphine was the
only analgesic that had a positive effect. And, Manfred didn't like the side
effects from morphine. If anything, Manfred relished being awake and alert.
Also, it was difficult to fly while taking regular doses of morphine because
the precision necessary for take-off and landing just wasn't there. It left him
too lethargic and inattentive. So, he would do what he had been doing since
he came back to Jageschwader 1 at the end of July: live with the pain.

Manfred could have kept himself from flying, but his drive to help his
men, the cause and also evaluate this new Fokker airplane was too strong.
Much like a race horse—and Manfred thought back to his beloved Santuzza,
that strong little speedster and jumper—he had to get his work in every day.
Besides, Manfred wanted to remain Germany's top ace. Voss was a friend,
but there are limits to what he was going to tolerate. Hunting partner or not,
he'd be damned if Voss was going to pass him in victories.

Manfred thought of his sister Ilse, who was also duty bound. They had
a lot in common. Beginning with his convalescence in the field hospital and
since his return to duty, she had corresponded with him, opening up her

heart about the rigors and stresses of her duties as a nurse. In addition to making him feel better about things, Ilse's letters made him appreciate Käte even more. Much of what Manfred had seen in the field hospital was revolting. As if seeing the men in the trenches from his low return flights wasn't enough, it was more than enough to see the amputees, the men wandering errantly from shell shock and smell the stench from festering wounds mixed in with the bedpans. So, his sweet sister, dear Ilse, had more courage than he, thought Manfred. She had to see men, their faces and their bodies in varying states of disfigurement, in ways that would make the average citizen cry out in horror, weep or simply vomit.

Manfred cleared his head. As he looked down, he saw a small patrol of what he thought were Sopwith Pups. Similar to the Camel, it had one fixed forward mounted Vickers machine gun that was synchronized through the propeller. Damn, he thought. The air war had become something totally different than what is was earlier in the year. The Entente was simply throwing airplanes toward the Germans. On the ground, they were hurling artillery and men at well dug in German positions. And, at sea, the German U-boats could not effectively temper the British blockade. Germany was, indeed, starving.

Manfred and his comrades indicated to each other they were going to dive down on this British patrol. Instead, though, Manfred saw that this British patrol was dropping down on some lower flying German planes. Needless to say, Manfred and his comrades instinctively knew that they had to help their comrades below, so they went down post haste.

Down and down they went. Manfred liked the feel of the new Fokker DR.I. It had superb control in a dive and lent itself to pulling out of one or easily changing course while in one in order to follow any sort of pattern one's prey might try. The fact that its rate of climb was superior instilled even great confidence in Manfred and Werner because this meant climbing to escape an attacker who simply couldn't keep up. Manfred was thinking that, indeed, Anthony Fokker had done well on relatively short notice. This new airplane, though small in stature, was formidable.

Quick into his dive, Manfred singled out a Pup and began the chase. The fellow was an able pilot who knew all the evasive maneuvers. He even tried to break off and make it back to Entente territory. His plan, though, was not to be. Manfred pulled in on him so that he was able to target him. Manfred fired, but this British pilot understood enough of the nuances of evasive flying that he was never in one flight path long enough for Manfred to take effective aim. The bobbing and weaving was bothering Manfred's equilibrium. And, the long dive had taken its toll on Manfred's head, which was throbbing. Manfred, though, was determined to make the kill shot. He focused, headache and all, in hot pursuit of his scurrying opponent. Manfred dove again, as the Tommie descended sharply. He fired a short burst, with some bullets tearing into the Pup's wings and fuselage. Manfred tried to do what he always told his men: hit the pilot first.

Out of the blue, Manfred had an idea, especially given that Anthony was making a moving picture with his camera. Manfred thought he would try to force this fellow down in order to take him alive. The British Pup pilot, on the other hand, had other ideas. Since his Sopwith was damaged, its pilot was determined to do as much damage as he could to the damned Germans. Even though he was flying ever lower in a forced descent, he was quite good with his evasive tactics. Besides, he began to strafe as many German soldiers as he could. As Manfred pursued him, they came upon a German infantry column, which the Brit made scatter helter-skelter for their lives. Men were diving here and there so the fearsome British .303 round wouldn't tear them to pieces.

This was to no avail. Manfred had triumphed with the Brit having to do a forced landing in German territory. Manfred watched as the Pup's pilot deliberately crashed his plane into a tree so that it could not be taken as a war trophy. Quickly, German infantry came upon the scene and captured the fellow. Manfred, glad to be done with flying and its accompanying nausea and headache, hurried back to land at the aerodrome in Markebeeke. He was looking forward to collecting some souvenirs and, as well, be in a moving picture with his big trophy, this British pilot.

"Nice work!" Anthony shouted to Manfred, while the people around him cheered.

With the large crowd gathering by his plane, Manfred was at a loss about what to do. Normally, he would relish the attention. Now, his nausea was such that he thought he might vomit in front of everyone. The mere thought of this made him panic. What would people think? How would it look for him, of all people, to vomit in front of a crowd? And with Anthony making a moving picture, to boot?

Manfred taxied his red Fokker toward the tents. As he stopped his engine, Menzke climbed up to help him unstrap, "You know, Menzke, I hope I am not sick here in front of everybody."

Menzke nodded and then asked, "What do you think, sir?"

"Maybe tell them the prisoner is arriving, so I can get to the privy," Manfred said *sotto voce* .

"A distraction, sir?" Menzke asked.

"Why not?" Manfred was really getting sick to his stomach.

"I can get you a minute or so. Stay here while I distract them, sir" Menzke smiled.

Menzke climbed down and addressed the crowd, "I see the prisoner over there. Follow me."

As Manfred got out of the plane, the crowd, rather naively, turned to follow Menzke. Manfred took advantage of the moment   to head for the privy, where he was sick for just a moment. Menzke apologized to the crowd for mistaking an approaching supply vehicle for one that was carrying the downed British flyer.

"This was an experience today," Manfred said aloud to Anthony as he approached him and the crowd from their rear.

"This all looked exciting. How was the plane?" Anthony asked.

"Like a monkey, the way it climbs!" Manfred was hale and hearty as he began his appraisal of the Fokker.

"And the two Spandau IMGs?" Anthony was positively beaming.

"The 7.92 Mauser gave our Tommie something to worry about. But, all joking aside," Manfred looked Anthony in the eye, "I have to say this is what we needed. Your design ideas, listening to our pilots — very important. And the 7.92 chopped his plane up quite well."

"This is good to hear. We'll talk more later," Anthony said as he motioned to one of his people to bring the camera over.

"The other planes are landing now," Menzke alerted everyone who turned to see the other pilots of Jasta 11 from his patrol starting to land.

As they turned to look, Manfred grabbed Anthony for an aside, "Quite nice, you know. Maneuvers like the devil. I'd like a little more power, but for right now, all things being equal, I was able to draw in on this Sopwith Pup and easily follow his evasions."

"Fuselage has that steel tubing — light and rigid — lets the wings do their job, *Old Man*," Anthony is serious, but still has a bit of the imp in his eyes.

Manfred was happy to see Anthony still open to wanting to improve things, which he was sure they would talk about later over dinner. As everyone watched the last of Jasta 11 land, a group of vehicles approached from the direction of the front. Manfred could see that they had the British flyer.

Manfred looked the British flyer in the eye, Anthony had the camera rolling and several flyers surrounded the Brit. Manfred saluted him and he returned the military courtesy.

"Lieutenant Algernon F. Bird," the British flyer went by the book.

"Manfred von Richthofen," Manfred smiled at him.

Anthony gestured to the pilots wearing the Blue Max to stand next to Lieutenant Bird. One of them offered him a cigarette, which he accepted. As the camera kept rolling, Manfred smiled and shook his hand. Of course, with no sound, no one would hear what they were saying to each other — and with no one present completely fluent in the other's language, things were kept fairly basic.

"Prussian … skill. Yes, Prussian skill," Manfred smiled in broken English.

"Listen, old boy — I'm no one's trophy," Lieutenant Bird asserted, but he smiled nonetheless.

"Ah, *keine Trophäe*," Werner Voss smiled and then laughed along with everyone else.

"*Ja, keine Trophäe*," was repeated with chuckles by all the fliers, as Lieutenant Bird was at a loss at what to do.

Manfred did not look at Bird, but, rather, looked him over as one would inspect a horse or something like that. While Bird understandably bristled at this. Manfred reveled in it.

"You know, chaps, Tommie is coming," Bird realized that he was going to be a prisoner of war. "*Tommie kommt. Ja, kommt.*"

Everyone laughed at this assertion that *Tommie is coming*. The mood lightened considerably as they stood around, sort of posing and moving for Anthony's camera as it took its moving pictures. Bird relaxed, as he knew he had made his point. He was hoping, at this point, for a prisoner exchange in the near future.

After a few moments, another vehicle approached with a major who spoke English, "Let me tell you, Lieutenant Bird—possible prisoner exchange, but right now you are being sent to a new camp for British officers, Holzminden.

Bird and everyone else knew that his fate—at least for now—was sealed. New camp or not, being a prisoner of war is always arduous, for it is demeaning. The treatment and living conditions are, in a variety of ways, inhumane.

After they saluted each other, Bird was taken off, with Manfred happy to have another victory along with all the publicity this was going to generate. Anthony had his moving picture of the event and Manfred was going to call Wagner & Son in Berlin to order his sixty-first victory cup.

*   *   *

"It's better that the Kaiser is coming tomorrow, Menzke," Manfred said as he waited for his telephone connection to Berlin.

"We'll be ready, sir. Today is quite the day for celebrating. Number Sixty-One!" Menzke was elated that his Captain had done so well.

As Manfred talked with his Berlin jeweler, Menzke was brushing Moritz. Menzke didn't like the sound of Manfred's voice as his conversation progressed with his victory cup maker. Finally, Manfred hung up and appeared disappointed.

"Sir?" Menzke asked as Moritz ran over the Manfred and circled him wanting to play.

"Well, no more victory cups, Menzke," Manfred began.

"Why not?"

"There is now a silver shortage in Germany," Manfred was bearing up to the reality of the war as it had now developed. He was reminded of a report he had read the night before. By now there were over 80,000 German casualties in the latest battle at Ypres that had begun six weeks ago.

Indeed, things were not going Germany's way.

Chapter Twenty

Manfred began a vacation—perhaps an encouraged convalescent leave—on September 6. Given that there was a war on, given that he was getting daily briefings on Jageschwader 1 and given that he was not one to rest on his laurels, it was less a holiday and more a reassignment of sorts.

He had sent Menzke ahead to set things up at his family home in Schweidnitz. Mamma and Menzke got on well. Besides, Manfred never trusted the shipping of his luggage to either the military or the shipping companies. Better that his stuff gets home through Menzke's efforts than it languish somewhere in Germany.

Manfred was up in his Albatros flying toward Schweidnitz. He was looking forward to being with his family. Ilse and Lothar were both going to be there. Lothar was walking again. Manfred was excited to see young Bolko. As well, Mamma and Papa would be there. So, it was a family reunion of the best type!

Manfred thought about the first ten days of his vacation, but was hoping for better things to come in the days ahead. The crush of his celebrity was not at all what he imagined it would be. Briefly in Berlin, he was smothered by folks who wanted him to sign their Sanke Cards. One fellow was so bold as to immediately try to sell them on the street while in sight of Manfred. He also received another bust of Kaiser Wilhelm. Although a great honor, at this point in his career, Manfred was more concerned about adequate equipment for Jageschwader 1 than token gestures from the leader of the German Empire.

Manfred then mused about his time a few days earlier on a hunting trip. During that time, he had made it clear to Menzke that all was not what it seemed.

"Yes, Menzke, we are on leave. I will admit that much," Manfred smiled as he put on his hunting clothes for the cool Bavarian dawn air above Coburg.

"Better to not get a chill, sir," Menzke handed him a sweater to put under his coat.

They were at the Schloss Reinhardsbrunn, one of two residences — the other the Fortress Coburg — within the vast estate of Carl Eduard, Duke of Saxe-Coburg and Gotha. The Fortress was an immense series of medieval walls and structures atop a mountain where it looked over Bavaria to the south and Thuringia to the north. The Schloss Reinhardsbrunn, by comparison, was built as an English country house, was over ninety kilometers to the north, where it, served as a hunting lodge for Carl Eduard.

"You know, Menzke, I might enjoy this hunt if it were under different circumstances," Manfred continued to smile to his loyal orderly.

"How so, sir? Is it the briefings we get from headquarters?" Menzke asked.

"Not at all. I like knowing what the Schwader is up to," Manfred clarified.

"Then what is it?" Menzke asked.

"I do not want to be indelicate, but I'll try to explain," Manfred began.

"Sir, I am discreet," Menzke assured him.

"Yes, you've been loyal and indispensable," Manfred assured him.

"Thank you, sir," Menzke was honored.

"This may be one of the most overpowering places I have ever been," Manfred wanted to get this out, which was rather unlike him. Menzke noted that his Captain was more emotive than he'd ever seen him.

"I agree, sir," Menzke sat on a chair and was focusing. He had rarely seen his Captain so sharp and attentive since his accident. It was good to see the *Old Man* in form, if somewhat different.

"This place is impressive. I understand that the Duke has his Fortress Coburg well to the south. Now, that one overlooks both the town of Coburg and large parts of both the Bavarian and Thuringian countryside. Impressive by itself."

"No doubt, sir."

"That place is the residence of the Duke — you know, Carl Eduard. We are at his other *château* — for hunting and entertaining," Manfred became more focused and intense.

"Yes."

"I mean, he is important. He is the Duke of Saxe-Coburg and Gotha, one of the venerable houses in the German realm," Manfred explained.

"I know this, sir," Menzke replied.

"You do know that the Duke is also a grandchild of Queen Victoria of England?" Manfred asked.

"Vaguely, sir. I never thought about it much, to be honest," Menzke admitted.

"Well, he is also Charles Edward, Duke of Albany, in England," Manfred went on.

"Ah, I see," Menzke said as a candle lit in his brain.

"You see why I got this invitation to hunt here. The Royal House of England was the House of Saxe-Coburg and Gotha until they changed its name last month to the House of Windsor," Manfred explained.

"And?"

"So, our host the Duke made a decision to side with Germany during the war and not England," Manfred kept his analysis going.

"And?"

"What better way for the Central Office for Foreign Services to reinforce the war effort than to have a German war hero go hunting with a noble who decided to renounce his British loyalties for his German ones?" Manfred looked tired.

"Sir, can I get you something?" Menzke was concerned at the sudden shift in mood and mien of his Captain.

"Ah, no, Menzke, no," Manfred said quietly.

There it was, the injury again. Menzke could see his Captain decidedly wrung out.

After a moment's pause, Menzke began, "The war is difficult for everyone, sir."

"I know. It really is," Manfred looked at Menzke.

"Well, sir, it is a very nice estate. I wouldn't mind if it were mine," Menzke sounded rather like an idiot, but it was just what Manfred needed, as he erupted into a genuine laughter, the likes of which Menzke hadn't heard since before his Captain was injured.

"Good one, Menzke. And I have to admit, hunting is hunting. Yesterday in the Duke's forest on horseback was wonderful!" Manfred continued to chuckle at his orderly.

Manfred, though, was back in the present. He took his Albatros down gradually as he approached Schweidnitz.

Two days earlier, Manfred had received one of those dreaded wartime telegrams. His comrade and dear friend, Kurt Wolff was flying Manfred's Fokker in battle when he was killed. Manfred telephoned the Schwader upon receiving the message. It turns out that his comrade had taken Manfred's Fokker up late in the afternoon in a duo with Lieutenant Carl von

Schoenebeck who was in an Albatros D.V. They encountered a squad of British Airco DH-4 bombers escorted by a group of Sopwith Camels. Some of the Camels split off to chase a squad of lower flying German Albatroses, while some remained to protect the bombers.

Wolff and Schoenebeck dove out of the afternoon sun as this British bomber group was trying to get home. They were outnumbered, but were undaunted because they had the element of surprise, especially coming out of the sun. Wolff pulled in on one of the Camels, but another was only a stone's throw away when it pumped the Fokker full of .303 Enfield bullets. Schoenebeck reported that Wolff went straight down, crashed and went up in flames.

Manfred had already sent Menzke ahead to get things arranged for his arrival in Schweidnitz, so he was alone when he got the telegram and made the telephone call to get the details of Wolff's death. All he remembered was that he went numb and then dropped to his knees, where he put his head in his hands and wept. Only twenty-two, Wolff would never again challenge Manfred with a flippant remark or energize the room with his light demeanor.

Manfred leveled his Albatros off at a safe three hundred feet as he went into Schweidnitz.

Since the town knew of his impending arrival, Manfred flew low over the rooftops waggling his wings to wave to his hometown citizens. Cheers went up, women waved handkerchiefs, men waved their arms and children jumped up and down. Manfred turned the plane into the gentle wind in order to take his red Albatros down onto the sport field just across town- from his home.

Lower and lower he went until he cut the engine and pulled back on his controls. His Albatros touched the earth of his hometown and rolled across the gentle grass of the sport field. Manfred turned and taxied to the other end, where his family, friends and townsfolk awaited him.

Menzke climbed up to help Manfred unstrap, "Good evening, sir!"

"Ah, Menzke—thank you for being here!" Manfred was elated, despite his headache.

Manfred stood up, waved to the crowd and climbed out of his red machine. People applauded, children waved flags and his family beamed to see him actually stand, move and wave.

"Hello, Ilse," Manfred hugged his sister who had run up to be the first.

"You look better than I expected," Ilse chuckled at her younger brother.

Manfred snapped the rubber bands under his chin, "These are much better than the bandage, I'll say!"

Manfred hugged his mother and was held by all his family.

"My baggage is here, I assume?" Manfred asked. Menzke nodded in the affirmative.

A few people patted Manfred on the back, but the usual German restraint held and the crowd let Manfred move toward the family car for the brief ride home.

"You going to drive, Lothar?" Manfred smiled at his brother.

"We are in the company of the woman of our house, dear brother," Lothar laughed.

"I was afraid of that," Manfred thought it was wonderful to be with his family.

"Let me drive. This is not an Albatros. Do you know what I mean?" Ilse smirked at her younger brother

"That's how it's going to be?" Manfred shot back

"You're the war hero, but I'm a better driver," Ilse winked at Bolko. Mamma and Papa laughed as they got in the car.

Manfred was home. He was with his family. Although never senti-mental, he felt a warmth and ease fill his person as Ilse began to drive the family to their modest estate. This was, though, short lived, as they passed a crippled veteran—missing his lower left leg and right arm—in ragged clothes sitting on a street corner with a cup in hand. Although the family saw through this fellow, Manfred was riveted and now reliving some of the horrors of his first night in the field hospital.

Chapter Twenty-One

The next morning came too soon. Manfred had the best sleep he'd had since his injury. The family was up, robes over nightgowns, sitting at the table in the dining room. Ilse had pulled her hair up in a makeshift bun held in place with one large barrette. Bolko was as unkempt as one would expect a young teenager to be when he was unhappy about being rousted before he felt it was necessary. Lothar, clean shaven with a sporting outfit on, had already been up. He had taken a walk down the street simply because he could now that his hip was nearly healed.

"We have acorn coffee, dears," Mamma smiled to Ilse, Manfred and Lothar.

"It's an experience everyone should   suffer through," Papa Albrecht said as he was reading the *Vossische Zeitung* with his hair tousled, slippers off under the table and robe not on squarely..

"No, Papa. It's an experience even the British shouldn't have to suffer," young Bolko cracked as he grabbed a cracker to spread a small amount of butter on it.

"I do have a surprise. I forgot about it last night in all the excitement, but I have this," Manfred, unshaven in only his nightshirt under a very elegant purple robe, held up a bag of coffee. "It's a half kilo that Duke Carl Eduard gave me just before I left."

Kunigunde, elegant in her matching robe, slippers and babushka, made a simple gesture and one of the servants took the bag to the kitchen.

"So, this morning, we break our fast in the manner of those in the royal household," Lothar nodded to his older brother.

Everyone smiled at this. Lothar added, "Papa, can I have *Aunt Voss* when you've finished reading her?"

Papa ignored him and grunted a bit.

The servant brought out six cups of coffee, one of which she set in front of each family member. The deep aroma of genuine coffee filled the dining room, with everyone taking a moment as if it were some form of Tibetan meditation.

"Almost as nice as the air on a hunt just before dawn," Manfred smiled.

"So, young warrior, how is your head?" Papa asked as he folded the newspaper, put it down and slid it over to Ilse while looking at Lothar, who scrunched up his nose.

"And what is this about your mysterious nurse? What's her name, Käte?" Ilse slyly smiled at Manfred, hoping that the rest of the family would get in on the fun.

"Some of the girls in town have asked if you are married," Bolko feigned innocence as he told Manfred this. "Are you engaged? Or still available?"

Manfred took a sip of coffee and reveled in the mix of taste and scent as he thought about answers to all these questions. He tipped his head up at the ceiling as if spying some distant peak in the Alps. Yes, he thought, family. Finally, he composed his answer.

"I might have expected such harshness if I'd been captured by the Bolsheviks on the Russian front," Manfred began in feigned seriousness. Secretly, he was delighted to have this moment of light-hearted fun with his family.

Before he could continue, Menzke appeared at the door of the dining room with a knock on the door jamb, "Sir, sorry to interrupt."

"Yes, Menzke—by the way, get some coffee. It's the real thing, blessed by royals, sort of," Manfred held up his cup to show him.

"Very good, sir," Menzke replied with a smile.

"What is it?" Manfred asked.

"The Albatros, sir. Just checked everything. She is safe. Fuel is topped off, oil is fine and the canvas is in place to keep the vitals dry. Perhaps I see a rain cloud on the horizon," Menzke reported.

"Excellent. Do you see this fellow, everyone? This is what an orderly is supposed to be," Manfred lifted his coffee cup to Menzke, who bowed slightly to acknowledge the praise.

"Thank you, sir," Menzke turned to go to the kitchen.

"Needless to say, *Old Man*, you've got some explaining to do. We've lined up that whole series of questions for you to pick off as if you were sniping at the target range. That is, if you're up to the task," Lothar looked Manfred in the eye, while Ilse hid a smile behind her napkin.

"Let me think this over while I have an egg and toast with a very little—my goodness—very little butter," Manfred said as he looked at the tiny piece of butter that was to serve all six of them at the table.

"Real coffee, just a tiny bit of real butter," Mamma smiled.

Manfred took a bite of toast along with another sip of his coffee. Then, he began to answer the queries about his purported romance with Käte, "Ilse?"

"Yes?"

"I have even more respect for what you do as a nurse," Manfred began what was a much more serious answer than his family had expected.

"Oh? It's nice that someone notices," Ilse looked at Manfred seriously.

"The image of the field hospital is still in the front of my mind," Manfred began to explain.

"Is this something we should talk about at the table?" Lothar asked as he moved his eyes toward Bolko to make Manfred consider what he was about to say.

"Very well, dear brother," Manfred paused, then changed to a much lighter response. "Käte Otersdorf is quite a beautiful woman."

Everyone in the family leaned forward to hear Manfred finish what he began.

"But, to be honest, she was simply taking care of me. Romance was far from my mind. The newspapers are crazy," Manfred continued to explain.

"I suspected this, son," Papa replied. "I didn't show it, but I thought you were finished when I heard what had happened. Even after I saw you in Courtrai—well, let me just say, I've seen head wounds go from bad to worse, and then from worse to the worst, the end."

"I've had procedures done now—let me think—five times. The wound is open, but not infected," Manfred was telling what he'd been through.

Everyone tried to be casual about it, but each family member was internally bemoaning how Manfred looked. His posture was different, while his movements were a little studied as Manfred seemed to protect the back of his head. His face would transform right before their eyes. Ashen one moment, then Manfred would look almost like his old self.

"Headaches, nausea?" Ilse was experienced in this sort of thing and knew what the long term symptoms were.

"Yes, for certain. But, not enough to keep me from flying. I had my sixty-first victory just two weeks ago," Manfred wanted to convince everyone he was fit both to fly and to command.

"Sixty-one, eh?" Papa commented.

"A Tommie. I chased him onto the ground. Captured. Anthony Fokker took moving pictures," Manfred smiled.

"So, he's a prisoner of war?" Bolko asked.

"Yes, sent to this new place, Holzminden," Manfred began to explain.

Papa looked at him and said "no" with his eyes, then he added, "There is a civilian camp there. Ten thousand French citizens."

The table became momentarily silent, but Manfred picked up the pace again, "I am fit to fly. As I said, Number Sixty-One."

Everyone just looked at him.

"They've sent me on leave, which is not necessarily a bad thing. But I have to tell you that I want to get back and help Jageschwader 1. There's a war on and Germany needs her young men," Manfred was self-conscious, maybe even a little embarrassed, as he was rambling, not at all like him. But, he decided to look committed as he took a definitive bite into his toast and then swigged down the last sip of coffee in his cup.

"Sorry to hear about Wolff, Manfred," Lothar changed the subject.

"Yes, quite the warrior. You never would have guessed it from his de-meanor. Looked like a poet or artist," Manfred held his hands in prayer as he said this.

"Sense of humor, too," Mamma added.

"Such irreverence—ah, he made us laugh!" Manfred laughed and, at the same time, wiped a tear from his eye.

"To change the subject, what are we to do today?" Ilse asked.

"Perhaps nothing," Papa suggested and Mamma nodded in agree-ment.

"It would be nice just to have tea, take in the sun—maybe some cro-quet," Mamma stood up and headed for the kitchen.

"Stealing more coffee?" Manfred quipped.

"It's my kitchen, *Old Man!*" She retorted as everyone laughed.

"What does Käte look like?" Bolko asked.

"Very beautiful. Brunette. Nice figure," Manfred was amused at his teenage little brother.

"Maybe too old for me," Bolko went back to sipping the last bit of his coffee.

"I'm sure. Besides, she's independent. No guarantee she would go for you," Manfred said off-handedly as he tried to reach for *Aunt Voss*, but Ilse kept it away.

"This is a trend I see developing," Papa answered while turning his eye on Bolko. "Women are becoming more independent."

"It's about time," Ilse said as she opened the paper.

"By the way, Manfred," Mamma said as she sat back down at the table.

"Yes?"

"People knew you were coming over and they gave me Sanke Cards for you to sign," Mamma pointed to cards on the sideboard.

"Not too many. Shouldn't be a problem," Manfred got up to get them.

"You know, Frau Schmidt—you know her," Mamma said.

"Yes."

"She left fifteen cards," Mamma explained.

Manfred picked them up and shuffled through them. I grabbed a pen from the bureau in the corner and sat back down to sign them.

"Fifteen? Well, she gets none. This is a war profiteer — makes me sick," Manfred sounded irked, but started to sign the cards.

Everyone looked at him, since his mood went so quickly from cheery to surly. Ilse was the first to speak.

"I'm going in to town. Just a short walk. Maybe someone can come along? Manfred?" Ilse asked.

Manfred ignored Ilse, as if he hadn't heard her. Everyone took notice, for this was unusual.

"Manfred?"

Still no reaction.

"Manfred? Do you want to come to town with me? A nice little walk?" Ilse persisted, but gently, as she lowered her voice.

Ah, no," as he kept signing cards, impervious to anything for the moment. "Too many things to do, Ilse. I'm busy!"

*   *   *

"So, Bolko is competitive, as you can see," Mamma said to Manfred just before lunch as she stood on the patio with Manfred while the two of them watched Bolko, Ilse and Lothar play croquet. Papa had gone into town, Menzke had promised Manfred he would take his   Captain's 1903 Mannlicher-Schönauer into the local gunsmith to have the trigger checked since Manfred remembered the last time he shot it, its pull had become inconsistent.

"It's normal in our family," Manfred smiled.

"Yes, competitive people do new things all the time," Mamma said.

"I never thought I would write a book," Manfred began.

"Interesting, isn't it?"

"By the way, the publisher, Ullstein, is sending Heidi back to take a few more notes to finish my *The Red Battle Flyer*," Manfred smiled.

"When is that?" Mamma wondered.

"She arriving tomorrow for a few days, staying at the hotel in town," Manfred leaned against the door jamb with one arm.

"Hmm...she's very pretty, if I remember," Mamma smiled.

"I remember — and yes, she is," Manfred looked at his mother.

They both broke out into laughter.

"I need you to help me in the salon. Some paintings need a little straightening," Mamma said as she took Manfred by arm and walked him into the salon.

"Yes, this is what sons are for, I imagine," Manfred smiled at his mother.

Kunigunde stopped and looked Manfred in the eye, "Tell me what happened, dear."

"What happened where?" Manfred asked.

"*Up there*," Mamma replied. "I want to know what happened to my son."

"I got hit. Not sure how," Manfred returned her gaze.

"Any idea?"

"Ground fire maybe, but I was up pretty high. Maybe even friendly fire—an accident," Manfred added.

"I've been worried sick," Mamma admitted.

"I understand. But, I'm almost back," Manfred smiled.

"Maybe you should quit flying," Mamma was very serious. "I mean it."

"What do you mean? If everyone were to quit when it's a struggle, tell me, Mamma: who would be left to fight?" Manfred was getting intense.

"I'm serious," Mamma relied firmly.

"We'd end up like Russia. Chaos everywhere!" Manfred was fixed and very serious.

"A lot of soldiers get relief—time away—you fight way *up there* all the time—every day!" Mamma pointed up to the sky as she spoke.

"I'm not one to do this just for the glory. There's real work to do here. I have more to get done!" Manfred was intense and focused. His eyes had a different tenacity, one that unsettled his mother. This look in his eye was new to her.

"You worry me, Manfred," Mamma said.

Manfred snapped out of it, shook his head and said, "I'm sorry. I feel confused. I don't know how I feel. "

*   *   *

After lunch, Manfred complained of a headache, so he went up to put his head down for a while. It was a restive, not restful nap. His yelling dream came, with the background of his half-asleep, half-awake consciousness filled with people screaming at him as he walked along that road with the jagged rocks.

"He really needs some rest, Mamma," Ilse began as she sipped some acorn coffee in the salon on the floor below Manfred's disquieting rest.

"Yes, but he's different, you know," Mamma responded. "In a deep, good way."

Kunigunde had seen that her son Manfred had grown. He was no longer the cadet turned soldier turned national hero. He had transformed himself into something deeper, one who had taken on major responsibilities to care for those who needed help, be they his family — with his autobiography to provide them income for the future — or his men — with him wanting to get back into battle as their leader and protector. Manfred wanted nothing in return. Rather, he did these things because he saw that he was the only person to fulfill these needs.

"He's got a new approach to things. Deeper, He's very moral," Kunigunde said to Ilse.

"Yes, I sense this, too, Mamma," Ilse turned her head toward the front of the house in response to singing that she heard.

"It's another school choir come to serenade Manfred," Mamma shook her head.

Albrecht came into the salon, "I'll wake Manfred. He ought to acknowledge them. You two greet them from the front porch."

Mamma and Ilse went to the front porch. They met the choir, which consisted of young school children dressed in their school uniforms, singing a song under the direction of their choirmaster. They each smiled and waved.

"This is lovely," Ilse whispered into her Mamma's ear.

Manfred appeared behind them, then stepped to the side. The school children stopped singing and broke into an applause when they recognized him. Manfred, though, was not pleased. He had a hard and rugged look on his face, with his eyes intense and fixed in cold concentration.

"No one understands," he began what was going to boil over into a tirade.

Everyone stopped dumb.

"I pass over the trenches. The soldiers stand for me with their eyes fixed on my airplane. Then, they clap and roar. We look into each other's eyes, them and me! There they are: filthy, ragged, ashen faces gaunt with hunger and no sleep. But we are one, as brothers and I am happy. They stand up, unafraid as the battle rages, and wave to me. This, Mamma, is my best prize, the men cheering me," Manfred said this last part as he held the Blue Max hanging just under his chin.

Chapter Twenty-Two

Up in the sky in his Albatros, Manfred had time to think.

By now, there were 125,000 casualties due to the Entente action at Ypres. He took his Albatros up higher over some clouds, thinking to himself, if he needed anything, he needed time away from everything and, conversely, he needed to get back to help Jageschwader 1.

With his recent appearances at a couple of cadet schools — to be seen and speak and be written about in the newspapers — the vacation part of his leave hadn't really happened. His time away wasn't really a vacation. There was the good time he spent at home in the family study with Ullstein's representative who was sent to help him finish his autobiography, *The Red Battle Flyer*. And, Heidi was well worth it. He even felt a budding romance there. He kissed her and she kissed him back. He wasn't sure there was an interest there or not. She used her coquettishness to keep him focused on finishing his book. He admitted to himself that he enjoyed walking her back to the Hotel Crown as the sun set on Schweidnitz. Yes, she was beautiful and engaging.

As Manfred approached Ottau bei Marienwerder, he saw a single flag on the local castle. He hoped this was a portent of good news, that there would be no crowd to greet him, that he could be, for this hunting trip, alone.

But, even those sweet moments with a beautiful young woman were not nearly enough. Werner Voss, all of twenty years old, was killed in action on the 23rd of the month. The details were still unknown, but Voss had gone up with one other flier late in the day, where he engaged seven British S.E.5s alone for ten minutes. Unknown at this time by the Germans, Voss had damaged each British plane with a stunning array of flying skill and combat tenacity. It was, indeed, an air battle for the ages, with Voss flying most of the time upside down, at odd angles, diving, climbing — to be sure, demonstrating his mastery of the art of battle flying. Voss was his own man, abrupt to many, irreverent to others, but Manfred liked and respected him — a genuine peer he could relate to.

Manfred brought the Albatros around just to make sure he knew the landing area and the wind direction.

As he looked over the small hamlet, he was relieved to see that there were no crowds. Indeed, Albert Mohnicke, the father of his Jasta 11 comrade Eberhard Mohnicke and the Forester of the Neu-Sternberg Forest Preserve, had understood what Manfred meant when he said he wanted privacy.

He decided to circle one more time.

Yes, hunting would help, even though his head was throbbing from the flight and his nausea was periodically making him feel as if he would mess all over his Spartan cockpit. The forest was part of a larger area, a prized place in East Prussia known as the Rominter Heath. The Kaiser built a hunting lodge here. It was a pristine forest with rolling hills of pine and spruce interspersed with meadows.

Just before he was to make his descent onto the field where he saw a small group of locals there to greet him, Manfred recalled that the war had reached this far into Germany in 1914. Less than one hundred kilometers from here had been the Abschwangen Massacre.

At the start of the war, the Russians, that time still under the Czar, pushed quickly into East Prussia. When they came upon the small village of Abschwangen, they passed on through. A few days later a German scouting party confronted a Russian vehicle and shot it up. Shortly after, the Russians came to the village and massacred a large number of male citizens. Of course, by now in late 1917, the Russians were pushed well back into their own country, but Manfred thought about the fact that the war, in all its manifestations, had reached deep into everyone.

Manfred took the Albatros down and down, soon to touch the ground, bounce and stabilize itself as he slowed. He taxied over to the small group of people at the edge of the field.

"Ah, Captain, it is my pleasure to meet you," Albert Mohnicke shouted as Manfred shut off the Mercedes engine. His greeting was accompanied by waves and smiles from the eight or so people who stood behind him.

Manfred undid his buckles, climbed out of the plane and reached out with his hand, "Hello, Mister Forester Albert Mohnicke. Captain Manfred von Richthofen."

Albert motioned to one of his assistants, who went up on the wing to get Manfred's pack and rifle.

Manfred noticed that he had a horse drawn carriage while the others had come on horseback.

"It is 1917 in the modern age and here we are with horses," Manfred smiled.

"Yes, we made sure to save the fuel for your airplane. You know, this is my first time up close to one," Albert admitted. Others in the group nodded in agreement.

Whatever it was, these simple village people put Manfred at ease. Although they didn't go completely away, his headache and nausea subsided enough for him to reply, "Let me show everyone the Albatros."

The people came and walked around the airplane. At first, they were afraid to touch it, but Manfred walked around telling each of them what the various parts were and what they did. They were impressed with the stretched material cover that enclosed the wings and fuselage, with several of them commenting on the red color.

Manfred got into the plane to show them how he actually maneuvered the plane.

"So, these are the rudders that let me turn left or right," he began his explanation.

The crowd was suitably mesmerized by this piece of modern technology.

"And these are the elevators that let me get up or go down. I have flown as high as five thousand meters," Manfred went on. "It is very cold. I wear winter clothes at that altitude."

"Ah," went the group.

"These are the ailerons," Manfred waggled them up and down on the front wings. "These let me tip the plane so I can turn or roll or even spin."

"Complicated," a voice from the group shouted.

Manfred replied with a chuckle, "I never thought of it that way!"

*   *   *

Dinner the night before was a welcome change from the black bread based meals Manfred was used to back in Markebeeke. First, there was a leek soup made from wild leeks found in a meadow between the large stands of trees that mixed in over the rolling hills of the forest preserve. There were green beans from Albert's private garden, along with wild greens taken from the fields. Albert and his wife were outdoorspeople *par excellence*, as they had made a stew from wild smoked boar, lentils and carrots. Albert apologized about the makeshift nature of the meal, but Manfred was glad to eat some meat, get some   fresh vegetables and actually have enough to make his belly bulge out. The spruce tea as a palate cleaner was a first for Manfred, something he appreciated at meal's end.

The night was peaceful, with the only sounds coming from the nearby woods, with the occasional hoot of an owl or baying of a wolf. Manfred fell asleep quickly, but was slightly restless as he was excited to go hunting. Manfred stirred and stretched in his bed. He laid there awake just before dawn. He kicked his legs up, swung himself up and sideways, and sauntered to the privy. A quick shave, some cold water splashed on his face and a quick wipe of the cold washcloth over his body made him feel zesty and alive. His head didn't hurt this morning and his stomach felt fine.

Manfred put on fresh underwear, pulled on wool socks and then pulled up his dark brown leather hunting pants. Before he put on his undershirt, shirt and tie, he made sure to tuck his hunting knife into the side pocket of his pants, along with two heavy duty workman's kerchiefs, one in each pants pocket. As he tied his tie, he realized that he was going to hunt alone, which had him both excited and mentally centered. He put on his loden green wool hunting jacket, buttoned it up, checked his lapels and put his binoculars on. He didn't put his hunting hat on, but rather decided, since he was going to have some breakfast, to leave it in the gun rack on top of his barrel in the small dining room in Albert's small forester's lodge.

"Do you like the Mannlicher-Schönauer?" Manfred heard Albert's voice behind him as he was sitting down to a preset table with a roll, some butter and a cup of porridge.

"Very much," Manfred began as he stood back up to shake Albert's hand and nod a greeting to Albert's wife, who, shy, was making some acorn coffee.

Albert sat across the table from Manfred, "I am sold on modern technology."

"Me, too," Manfred said with a mouthful of porridge. "Forgive my manners, but the food here is …"

"…yes, everyone says that," Albert laughed as he finished Manfred's thought for him.

"The Mannlicher-Schönauer is a beautiful weapon. Very smooth action. I just had my gunsmith check it, as the trigger pull was inconsistent."

"What was it?" Albert wondered."

"He smoothed the sear. Found a rough spot. He also trimmed a spring to lighten the pull a half kilo," Manfred explained.

Albert nodded, "Anyway, I like the modern technology. It's better, but a number of hunters come here with their drillings."

"Yes, the two shotgun barrels on top of a single one shot rifle barrel. We have a few at home. A good weapon, but my Mannlicher-Schönauer — it's simply wonderful. —and, much better as a rifle."

"You are on your own this morning, as you requested. I will blow the hunt horn in a few minutes. Once we hear shots, we'll bring the cart to bring your quarry back," Albert explained.

Manfred nodded, barely able to contain his excitement. He put on his hat, grabbed his rifle, centered his binoculars and checked his ammo pouch. He had a dozen rounds, with his Mannlicher having three in the clip. He checked his safety, shouldered his sling and headed off into the woods.

It was a typical East Prussian autumn morning. Clouds, which Manfred thought — at times — should be Germany's national symbol, were light and flowing, but heavy enough to keep the air grey and the sun something of a distant relative. The air was crisp, but not cold enough to see your breath.

As he left the lodge area, Manfred headed out on the path that Albert had suggested. He walked down a dirt road for about one hundred meters and then veered off up into a large stand of trees. Manfred felt his breath as walked up the gentle rise into the trees. He realized that his conditioning had declined while recuperating from his injury, a wound that prevented him from being physically active in any serious way. By the time he was in the middle of the tree stand, Manfred was taking some deep breaths to catch his wind. He stopped and looked up.

The sun came out momentarily and cast beams of light down to the ground. Manfred looked down and took several deep breaths as he scrunched the pine needles that covered the canopy's floor. He stared at the moss on the trees and noted the ferns here and there. He then looked up where his attention was caught by a raptor he could see through a large opening in the branches. Its wings were out as it soared in a large curve into the westerly wind. Other than that one bit of wildlife, Manfred saw little wild life, as he expected in an evergreen forest.

Manfred began to walk again toward the summit of the rise. As he reached the top, he took his binoculars to look down through the trees of the east side of the hill. He imagined he would find no elk or deer here, but expected to find a spot on the edge of a meadow where he would hope they might stumble by. Walking downhill, his legs loosened, his breath became more balanced and his confidence came back. He stopped, unshouldered his Mannlicher, wrapped his left arm in the sling and took mock aim. His hold, which he hadn't practiced in few weeks, was surprisingly steady. Well, he expected it was good enough to let him hit whatever he aimed at!

The large stand of trees and the hill gave way at the bottom to an open meadow that was dotted with the occasional larch. The autumn grasses were still predominately green, but some of it was browning as summer was now well past. His boots were covered in dew, as were the damp bottoms of his waterproof leather pants. A large branch looked just about right, so Manfred picked it up, took his deer horn knife to hack, cut and carve it into a walking stick. By the time he finished, he realized that a doe and two nearly grown fawns came out of the wood on the far side of the meadow. They took one look at Manfred and disappeared from whence they came.

Manfred walked across the meadow to where he thought he spied a trail into the next stand of trees. He was wrong, but saw that it was a drainage rivulet formed by the regular rains in this part of East Prussia. It descended from a much larger hill—really a small mountain—that Manfred decided to avoid by walking around its large base—a path dotted with trees, brush and some open grass covered areas on the edge of the large mountain to his left and a smaller wood covered hill to his right.

After a while, Manfred sat on a large flat rock. He looked at his pocket watch. He'd been out for two hours already, even though it seemed like just fifteen minutes. Maybe he'd find no game, but at least he had time to get some much needed hiking that was helping him to clear his mind. Kurt and Werner were gone, the Entente was pressing hard at Ypres, British fliers were beginning to assert their continual presence in the skies above Belgium—all this faded away as Manfred got up to walk a little further.

Step after step, Manfred entertained speculation about what he'd do after the war. He decided that he could not be a commercial pilot. Passengers, packages and mail just didn't suit his temperament. He laughed out loud when he realized that if Werner were a commercial pilot, he might throw his passengers from the plane! He envisioned Lothar better suited to this, but perhaps more able to share a drink or two with the passengers than focusing on actually taking off with the intent of getting to the planned destination. Yes, he thought, Lothar had a side that only he really saw, since he hid it well from Mamma and Papa. Lothar had a social ease about him that could easily turn into the love of easy times.

Manfred could see himself as a big game guide to Africa, even though he'd never been there. Maybe even a forester, like his host, Albert Mohnicke. The Richthofen family was aristocratic, but that title brought neither self-sustaining landholdings nor wealth in the form of securities or cash. That was why he consented to write his autobiography for Ullstein. He knew it would sell, which, in case of his death, would provide for his family. Perhaps there will be another book after the war, but Manfred could not see himself working for business — unless, of course, it was for Anthony Fokker in airplane development. Now that was an idea!

Marriage? After the war, certainly a possibility. It distressed Manfred that he'd have to break through that national hero thing in order to find someone who would love him for who he really was. What with all the fan mail addressed simply to "MvR, Schweidnitz," he knew that he might have to wait a year or two for the fervor to die off. Manfred did not relish life in the limelight of public celebrity — and he genuinely didn't want to raise children in such an environment. But, he mused, she would have to be beautiful and love being outdoors!

Manfred figured by now he'd covered eight or nine kilometers. It was now past eleven, with the sun overhead, if the clouds would permit. Manfred spied the edge of a large flat rock ahead, one that was covered in brush, downwind and flat enough for him to sit or even lay on. After he got to it, he cut down a few branches to give himself a clear view across the large field that went for two hundred meters to the other hill at its far side.

At this point, Manfred was hungry. He was about to take out a piece of bread he'd wrapped in paper, along with small piece of cheese that Albert's wife had handed him with a smile. Instead, he looked across the meadow, where he saw a large stag, a beautiful elk with large spatula horns, a rack that would make any trophy hunter proud. Only this, in these times of famine and shortages everywhere, was no trophy hunt. Any bit of meat you could find was essential for survival.

Manfred was seated, so he dare not draw any attention with unessential movement. He undid his safety, quietly chambered a round by cycling his bolt and wrapped his left arm into his sling. A quick turn of his sight to bring things into focus and he was now pulling in on the elk, which was unaware of his presence. The elk, a browser was nibbling at some branches of large shrubs. After a moment, he turned sideways, which gave Manfred the perfect moment to aim at the rear center of the elk's shoulder. A gentle squeeze and the elk went down right where he stood! The report echoed through the mountains. Manfred was up. He broke off a branch and stuck it in the ground it in front of the rock where he had fired. He took his new-found walking stick and headed across the meadow. He thought his shot was about one hundred and seventy meters. Not too bad for a wounded warrior. He even ignored the throbbing headache begun by the concussion from his Mannlicher. There would be elk on the table tonight.

As he sauntered toward his dead quarry, Manfred noted exactly where the elk was in relation to the mountains and meadow. When he got to it, he realized that this had been one great month for hunting. To date, he'd taken a ram, three large deer and this elk. Manfred broke off a small branch, which he placed as *the last bite* in the elk's mouth. He broke off a larger one, which he put on the elk's abdomen. His instinct was to field dress it to cool off the meat. His knife was good enough that he could cut from the stag's anus to his breastplate, thereby releasing   everything in its   the abdominal cavity. Then, it was a matter of skinning and quartering the beast into pieces he could pack and carry. But, there was no way he could dress the animal and carry it back to the lodge. It was too large and he had no pack. Instead, he once again took note of where he was and headed back to get the wagon.

Once he reached the edge of the field, he chose his return the way he had initially came through the narrow valley between two mountains. He was winded, but elated, so he pressed on. After thirty minutes, he was relieved to see Albert and two grooms coming in the wagon pulled by two horses.

"Hello, Albert! We have success!" Manfred shouted.

"Yes, we headed out this way even before   we heard your shot. My wife—well, she sees in her mind's eye and told us we would have elk tonight!" Albert replied as the two grooms saluted Manfred and shouted, "Good work, Captain!"

They got to the elk in about twenty minutes. Manfred sat on the front seat alongside Albert. The groom sat in the back doddering on about Manfred's one hundred and seventy meter shot—one shot for a clean quick kill. It took all four of them to get the elk into the wagon. It was more than an hour-and-a-half to get back to the lodge. By then it was late afternoon.

"Before we do anything, let us get the branches," Albert, Manfred and the two grooms each cut branches from nearby trees. They laid them on the ground, then lifted the elk from the wagon and set it on them. Manfred set one branch on the elk's abdomen, while Albert set one in its mouth as *the last bite.* One of the grooms took a twig, bloodied it from the wound and dabbed a little blood on Manfred's hat. Albert said something about honoring nature, then blew his horn to signify the end of the hunt.

"Thank you all for your help," Manfred said.

"Let us get a picture, Captain," Albert said as he took out a camera from his bag. Manfred stood behind the elk in his leather pants, loden green coat and hat with binoculars around his neck He put his hands in his pockets.

"You look like a hunter, Captain," Albert smiled. His wife came out to see all the commotion.

"Good eating tonight," she laughed when she saw the elk.

"What camera is that?" Manfred wondered as he tipped his hat to the lady.

"A Nettel Piccolette — very nice, easy to handle," Albert was trying to frame the picture and focus while he talked.

Having heard the horn, a few villagers came by to see if they could get some meat once the elk was dressed.

"Small camera. I like that," Manfred looked into the lens.

"Very good, Captain. Can I invite you to help us dress the animal? We'll give the kidneys and liver to my friends who've come by," Albert said as he put the camera back in his bag and nodded to the villagers.

"Nice to share, I think," Manfred answered. "No trophy animals these days. Strictly for eating, eh, Albert?"

"I dare say."

Chapter Twenty-Three

"Another cup of tea, Captain Baron?" The waiter in the restaurant of the Hôtel Continental asked Manfred as he sat in a table at the end of the long Baroque interior.

There was no response. Manfred was elsewhere.

"Sir, more tea, another cake or some cookies?" The waiter asked again as he stepped into the middle of Manfred's field of vision.

"Oh, sorry. Just thinking. No, thank you," Manfred said as he took the final sip of tea in his cup.

Just before he came into the restaurant, Manfred stopped some flyers on his floor to mention that their jackets were unbuttoned, "You know, gentlemen, this is not proper."

Well lubricated, the flyers chuckled, but said nothing before they turned and entered the stairwell to make their escape.

Two other flyers stopped, stood at attention and saluted Manfred, "Good morning, Captain!"

"At ease, lieutenants. You are with?" Manfred asked.

"We are finishing flying training, sir," one of the men offered up.

"We need good men," Manfred began.

"Yessir!"

"You know, hunting in a Fokker or Albatros is only partly the machine. The airplane is small. It's advantage is that it is quick and excellent at turning. No real size to the airplane, you know. Really, just the bullets and machine guns."

"Sir!"

"It's the pilot, boys. The battle flyer that makes a difference. There is a war on. People are sacrificing. The famine. Men at the front. Unbelievable conditions. Nurses in the   hospitals working around the clock," Manfred was lecturing, but not yelling. Part of him was too tired to yell. "It's bad, gentleman. Germany needs you."

"Yessir," the men said in a much more subdued tone.

"Carry on," Manfred saluted them, wondering what he was doing here in Berlin.

As Manfred took the elevator to the lobby, alone in that tiny descending room, he felt odd. He wasn't sure, but everything seemed grotesque. The airplane manufacturers, the flyers, the available food and drink — it wasn't fair that they were here in this luxury hotel, yet not far from here were bread lines where people held signs of protest, "We need bread!"

And there were the invalids. Men missing parts of arms and legs, men blinded, men simply distorted from shell shock — all trying to make their way in the capital of the German Empire, which was turning a constant blind eye to the waste products of the war.

So, Manfred had come into the restaurant for a simple late-morning snack. As he sat alone, questions about the war boiled in his mind. And today of all days, he was upset about the conduct he saw at the hotel. It was a disappointment to him because of all the carrying on.

"No, thank you, Maurice," Manfred thanked his usual waiters at the restaurant. "I think I'll get out for a walk."

"Very good, sir. It is a wonderful day. I came down Friedrichstraße this morning from above the river where I live. Just a wonderful day. You'll enjoy it."

Manfred walked through the lobby, a place he enjoyed. Its eclectic mix of various furniture and décor made him feel at ease. As he exited, he turned south, crossed the street and caught the first side street to the east, which took him right to Friedrichstraße, where he turned right and continued south.

As Manfred walked, he was continually stopped by autograph seekers. To be more specific, he was asked to sign their Sanke Cards.

"Yes, you're welcome!" Manfred would smile time after time as he was thinking how tedious this had become. Just once, he thought, he'd like to say, "Everybody, leave me alone! I just want to be alone!"

Last night had been especially restive. The nightmares returned with a vengeance. He woke himself out of a rough sleep three or four times. After the second time, he turned the light on, tried to admire the Rococo décor of his suite and forced himself to stay awake simply to avoid having the dream again. There he would be, walking down the road covered in jagged stone, naked, authority figures yelling at him. The problem was, this dream was unresolvable. He wasn't sure what these people wanted, nor was he sure why he was so filled with a raw and overpowering guilt. But, it was enough to frighten him so that he did not want to go back to sleep. For several moments at the hotel, he seemed to confuse the grotesqueness of the dream with the ugly reality he saw with the flyers. At times, Manfred, then, was confused.

Now that he was on the street, he realized that not only did he need to escape the Hôtel Continental, he needed to escape everything!

The men—better, the boys—back at the hotel bothered him. He wondered, how could they be so irresponsible? And how could the people on the street be so happy when the war was not really going as planned?

He recalled as he came into Berlin several days earlier that there were protests about the famine. Signs read "We need bread!" and "We want coal!" These were simple enough messages, but no one here was listening. The cripples from the war, too, were too much to ignore. He thought he saw them in his dream. He wondered about these men who had given greatly for the war effort. Were they hoping to make a living by begging? Or had they given up, propped themselves up against a wall, where they sat as empty shells, despondent and hopeless?

Manfred had an inkling of fresh hope, though. His brothers were in regular contact, one happy with him, the other, rather humorously, wanting more. Lothar returned to command Jasta 11 a week earlier. He was in fine form, once again. By contrast, Bolko had wanted Manfred to come to his cadet school, but Manfred hadn't had the time. He wasn't so happy with big brother.

Nonetheless, Manfred was going to a place he just loved in Berlin. The intersection of Unter den Linden and Friedrichstraße was all that was alive about modern Berlin. As he reached it, Manfred paused to look around.

"Excuse me, Captain Baron von Richthofen, might you sign my card?" A young girl held out her card with a pencil.

"Of course," Manfred bowed his head slightly as a gentlemanly gesture of respect and signed her card.

"Oh, thank you, sir!" The girl simply beamed at Manfred, who felt that this was the sort of sincerity that was lacking back at the Hôtel Continental among the flyers.

Manfred took a deep breath, looked around and took in the vitality and vibrancy of the intersection. He saw the Café Bauer, the Café Kranzler and his favorite, the Victoria Café. He loved the architecture here, with many Germans saying that it eclipsed the classical facades of Paris, herself. Maybe not, noted Manfred, but it was still fabulous. Manfred looked up high on the Victoria Café building. There was the Stollwercke Chocolates sign. The hustle and bustle here was refreshing, Manfred thought. Why, there was every mode of transportation you could want. Horse and carriage, automobiles, streetcars, entrances to the subway and even omnibuses.

Manfred crossed Friedrichstraße so he could go to the Victoria Café. Several gentlemen tipped their hat while he crossed. He met their eyes with a slight bow of his head. He entered the Victoria.

"Sir, how many?"

"Just one, please," Manfred smiled.

"Very well. We have this seat right at the window, the view is always interesting here, Captain Baron," the waiter pulled a seat out for Manfred who sat down.

"I like this view. Very nice," Manfred said. His head was starting to act up, although his stomach was calm.

"Here is the menu, sir," the waiter smiled.

"No need. Hot chocolate and the anisettes," Manfred was looking forward to this.

"Here is today's *Aunt Voss*, while you wait," the waiter handed Manfred the latest copy of the *Vossisches Zeitung*.

"Thank you," Manfred looked at the newspaper while the waiter turned to put in his order.

"Let's see," Manfred said aloud to himself as he looked the paper over. "The Kaiser is still in charge. Russia is to the East, France and Belgium to the West."

An older couple at the next table overheard this and laughed. They recognized Manfred and were put at ease seeing that Manfred had a sense of humor and charm. Manfred smiled at them, "Let's get the basics right before we do anything else,"

They waved politely, "It is our honor, Captain."

"The honor is mine to serve, kind people," Manfred was always gracious.

They returned to themselves in order to let Manfred enjoy the hot chocolate the waiter brought to him. He loved the elegance of the Victoria, the street life of this intersection and chocolate, which was slightly bitter and sweet, the perfect dessert. He dipped one of the anisettes into his cup and took a bite. Certainly, he thought, this was better here, sitting alone, away from the juvenile flyers at the hotel. He was thinking about two days ago when he had gone to nearby Schwerin to see Anthony at the Fokker factory.

"So, how is the head, Manfred?" Anthony asked.

"I am here," Manfred answered.

"I can see that," Anthony looked carefully at Manfred's sunken eyes and thought that he seemed a little pale.

"Things at the front are heating up. They are pushing forward at Ypres, aiming, we are sure, for the ridges at Passchendaele," Manfred was quite serious.

"What is going on? You seem so serious," Anthony observed.

"Well, between us, the war is difficult. I think you understand that," Manfred began to tell Anthony some rather blunt things.

"Well, let's walk through the factory here. No one can hear us. The men are too busy. Tell me your thoughts," Anthony offered.

"I'd prefer to talk in complete privacy, Anthony," Manfred countered.

"This is fine. My office, then," Anthony offered.

"By the way, how've you been?" Manfred asked.

"Busy. Little time for sleep. The government has forced me into a co-operating with Junkers," Anthony began to complain.

"So, you have to work with Hugo, eh?" Manfred asked.

"Can't stand the guy. I prefer to work on my own," Anthony was forcefully blunt as the entered his office. Manfred refused a chair and didn't want a drink, "Whatever it is, Manfred. Share your thoughts with me. You know we can be discreet with each other."

"You know, this all metal plane, the Junkers J1, it's …"

"Yes, yes, yes! I know it's a big advance — a step forward," Anthony interrupted tartly as he was getting impatient talking about Hugo Junkers and his forced business marriage to his company.

"It's heavy, I've heard," Manfred said quietly.

"If we could use aluminum in sheets, which we can't yet do, it would be a superb plane," "Anthony poured himself a drink. "Scotch, Manfred? The real thing."

Manfred laughed out loud, "You're so cosmopolitan, Anthony."

Anthony took a healthy swig. Looked Manfred in the eye and laughed. "Tell me what's on your mind, friend," Anthony was finally settled.

"So, the plane is not enough," Manfred laid it out right on the table.

"You've had victories in it," Anthony rebutted.

"Yes. But we're short on power. Maybe too much drag from three wings?" Manfred had a thought.

"No doubt, but speed is traded off for maneuverability," Anthony explained.

"And rate of climb?" Manfred asked.
"Certainly," Anthony took another sip.

"I understand — and you've done well on short notice. But, this is not abstract design. We have to fly these against the British in combat," Manfred explained.

"I appreciate that, Manfred. I do understand. Real men, real lives. The survival of Germany," Anthony was serious.

"We need more speed with the same quick abilities," Manfred smiled at his friend. "You are a talented fellow, Anthony. I have faith in you. You'll figure it out."

Anthony shook Manfred's hand, "Thank you, Manfred. From you that means everything. I don't get many compliments these days. And Ludendorff, well …"

"Yes, Ludendorff," Manfred raised his eyes to the ceiling of Anthony's office.

"Captain, can I get you anything else?" The waiter at the Victoria interrupted Manfred's chain of thought as Manfred was actually looking up at the decorative ceiling of the Victoria.

"Ah, just day dreaming. The afternoon, you know," Manfred tried to recover his senses.

"It is nearly five o'clock, Captain. You've been here a while," the waiter explained.

"Oh, well, I would like to buy some Stollwerck Chocolates and have them sent to my home, to my mother and sister," Manfred explained.

"Yes, sir. Small, medium or large?"

"Large to this address in Schweidnitz," Manfred handed the waiter his card. "Here are the Marks to cover that and the rest for you."

"Thank you, sir! Very generous," the waiter beamed.

Manfred walked back to the Hôtel Continental. It was not yet dark, but the streets darker than earlier as the sun was low in the sky and the buildings cast dark shadows everywhere. It was still Berlin, though. Busy, busy, busy. People were hurrying home for dinner. When Manfred entered the lobby, he saw the mother of an old friend from Schweidnitz.

"Dear boy, please have dinner with us," Frau Schmidt asked.

"I will be there," Manfred replied as he went up to his room to freshen up. He shaved again, took a quick bath and dressed for dinner. He put on his dress uniform and went down to the restaurant.

Everyone turned to look at Manfred as he entered the archway of the restaurant. He cut a fine figure with his dress uniform. Woman loved his chiseled face. He looked every bit the Prussian warrior and national hero. A few youngsters came up to Manfred, smiled and held out their Sanke Cards, which he consented to sign with just a nod of his head. Frau Schmidt noticed that Manfred was much more serious than usual.

Manfred, by contrast, was irritated that there was an air of frivolity throughout the hotel, including that night in the restaurant. Filled with flyers, the restaurant was louder than normal. This bothered Manfred's head, which began to throb. It also bothered his psyche, which was offended by the ease at which people seemed oblivious to the war, to the sacrificing of the troops and the near dire situation Germany was in. Manfred kept this bottled up inside. He smiled through dinner, was very polite, made a few jokes, but never felt quite right.

"Dinner was lovely," Frau Schmidt commented.

"Yes. You know, the men at the front are sacrificing," Manfred said quietly. He realized that most people don't have the necessary self-control for undertaking something as serious as war. That was it. The lack of self-control distressed him tremendously.

"We are aware," Frau Schmidt was sympathetic, but taken aback at Manfred's abruptness, which came across as more accusation than conversation.

Manfred, in an act that was not only atypical, but, perhaps, something that denied all social convention, bent his torso forward and laid his head on the table for all to see his wound. Everyone at the table was aghast.

Manfred then lifted his head to look unapologetically at each individual at the table, perhaps with an air of misguided assertiveness.

"This is what I am talking about."

Chapter Twenty-Four

"The Circus looks good, sir," Menzke informed his Captain.

"Excellent, Menzke. We had very short notice to move the Schwader seventy kilometers south to here in France."

"Yessir," Menzke acknowledged.

"The trains are all jammed right now. Passchendaele falling to the Entente on the southeast of Ypres didn't help much," Lothar chimed in.

"We have to get *up there* now. It's mid-morning," Manfred was smiling, perhaps more at Moritz who was jumping around as Manfred was buckling up his heavy pants over his leather flight jacket.

"It's cold up there, more than usual with his being late November, sir. Do you want the extra scarf?" Menzke asked.

"No, I'll be fine," Manfred assured Menzke.

"It's all right. We get used to this sort of thing," Lothar added as he turned toward his mechanics moving his plane by swinging the tail around. "I'm coming over in a minute!"

"You know, Lothar, the French air here above Avesnes-le-Sec will do just fine for killing more Tommies," Manfred was about to climb into his Albatros DV5.

"No doubt, dear brother. Too bad we've had to ground all the Fokker's earlier this month," Lothar remarked.

"Better to figure out why they were getting strut failure than fall apart while *up there*," Manfred climbed into his plane while Lothar sprinted to his Albatros DV5.

"We are ready, sir!" Menzke shouted as he helped Manfred strap in. The planes began to fire up. Manfred waved to Menzke to turn over the propeller.

Menzke thought about his Captain. His concern had been growing, but he dare never tell a soul. Manfred could still shoot and fly. In those skills, he was transcendent. If you flew against him, the chances were likely he would shoot you down.

But, Menzke noticed something that everyone else seemed oblivious to. Perhaps they were too busy, too preoccupied or simply wanted to keep up appearances of business as usual. Menzke wasn't sure the reason. Manfred now looked older than his twenty-five years. Much older. He even moved differently. At a studied pace. His youthful vibrance was gone. It was not simply his sunken dark eyes and sometimes ashen face. No, it was deeper. It involved his Captain's entire person. Gone was his youthful elasticity and spontaneity. He seemed a weakened copy of his former self.

Manfred confided in Menzke the night before that he really didn't enjoy his vacation. Even a humorous mistake on the national level wasn't as funny to him as much as confirming for him what a bunch of idiots he thought the press were.

In mid-October, Manfred was with Menzke back at the Schloss Reinhardsbrunn—again, one of the two residences Carl Eduard, Duke of Saxe-Coburg and Gotha. He was there as the best man for his comrade Captain Fritz Prestien, who was marrying Wally von Minckwitz. She was the daughter of the Chief Court Hunt Master of the Court of Saxe-Coburg and Gotha. That was not a bad position to hold, Manfred thought. Fritz Prestien was on the staff of the Inspectorate of Military Aviation in Berlin. Not a bad friend for Manfred to have. Overall, though, it was a *society wedding*. As such, it was covered by the press. The wedding went very well, but the reporting was not so good. A reporter from the *Gothaisches Tageblatt* mistakenly reported that Manfred was the one who married to Fräulein Minkowitz. The news of Germany's greatest war ace getting married sent all of Germany atwitter. Even Manfred's father got the news from his wife and remarked, "Why don't I ever know anything? Ah, youth!"

Humorous? Maybe so, but Menzke saw that Manfred was just more serious than he'd been before his head wound.

Inside, Manfred was seething with concern. The war wasn't going so well. The Entente won the battle at Ypres on November 10 by capturing Passchendaele. Casualties were over a half million, maybe more, when you added up the toll from both sides. But, soldiers being dispensable to the generals, it was a victory for the Entente. It was a scant amount of territory gained, but it did disrupt the German supply lines at the front. Then, on November 10, the Entente launched a new offensive at Cambrai. This was the reason that Jageschwader 1 was moved south out of Belgium to nearby Avesnes-le-Sec in France. Although they moved quickly from Markebeeke with seven planes flying down, it was catch-as-catch-can with the rest moved on trains.

This was a movement not so much out of desperation, but of military necessity as the Germans were planning a counterattack. The Entente had used infiltration tactics to bypass German strong points on No Man's Land in order to funnel men and some materiel into German held territory behind the front line. However, they hadn't done enough to reinforce these gains so that the Germans planned a response that they thought would be successful.

Manfred taxied his Albatros while Menzke leashed Moritz to walk back to the tents. Manfred gave it full throttle and pulled back on the controls as his Albatros was at the end of its acceleration on the ground. The plane lifted off. He began his climb to five thousand meters as the rest of the Schwader did the same.

Manfred was fighting off a severe headache. He tried taking several aspirin with bread and tea to calm his stomach. He did this an hour before he took off, but the aspirin had little effect. For some reason, the head pain seemed of a deeper unreachable sort, with his nausea coming and going regardless of what he put in his stomach. He took some comfort in his new quarters in the Château Dejardin, a wonderful building designed by the chief architect of Louis XVI, Ange-Jacques Gabriel. The Château's rusticated façade on the ground floor gave way to large floor to ceiling windows on the first floor, surmounted by smaller attic windows on the floor   above, with dormer windows punctuating the roof. Needless to say, Manfred liked the building. Part of him wanted to relax, to let go. He knew that he needed to get away. He even thought he could pretend he was in the early 19th century when in his quarters in the Château. He and Lothar had joked about whether to call it a Schloss or a Château. Then, in the middle of their joking, Manfred became dead serious as he thought of the forced labor on the railroad last winter, those poor starved French adolescents. So, it seemed as though he could never relax. It wasn't his injury, either — so he told himself. Rather, Manfred was intent on carrying Germany to victory all on his own.

As he approached altitude, he looked around and saw other airplanes reaching height so that they could assemble into an echelon. Manfred was intent on getting a victory today, the 23rd day of November, but he briefly flashed back to his conversation the day before with Lothar.

"Can you see it from their perspective?" Lothar asked as they just finished setting up in the Château Dejardin and were leaving to walk to the aerodrome.

"Yes and no. I mean—well, I'm fine," Manfred insisted.

"I understand how you feel," Lothar replied. "I really do. I, too, want to get some more Tommies, shoot down more Big Vickers—the whole thing," Lothar assured his brother, who was now known in his family to go off while in the middle of seemingly innocent conversation.

"They've offered me a desk job with a serious promotion," Manfred looked Lothar in the eye.

"How serious is serious?" Lothar smiled at his older brother.

"Serious serious," Manfred chuckled. "You could not salute me enough."

"Well, let's think about it. You're one of the few things that has gone right in this war for Germany," Lothar grabbed his brother's arm as the two walked toward the aerodrome. The crisp November air made their nostrils feel fresh and their brains alert.

"Really? You mean, getting shot in the back of my head most probably by friendly fire is …"

"I get your point. But, you didn't shoot yourself," Lothar tried to keep it light.

"So, I said *no*," Manfred chuckled.
"*No* to the serious promotion?" Lothar asked.

"Yes."

"It would mean you couldn't fly, right?" Manfred was just checking.

"Yes. No more flying," Manfred answered.

They walked in silence, then Lothar concluded, "Defiance. It suits you."

"You think so?" Manfred asked.

"You would have made a fine Bolshevik," Lothar continued apace.

"Yes, Lenin, Trotsky and von Richthofen. I like the sound of that. What a wonderful group," Manfred laughed.

"I think I've figured out the real reason you paint your plane red," Lothar was happy to see his brother laugh.

"I'm glad we've had this little chat," Manfred looked around for Menzke.

But, that was yesterday.

The planes assembled in an echelon. As they made their last leg of the climb, Manfred was headed due east. He mused that the countryside was beautiful, with the landscape greying and browning just as it always does this time in November. It would have been a perfect morning to hunt. But, hunting, he thought to himself, was another time and another place. The handful of planes that went up on patrol turned southwest for their part in the war effort. It was, indeed, very cold, so Manfred pulled his inner scarf over his mouth. His head seemed to settle so perhaps the aspirin was working. Manfred scanned the skies and signaled to the planes on each side of him that they would continue forward.

After fifteen minutes, once they had gone, perhaps, thirty kilometers, they all signaled each other at the same time. Down they went about two thousand feet toward a group of Airco DH.5s. With a sole pilot and one forward mounted fixed Vickers, this plane was no real threat. Within a minute, Manfred and his men were in pursuit of the Brits. Two had broken off, zoom dived and tried to outflank Manfred's patrol from the east. This didn't work, as the DH.5s didn't have enough speed to get high enough to attack. They found themselves below the Germans and now open to a roll followed by a dive. Manfred executed his pursuit curve perfectly as he pulled in on one of British planes. The fellow was cognizant that there was a red German Albatros behind him and he was heading towards No Man's Land as fast as he could. Manfred followed. The Brit dove again toward No Man's Land. Manfred dove after him, while Lothar peeled off to give chase to a Bristol two-seater, the F2B.

The fellow pulled up in a zoom dive again, but Manfred gave pursuit at just the right distance and speed to actually tuck in a little closer behind him. He centered in and fired a short burst. Manfred was sure that he'd hit the fellow's tail. The Brit tried to roll to the left, but Manfred pursued. He rolled right and headed directly west. The problem the fellow was having was that he was running out of space to descend. Manfred shot again and soon again. The British plane was now damaged as they came to No Man's Land. Manfred pulled up in an Immelmann in order to avoid enemy ground fire. Within a few seconds he was going in the other direction, while Lothar, too, successfully shot down the Bristol. Manfred's prey landed very awkwardly toward the British side of No Man's Land.

"Not bad for someone whose head is not quite right," Lothar laughed as they met after getting out of their planes.

"This was Number Sixty-Two, sir," Menzke smiled.

"Yes, I think we were over near Bourlon Wood, if I remember my map correctly. Anyway, Tommie was able to land, but I shot the plane quite a bit," Manfred sounded triumphant.

"Nice to see you haven't lost your touch. Precise and economical," Lothar was happy to see Manfred fly like his old self.

"You sound more like a music critic: precise and economical," Manfred mocked his younger brother. "And you got the Bristol?"

"Absolutely!"

As the two of them arrived back at the Château, Manfred looked around, bent over in some bushes and vomited.

"Are you all right?" Lothar asked.

Manfred wiped his mouth with his handkerchief, stood up and looked at Lothar, "You know how when you have the stomach flu and you feel better after vomiting?"

"Yes, unfortunately," Lothar replied.

"This isn't that. I vomit and still feel turned inside out. I need to lie down in my quarters for the rest of the day," Manfred admitted to Lothar as the two of them walked into the Château. "Let's keep this between us."

"Of course. By the way, the French had good architects, I think," Lothar smiled as they walked up the steps into the building.

"I appreciate your good sense of humor, but my head and stomach are reeling," Manfred admitted to his brother as he shut his door, slipped off his uniform and curled up under a blanket on his cot in the fetal position, sick and uncomfortable as hell.

Chapter Twenty-Five

The cold was brutal. It was the coldest winter in ages. As such, the air war was sporadic, with it being simply too cold to fly with any regularity. The cold meant that the men in the trenches suffered and the famine in Germany seemed doubly bad — if that was   possible — because people simply needed more energy from food to survive the cold and there wasn't any extra.

Manfred put his head back on the rest of his couchette seat of the eastward bound train. He turned his head to the right in order to avoid putting pressure on his wound, which was still open to the bone.

"Here we are headed east … again!" Lothar said as he was looking at today's edition of *Aunt Voss*. The train was just pulling out of Berlin Friedrichstraße Station.

Manfred lifted his head, turned it toward his brother and smiled, "Seems like old hat, you know."

"I remember the Kaiser said the troops would be home by the time the last leaf fell," Lothar said.

"I think he forgot to mention the year, perhaps 1921 or something like that," Manfred was sardonic.

"Well, the whole thing has been one surprise after another," Lothar added as he went back to *Aunt Voss* .

"Yes, war is like that. Much of the unexpected," Manfred laughed as he put his head back sideways on the seat rest.

Lothar watched him close his eyes, something he was glad to see. He had seen his brother suffer too much. Manfred was able to bear up under everything—getting shot in the head, coping with several surgical procedures and getting back to both flying and command—as if he had simply been away on a brief vacation. So, to see his older brother actually relax with a smile on his face was a welcome sight.

Manfred sat bolt upright, "I did send Mamma the telegram, right?"

"Yes, she knows we're headed to the peace negotiations at Brest-Litovsk," Lothar assured his brother.

Manfred put his head back sideways on the rest. Lothar turned a page of *Aunt Voss*. A few minutes passed as the train was now out of the station and picking up speed. The gentle chug-ga-chug of the wheels as they went over the seams in the rails was soothing to both brothers.

"You know," Manfred sat bolt upright again.
"I know what?" Lothar smiled as he flapped his paper and looked across the car at his brother.

"See, it's this way. I haven't told anyone this," Manfred began.

"It's safe with me," Lothar was amused at his older brother's almost impish naiveté, something he hadn't seen in Manfred in years. Lately, there were moments Manfred was like a child. He would become enthused and talk about things like a young boy talking of a new discovery that he is certain is something new to all of humanity.

"They've figured out what was wrong with the Fokker DR.1. Anthony explained to me that the varnish on the struts was hastily done."

"So, moisture … "

"… moisture could weaken the wood," Manfred completed his brother's thought. "So, we get the Fokker back for our spring offensive, pull those divisions off the front with Russia, and we can hit the Entente and the Americans hard."

"This makes sense," Lothar put the paper on the seat beside him.

"And, Anthony is working on a new plane, better than the DR.1," Manfred was elated, much as he used to get prior to his wound.

"Well, I have twenty-six victories. You have what? Thirty-two?" Lothar teased.

"Sixty-three," Manfred looked his brother in the eye.

"Oh, yes. That's right. By the way, you never did tell me about that trip to Speyer the second week of the month. To the Pfalz Works," Lothar was prying.

"Ah, well … it was cold. Great train ride down from Cologne. I sent Mamma a telegram. You know: *Going to Speyer to see an airplane factory … Will spend Christmas with JG1, along with Lothar and Papa. I sent Bolko a present.*"

"Sure."

"So, the powers that be had plans for me. I would have preferred to stay in Avesnes-le-Sec, but I had orders to go test the new Pfalz in Speyer. The trip down from Cologne, though. Oh, yes. Through the Rhenish Slate Range south of Cologne along the Rhine. Powerful. Just wonderful views. A dusting of snow, big rolling white and grey clouds — like cotton balls. The Rhine split the Rhenish Massif into something that should be on a Sanke Card."

"And Speyer?"

"Speyer was beautiful. You ever been down in the southeast?" Manfred asked his brother.

"Once or twice. I can't remember," Lothar was entertained by his brother's animated story.

"Well, let's see. Yes, Speyer. Even passing through Mannheim. Nice. But, the Pfalz representative met me at the station and took me around Speyer. Charming. Very medieval little city. The cathedral, *Romanesque*. The representative kept saying that over and over. *Romanesque*. Also, the Old Gate is still right out of the Middle Ages. I liked Speyer. Picturesque — yes, that's the word."

"What about the plane?" Lothar wanted to know

"Ah, that's a different story," Manfred was derisive.

"Really?" Lothar asked.

"The Pfalz DR.1. A big 160 horsepower Siemens-Halske with 11 cylinders — a rotary engine. Two twin fixed LMG 08/15 guns," Manfred said.

"I like the fire power," Lothar commented.

"It climbs really well, but it's heavy and sluggish. Not too good for air battles," Manfred said.

"That's too bad. We could use some help, I fear," Lothar got serious all of a sudden.

"No doubt, dear brother. No doubt. But, there is good news on the horizon. *Idflieg* is having a competition in January. Everyone is to submit a new plane," Manfred explained.

"This is encouraging," Lothar smiled.

"Yes, yes. Fokker, Albatros, Euler, DFW, Siemens-Schuckert and Pfalz are working on new things," Manfred opened up to his brother.

"Good."

"I met the Everbusch brothers, Alfred, Ernst and Walter," Manfred went on. "They believe in Pfalz, but I'm not too convinced," Manfred sat back in his seat.

"Just slow and sluggish?" Lothar wanted the details.

"It's the older Pfalz D.VIII. They put on another wing to make it a triplane, since that is the current fad."

"I see."

"The engine rotates clockwise, but the crankcase—you know—with the attached propeller—well, they go counterclockwise. No gyro forces from the engine, which is good at full throttle," Manfred went into the details that Lothar was looking for.

"Clever design," Lothar commented.

"Yes, but the engine fails after eight hours or so. We have bad oil here in Germany. So, with castor oil, not much longevity," Manfred admitted.

"It won't do well at the January competition in Adlershof. Too sluggish, slow—just not reliable," Manfred sounded definitive. Lothar nodded and Manfred put his head back on the rest with his eyes closed.

The door to their couchette slid open. It was Lieutenant Fritz Prestien, the fellow Manfred had been the best man for back in October.

"Can I have my wife back?" Fritz joked, directly referring to the mistaken newspaper article that had Manfred marrying Wally instead of Fritz.

"Sure thing, Fritzi, but I have to say, she does fly well," Manfred retorted with a sly grin.

"How are you, Lothar?" Fritz asked as he sat down next to Manfred.

"Well. Looking forward to seeing winter in Brest-Litovsk. You?" Lothar asked.

"Well. Married life agrees with me. Wally sends her regards to you both," Fritz replied.

"So, what brings a representative of the Inspectorate of Military Aviation on this mission of peace?" Manfred asked.

"Ah, good question. I think just some official presence. Adding some weight to our side. I'm to be there just a few days. Not like the Richthofen brothers," Fritz smiled, but then got a serious look on his face.

"Why so serious?" Lothar asked.

"The final report on Voss will be finished within the week. I've seen a draft," Fritz opened up. Both Manfred and Lothar leaned forward, intent on hearing him out.

"So?" Manfred asked.

"Ah, Bubi went down quite the hero—and I don't mean that as propaganda," Fritz clarified.

"What have you people discovered?" Lothar asked.

"So, it's like this, as far as we know. Voss led an afternoon patrol of Jasta 10. He had two wingmen. Lieutenant Gustav Bellen and Lieutenant Friedrich Rüdenberg, each in a Pfalz. Voss, in a Fokker DR.I, flew well ahead—alone—he had the faster plane."

Yes," Manfred acknowledged. "This makes sense."

Lothar nodded.

"Now, there was a second patrol, also from Jasta 10. This was led by First Lieutenant Ernst Weigand in an Albaros D.V. Three Pfalz D.IIIs accompanied him, Lieutenants Erich Löwenhardt, Alois Heldmann, and Max Kuhn, each flying a Pfalz DIIIs," Fritz got into detail.

"Yes, I've flown the Pfalz. Not to my liking," Manfred commented.

"A common judgment, I might say. Anyway, Bubi flew well ahead. He was alone against Seven Royal Aircraft Factory S.E.5s," Fritz gave more information.

"He should have flown home," Lothar interjected.

"Probably so," Fritz agreed.

"Seven to one—not good odds," Manfred observed.

"Voss gave them hell for over ten minutes. We've heard he impressed the British. It was a great example of flying. He was upside down and sideways most of the time," Fritz explained.

"Bubi could fly," Manfred was forlorn hearing about his comrade's end.

"Where were his wingmen?" Lothar asked.

"That is the question we've been looking into, still. You know, Bellen was dismissed in October and Rüdenberg was removed from active duty in November. I think he went back to university," Fritz said.

"Mild sanctions," Manfred offered his opinion.

"No doubt. No doubt," Lothar agreed.

"Sad affair. The whole thing," Fritz concluded.
The three of them were silent for over a minute. Then, Fritz asked Manfred, "How is the head?"

"Not bad," Manfred lied. "I wish I were still flying."

"Winter. It's cold and things have come to a halt," Fritz got up.

Manfred and Lothar stood up and shook hands with him.

"I didn't mean to bring bad news, but I thought you wanted to know that Bubi was a real hero," Fritz started to walk out.

"We had no doubt," Manfred said. He slid the door closed.

"We could use more men like Voss," Lothar concluded.

"Certainly, we could," Manfred concurred.

"I was disappointed in Christmas dinner, as was Papa," Lothar changed the subject.

"Yes, we should have gone home with Mamma and Ilse and Bolko," Manfred offered up.

"All that talk of the old days and heroic fighting from new fellows who weren't even there," Lothar was disappointed that some of the new battle fliers were interested in posturing than real action.

"Real service takes a good heart and good courage," Manfred said.

"Not to change the subject," Lothar began.

"But, you want to change the subject," Manfred smiled at his brother.

"Sure. Here it is. What do you think the Bolsheviks will be like?" Lothar wondered.

"Good question. Can we rely on the papers to tell us?" Manfred was lightly sarcastic as he stood and looked out the window at the snow covered landscape.

"Probably not. They say, for instance, you are a national hero," Lothar teased.

"Well, what do they know?" Manfred smiled.

"Precisely my point. But, seriously, what do you think the Russians, the Bolsheviks will be like?" Lothar asked.

"Russia, I think, is in chaos. It's a big place. Huge. Someone from the General Staff told me that Moscow is closer to New York City in the United States than it is to Vladivostok on the far western side of Russia," Manfred began his thoughts.

"I didn't know that," Lothar admitted.

"Huge piece of land. The Czar lost his grip. I think people stopped believing in something, which gave the Bolsheviks an opening," Manfred went on.

"They have all this equality talk," Lothar replied.

"We have the same thing. The Kaiser had me speak at that munitions factory before Christmas. The workers were on strike," Manfred offered up.

"Yes, you spoke of this before," Lothar commented.

"The workers are upset. I can understand this. We have food shortages. They work long hours," Manfred explained.

"I understand, too," Lothar replied.

"They talked about fairness. I talked about the war effort. They listened. Wanted to shake my hand, you know," Manfred went on.

"They went back to work?" Lothar asked.

"Yes, but maybe only because I was there. I think they went back on strike after I left," Manfred added.

"These are different times," Lothar went on with the topic.

"Yes, times are different. Look at Germany. Seriously, look at Germany," Manfred began to put forward his latest conclusions.

"I'm not sure I understand what you are trying to say," Lothar admitted.

"I see the injured from the war. Don't you remember when you were in the hospital?" Manfred asked his brother.

"I try to forget. I really do," Lothar shook his head. "Like a nightmare."

"Oh, no doubt. Hideous!" Manfred remarked sharply.

Lothar just nodded.

"Germany is different. The crippled veterans. Not to mention all the dead soldiers. Add in the rest. I see the food lines and protests. People holding signs. Protesters. Workers on strike. Who could have predicted all this?" Manfred asked.

"They said the war would last a few months and that we would win," Lothar was thinking about everything that Manfred had just said.

"Yes, they did. But look at what has happened," Manfred looked Lothar in the eye.

"The war is a mess for ordinary life," Lothar was in deep thought, provoked by his brother's conclusions.

"Yes, it is."

Chapter Twenty-Six

"How much longer are we going to have to stand here?" Lothar asked Manfred as the two of them stood at parade rest in a long line of Germans behind their negotiating team seated at a long conference table with the Russians on the other side of the table and the room.

"Who knows? It's been a long day. I hope dinner is soon," Manfred whispered.

"Dinner last night was illuminating," Lothar replied.

Last night, Manfred and Lothar sat at the table with Germany's representative to the conference, Foreign Secretary Richard von Kühlmann and one of the Russian delegates, Anastasia Bizenko. Manfred was quite taken with her after he heard her story. He learned that she was a veteran of the revolutionary movement for over a decade. With pride, Anastasia explained she was part of the failed Revolution of 1905. She spent time in a Siberian prison camp, as she explained, for murdering Russian War Minister Viktor Sakharov. Unashamed of her own actions and unimpressed with the show of German military pomp, she calmly talked about how she approached Minister Sakharov in a receiving line, held her pistol under a handkerchief and shot him dead.

Anastasia Bizenko was of average height and wore the clothes of an ordinary Russian workwoman. She pulled her hair back, which accented her attractive face. Manfred was attracted to her. She was bold and independent, spoke forthrightly and was, Manfred thought, beautiful, even if a bit older than he. That she was in a Siberian prison camp and now a member of the Russian delegation was — again, for Manfred — impressive.

Lothar could see why Manfred was physically attracted to Anastasia. She was a good looking woman, once you got beyond all the revolutionary trappings. However, Lothar was more than surprised that Manfred would settle — at least for this moment — his attraction to the opposite sex on someone so different than he.

"The Bolshies are a different lot," Manfred said as he focused on Anastasia at the negotiating table.

"They smell like farmers and factory workers," Lothar whispered.

"Smart, though. I can see it in their eyes," Manfred said as he nudged his brother to pay attention to the proceedings.

Adolph Joffe was a soft-spoken man. He professed non-violence as a goal for the entire world and wanted to eliminate exploitation as the governing principle of human interaction. Manfred thought to ask him why the Bolsheviks relied on their rifles to get control of Russia, but felt it would be beyond his current charge at the conference.

Manfred and Lothar struck up an immediate friendship with the head of the Austro-Hungarian delegation, Austrian Foreign Minister Count Ottokar Czernin. As Manfred thought about their new friend, the negotiators adjourned at the table, with people getting up, stretching their legs and talking about dinner.

Lothar looked at Manfred and mouthed, "Privy. Back in a moment."

As Manfred was walking out the large chamber, he felt a tap on his shoulder, "Would you and your brother join me for an apéritif?"

"A welcome relief!" Manfred remarked to Count Czernin.

Grabbing Manfred's arm, Count Czernin spoke *sotto voce* as the two of them walked a large salon, "I'm not sure this phase of the talk will end with anything concrete."

"As a break, I wish I could take you up in my Albatros," Manfred offered.

"I appreciate that, young man. At my age, well—it would be a welcome relief. Would I survive it?" Count Czernin was in a better mood than Manfred would be if he had been at the negotiating table all day.

"We'd see to it, sir," Manfred felt relaxed around the Count, who was sincerely interested in flying.

"Try this, *vermouth*. A nice prelude to dinner," Czernin took two glasses off a tray held out by a passing waiter. "And call me Otto."

"Manfred, please," Manfred smiled at the Count.

Lothar came up from the side and took another glass, "I could get used to this *vermouth*."

"I'll grant the Italians that much, but no more," Czernin joked.

Manfred looked across the room staring at Anastasia Bizenko, until Lothar interrupted him "I'm not sure a Bolshie is the right choice at this point in your life."

"Nice looking woman, I admit," Czernin offered up.

"Another time, maybe," Manfred decided to change the subject. "Flying would do you good, Otto. Hunting would do Lothar and me some good."

"Let me think on that last one. By the way," Czernin pulled both Lothar and Manfred in with a subtle gesture of his head.

"Yes," Manfred answered for the two of them.

"These talks are close to an impasse. Your Foreign Secretary confided in me that he was horrified at the stringent terms the General Staff has put forward to the Russians."

"Oh?" Lothar queried.

"The German General Staff wants a good deal. Russia pulls out of the Entente. Russia gives the Baltic States to Germany. The southern Russian Province of Kars Oblast goes to the Ottomans. Ukraine becomes independent. And, Russia gives Germany repatriations: six billion German Marks in gold," Czernin explained quietly.

"What did Russia ask for?" Manfred wondered.

"Stop the war, but nothing else. No territory surrendered," Czernin had a serious look on his face.

"They aren't in much of a long term position to ask for that, are they?" Lothar observed.

"No, but we need to get this done in good time so we can pull everything off the Russian front and move it west. This spring and summer will decided the war — especially now that the Americans are coming in," Czernin admitted.

"Everyone understands that. Maybe that's why they want to slow things down," Manfred suggested. "Keep our forces here in the east."

"Who knows? There are many unknowns," Czernin admitted.

Manfred liked Otto. He had a lean quality about his appearance that carried over into his manner. Here was a man he could relate to in that there was little padding, little flourish, little pomp. Czernin got down to business, but only in the most refined, polished and courteous way. He also was fascinated with flying.

"We're testing a whole lot of new planes in a short while in Adlershof. A competition to see who gets the new contract for the latest battle planes," Manfred started to explain.

"Competing designs. I like that," Czernin was excited to talk about the latest developments in flying machinery.

"Progress is made all the time. Higher, faster, longer durations in the air. All this is something to look forward to," Lothar added.

"How high? How fast?" Czernin wanted to know.

"We're going to bring oxygen tanks up because we're going to be so high," Manfred started to answer Czernin's question.

"How high is that?" Czernin pressed Manfred for answers. He was excited to talk about *up there* .

"Seven, eight or nine thousand meters will be probable, eventually. And this is an advantage in air battling because you can drop down on the enemy battle fliers," Manfred explained.

"Yes, *falcon tactics*, eh?" Czernin was showing what he knew about a topic he loved.

"Certain. But, we also will be going faster. Two hundred kilometers per hour and above for cruising on the level," Lothar chimed in.

"This is amazing. I remember the Wright Brothers, what? Just over a decade ago," Czernin said.

"Progress is happening all the time," Manfred added. "Let me tell you, Count—the Fokker with its three wings—it's not as fast as we want, but it can do things we only dreamt of even a year ago."

"This is true. We are testing new planes all the time," Lothar added.

"The war has brought about a lot of change. Progress in some technology. Do you think?" Czernin asked both brothers.

"Our sister works as a nurse," Manfred began to explain.

"No need, my friend. I have friends whose daughters are nurses. I understand. Not a pretty job," Czernin shook his head.

"No, not at all," Lothar chimed in.

"And, the war is—well, I think both sides are … I'm searching for the word," Manfred waved his hand in the air.

"I don't want to say *desperate*, do I?" Czernin smiled with tight lips at both brothers.

"Not advisable," Manfred said.

"Any of that chivalry left in the air battle?" Czernin asked.

"Early on, when my machine gun jammed, a British Tommie actually waved to me and let me go," Lothar reflected back.

"What a warrior — to be such a gentleman in battle. I wish we could meet this man!" Czernin was elated.

"I understand, Count. But, the war is fiercer now. Both sides have anti-airplane fire. This means we have to fly much higher to avoid being shot down by the ground artillery," Lothar explained.

"Hmm…not very nice, eh" Czernin asked.

"Not at all. Not at all," Manfred answered.

"By the way, who is that gentleman across the room with the drawing tablet?" Lothar asked, changing the subject.

"That's the famous artist Emil Orlik," Count Czernin answered. "He's a *modern artist*."

"I really don't understand modern art. Professor Busch I could understand," Manfred commented.

"Yes, Busch and Orlik — worlds apart, Manfred," Czernin observed.

"Ah, I'm not sure I grasp it," Lothar smiled as he took another sip of *vermouth* .

"Traditional art and modern art. Orlik's here to do sketches of all the major participants — on both sides," Czernin added.

"Remember our comrade Schäfer?" Manfred seemed to go off topic.

"Certainly, how could you forget Karl," Lothar responded as Czernin listened to see where the conversation was going.

"He knew art. He was studying in Paris when the war began," Manfred completed his thought. "He understood modern art."

"A lot has been interrupted, my boys," Czernin understood the point Manfred was making.

"He's dead. Killed last summer in an air battle," Manfred said quietly. "It was last June, right, Lothar?"

"Yes, last June. He was fluent in French. Quite a fine mind," Lothar added.

"Pity," Czernin replied. "This is very sad. Let an older gentleman change the subject. Did you take my advice to escape the boredom of this meeting?" Czernin asked both brothers.

"Yes, we have permission to go on leave to the Czar's hunting lodge in the nearby Białowieża Forest," Manfred pulled their leave papers from inside his jacket to wave them in the air with a smile.

"Outstanding! This will be wonderful for you both," Czernin advised the brothers.

"I understand a good many of the wisent have been killed off by hungry German infantrymen," Manfred looked concerned.

"Yes, so I've heard, as well," Czernin shook his head.

"But, we have snow, plenty of cold — it will be good to get out," Lothar changed the subject.

"Of course, of course. I wish I could accompany you both, but we have work to do here," Czernin seemed disappointed that he couldn't go with Manfred and Lothar.

Chapter Twenty-Seven

Manfred didn't sleep at all as he was so excited.

The two brothers took the train from Brest-Litovsk earlier that day. They travelled the one hundred and twenty kilometers in four hours to reach the decorative train station next to the deposed Czar's hunting lodge. The structure was a simple wooden platform surmounted by a single story wooden arcade with a slanted single peak roof. The wooden lattice work that made up the balustrade and faux entablature cemented the effect of giving arriving passengers the appearance of arriving at a fairy tale place.

Manfred and Lothar, enchanted by the station, got off the train with their large bags. German infantry soldiers at the station saluted both officers, then recognized Manfred as the hero battle flier. Two of the men produced Sanke Cards for Manfred to sign. One had a group photo of Jasta 11 and wanted Lothar's signature, too. The men helped the brothers load their bags on a horse drawn sledge to take them to the czar's lodge.

Manfred's initial impression of the Białowieża Forest did not disappoint. The mixture of tree types, the vast snow covered expanses under the canopy of evergreen and now barren oak enthralled Manfred. He hoped to see some wisent, but was not disappointed because he knew the occupying German infantry had shot a good many of them in their quest for fresh meat.

The lodge was impressive, even though it had a reputation of being simple, and by Russian court standards, stark. It was only two stories, but was surmounted by an attic under a variegated copper covered Mansard-style roof. It was a long structure, with a single hunt tower, situated on a lake and had a garden, asymmetrical and meandering, very much in the English manner. It had one hundred and twenty rooms, which caused Manfred and Lothar to both wisecrack about the *modesty* of the lodge.

The brothers were surprised that some of the Russian staff were still there and had attempted to maintain the lodge very much as if the Czar was still in power and still in control of the forest. A very elderly man approached Manfred and introduced himself in broken German with a smattering of French. Manfred could discern that at one time this fellow, Grigory, was once the hunt master and possessed an encyclopedic knowledge of the forest. He, too, had some Sanke Cards of Manfred and Jasta 11, which he asked the brothers to sign.

Some infantry officers and a few of their men were quartered in the lodge, but the majority of men were camping a few kilometers away. As such, staying at the lodge had the sense of being away from all of civilization at a place that was idyllic, a winter-style Elysium. The whole experience rejuvenated Manfred, who had to tell himself that this experience was, sadly, only to last a few days.

Dinner that night consisted of black bread, pickled beets and roast wisent, slowly cooked in one of the kitchen's large ovens from late that morning. Manfred fought his urge to stuff himself, but did have a second cut of meat, as did Lothar. Manfred had some cognac after dinner and was surprised that his head did not explode in its usual raging pain. Moreover, he was doubly surprised that he had minimal nausea throughout the evening.

Manfred and Lothar were given two Mauser rifles by the officer in command of the lodge. He explained that they had each been sighted in, so that the distances on their newly added tangent rear sights were accurate. He gave the brothers each two dozen rounds of full ball 7.92×57mm Mauser cartridges. Each brother laid out his clothes and was happy to see the commander give each of them a pair of snow boots and a heavily furred Cossack style hats with generous earflaps.

Lothar fell asleep right away, but Manfred, who hid how he was feeling, was just too excited to sleep or even lie still in bed. Around two in the morning, Manfred found himself with his night coat on standing in untied boots on the porch of the lodge. The crisp air cleared his nostrils and made him feel even more awake. It was snowing, which made Manfred feel as if he were standing in a paperweight snow globe. It didn't feel real. Manfred was brought back to reality by a tug on the side of his night coat. It was the old man, Grigory.

Grigory smiled at Manfred and began to talk about the Białowieża Forest in his broken German, intermingled with rather good French, with an occasional English word thrown in. Given the language barrier, Manfred was amazed that he learned so much about the forest.

Grigory explained that the forest went back to *before time*, perhaps as much as five or six thousand years — maybe even more. He began by lamenting the fact that the Germans had shot the ancient European bison, the wisent, to near extinction. As a man of the outdoors, Manfred shared his disappointment in the uncontrolled shooting the Germans did to feed themselves such excellent tasting meat.

Manfred explained to Grigory that even though he'd only seen it for a few minutes, he felt blessed to see the forest in all its magnificence. As Manfred finished his sentence, the snow came down with a new fierceness, so Grigory motioned for Manfred to follow him inside, where they sat in a salon right off the foyer.

Grigory told Manfred about some of the large flora in the forest. It had both evergreens and leafed trees. There was the visually and spatially dominant oak. With black alder and dwarf birch that were now leafless in winter. There were pine and spruce, too, with their eternally green and blue boughs of needles. Grigory wanted Manfred to know that the forest floor was blocked here and there by fallen oak, so the use of a horse drawn sledge required good judgment and foresight.

Grigory became more animated as he talked of the fauna of the forest. He talked of the elk, the bobcat, deer, grey wolf and European lynx. He saved the best of last as he described the wisent, until he started to cry about the fact that it was nearly gone from the woods. Manfred realized that a continuity with ancient times, times that predated the Norse myths and the Germanic hero Siegfried, was nearly broken.

Manfred thanked Grigory. The old man shook his hand and bowed to him, "Yes, Baron, you are noble."

Manfred dozed in a warmth until he heard a knock on his door at six in the morning. He shouted that he was awake and started to stir. As usual, his neck was stiff as hell, something he always woke with since his injury. He reached his hands behind his head and began to massage his neck muscles. After a few compressions with his hands, his neck moved more easily so Manfred sat up on the side of his bed. He stood up, walked to his privy, relieved his bladder and proceeded to shave. He then splashed cool water on his face and the top of his head, careful to avoid getting his still open wound wet.

As he was putting on fresh underwear and stepping into his wool hunting pants, he heard a knock at the door. Lothar was ready, standing there with a big smile on his face, "This is to be a momentous day. It is as if we are czars."

"Indeed, dear brother, it is as if we are Russian royalty," Manfred slipped on his sweater and grabbed his winter coat.

"There is breakfast, I think," Lothar said as Manfred closed his door.

"I smell something good," Manfred grabbed his brother's arm and they walked down the hall toward one of the lodge's dining rooms.

A few infantrymen were having black bread with butter, boiled potatoes, and oatmeal. They stood up as Manfred and Lothar entered, but Manfred waved them down, "We are not officers today, gentlemen. We are royalty going to hunt."

The men nodded and smiled in approval. One of them held out a pot of coffee.

"Thank you," Manfred said as the two of them decided to sit with the men.

"It is a fresh morning, sir," one of the men said to Manfred.

"How much new snow?" Lothar asked.

"Maybe twenty centimeters," another of the men answered.

"Nice for the sleigh, but not too much for the horses," Manfred concluded.

"Yes, the horses here are Russian Ardennes. These are beautiful work horses. Feathered fetlocks, shorter legs, but very sturdy. Not affected by the cold. We've prepared your sledge with four horses, so you can load and pull in big game today, sirs," the third of the men smiled.

Manfred swigged down his coffee and felt its warmth wake him up even more. Lothar put some bread in his jacket pocket as the two brothers stood up.

"We thank you soldiers," Lothar said as he followed an excited Manfred out toward the front porch.

It was still dark out, but with the snow covering everything, it was easy to see. The rifles were standing behind the seat of the sledge in oilcloth gun sacks. Two of the horses were chestnut, one was roan, while the fourth was black and white.

"The horses look noble, even though we have a simple sledge," Lothar observed.

"This is a day of a lifetime, to hunt like this in a forest like this. It goes back thousands of years," Manfred replied to his brother.

"You'll have to update me on the forest. You seem freshly informed," Lothar said.

"You do have the cartridges, right?" Manfred asked Lothar.

"Yes, I have mine. You?" Lothar asked.

"No doubt, dear brother. No doubt," Manfred got up on the seat and Lothar sat next to him.

As they were about to pull away from the front porch, Manfred looked toward the door, where Grigory waved at them both. Manfred waved back and said to Lothar, "Interesting man. He was the former hunt master. He's close to ninety now, but we spoke at length about the forest last night when I was too excited to sleep."

"That explains it," Lothar waved to Grigory, who reciprocated as Manfred clicked his cheek and shook the rein to pull away. They began down one of the long roads into the woods.

"I want you to promise me one thing," Manfred said softly as the sleigh glided noiselessly through the fresh snow above the hard pack below it.

"What's that?" Lothar asked.

"If we see a boar," Manfred started to explain.

"Yes."

"I get to kill it," Manfred smiled with the confident determination that Lothar used to see in his face all the time.

"That's fine with me," Lothar said as he wondered what Manfred was thinking.

The two of them drove on for several minutes. They finally left the longest road through the rambling English garden and slid into the forest. Lothar looked up at the tall oaks, spied a stand of spruce in the distance and pointed to a fallen oak trunk off the side of the trail.

"These are massive oak trees," Lothar commented.

"Grigory was telling me some of these may be four or five hundred years old," Manfred said softly as he pulled up on the reins and brought the sledge to a halt.

"I see," Lothar said.

"Yes, with the snow blanketing everything, it is perfectly quiet," Manfred whispered as the two of them sat there for a few minutes.

"Let's go up to that rise ahead and walk a bit," Manfred suggested.

"Fine with me," Lothar replied as he reached for one of the oil sacks with a Mauser in it.

Manfred drove the sledge ahead, gently pulled on the reins and got off. Lothar took Manfred's rifle and got it ready, while Manfred tied up the Russian Ardennes with a rope. He fastened the middle of the front halter to a nearby branch of a black alder. He took his rifle from Lothar, took a stripper clip from his pocket and pushed the five rounds into the receiver. He swung the gun up, swung it down into the woods away from Lothar and turned to his brother.

"Nice feel, the Mauser. These two rifles look to be in very good shape. Not a lot of infantry abuse," Manfred judged.

"I think so. Let's walk that way," Lothar said as he pointed to the north.

The fresh snow was light and fluffy, almost like feathers from a comforter that had popped open unexpectedly. Underneath, though, was semi-hard snow that let their boots sink down another ten centimeters or so. It was deliberate walking, then, but the two brothers were enchanted to be where they were with a full blown war going on elsewhere in what they considered to be the civilized world.

"I think something is up ahead behind that stand of bushes," Manfred whispered to Lothar as the two of them crouched behind some snow covered boulders.

In a few minutes, two wisent appeared from behind the stand of bushes. They each stood just two meters tall, with thickly tufted dark brown coats. The male had horns, while the slightly smaller female, hornless, had a slightly darker coat. Given the slight westerly crosswind, the two beasts were unaware of Manfred and Lothar.

"Impressive," Lothar said as he began to raise his Mauser.

Manfred gently put his hand on Lothar's barrel, "Maybe not these today."

Lothar lowered his barrel, "Why not?"

"Not many of these left," Manfred began to explain. "You know, our infantry has killed almost all of them throughout the forest."

Before he responded, Lothar thought about it, "I understand. You are right, brother."

"Maybe we find some elk, eh?" Manfred smiled as he kept his voice low.

"Let's watch these two for a few minutes," Lothar lowered his rifle and returned it to his shoulder on its sling.

Manfred nodded, but then turned his head around as he looked defensively for a boar who was about to rage on the two of them.

"What are looking for?" Lothar asked.

"Nothing. I think it's really nothing," Manfred was trying to come to grips with his changed perception of the woods, the stresses of his command and the pressures on Germany to succeed with her back up against the wall.

"Relax and enjoy the wisent," Lothar turned his gaze toward the two brown beast who had just become aware of them.

In the blink of an eye, they were gone.

"Well, that solves that," Manfred said as he stood up and shouldered his Mauser with its sling.

The walk back to the sledge took about ten minutes. Their horses were quietly waiting for them as they untied their rope, got back up on the seat and, this time, had Lothar take the reins and move forward along the trail through the forest.

After another half hour of walking the horses, Manfred turned to Lothar, "We've been out quite a while. My watch says it's nearly eleven."

"Maybe give the horses their snack and us the same," Lothar pulled the horses gently to a stop.

Manfred got the four feedbags out of a burlap sack, checked to see if they had been loaded with some oats and fastened the bag around each horse's muzzle. Lothar was eating some buttered black bread with some cheese.

"Hungry?" Manfred asked.

"Surprisingly so," Lothar laughed.

"Me, too," Manfred took his bread, butter and cheese out of his pocket to take a bite. He also grabbed a canvas sack behind the seat and pulled a corked but open wine bottle out. He took a sip and handed the bottle to Lothar.

Lothar took a sip as he tipped his head back and let the wine pour into his mouth, "A nice touch. This tastes good with the cheese and bread."

"Yes, we are lucky. Words really don't do this place justice. Even if we don't bag anything today, it is fabulous," Manfred took another swig to wash down the dry bread and hard cheese.

"We'll get lucky. Don't worry," Lothar sounded confident as they proceeded to finish their snack, get the horses ready again and move forward with the sledge.

Lothar stopped the horses at a fork in the trail, "This way goes deeper into the forest, that way loops around and rejoins back there about fifty meters. What do you think?"

"Let's loop around. We can move the horses a little faster so we'll have time to hike out for some elk," Manfred advised.

An hour back toward the lodge, they stopped and hiked into the woods. They saw nothing, so they turned around and made their way back to the sledge and horses. As they walked over a rise in the forest floor, Manfred dropped to his knee and unshouldered his rifle. He quietly slid the safety off and worked the bolt to chamber a cartridge. Lothar did the same. One hundred meters through the woods were a herd of elk, perhaps ten of them.

"Rare to see this many together," Lothar mouthed almost silently to Manfred.

"We fire on three. You to the left, me, the right," Manfred said as he sighted in. Lothar did the same: sight picture, front post through the tangent sight, bison and, finally, front post with bison behind it. "One, two, three."

Each brother felled stag, clean shot to the central rear shoulder, through the heart. The other elks scattered.

"Nice shot!" Manfred said to Lothar.

"Did you doubt?" Lothar cracked.

"Most of the time," Manfred stood up and the two of them hurried to the sledge. The horses, used to hunting, hadn't stirred a bit.

"We can use this large piece of canvas to drag them one at a time up the back gate of the sledge," Lothar said.

"Let's not take the sledge off trail. If we sink it, we'll have to unhitch the horses and walk them back to the lodge.

Lothar looked at Manfred, "Too bad we can't stay here for a few months."

"The Bolsheviks wouldn't like that."

"Ah, I forgot about all that for a while."

"Me, too," Manfred smiled. "Me, too."

<h1 style="text-align:center">Chapter Twenty-Eight</h1>

Manfred and Lothar were again standing behind the German side of the negotiations at the Brest-Litovsk. Manfred looked refreshed—at least to Lothar, who was happy to see his brother more energetic and more like his old self, in a lighter mood.

They had conversation on the way back to Brest-Litovsk.

"I have to admit that I have reconsidered that promotion the General Staff has offered me," Manfred admitted to Lothar.

"What brings on this possible change of mind?" Lothar asked.

"Just relaxing and thinking. You know how it goes. Thinking of everything back there at the Czar's lodge. The bison, the elk—and, all those animals we didn't see. Bobcat, grey wolf, raptors—the whole lot of them. I'm just rambling now. But, let me tell you, this was the first time I've really relaxed since my injury. It was nice—comfortable sitting in front of the fire last night after dinner."

"I can understand that," Lothar replied. "I remember times before the war. Life was better then."

"I don't mean I'm getting soft. Never that. Hell, Lothar, you've been in convalescence for months. You know what I mean," Manfred opened up to his younger brother.

Lothar didn't respond, he just nodded to Manfred.

So, standing at the conference, making a show of German military might, of Prussian discipline, Manfred leaned over to his brother, "I spoke to Anastasia. I asked her about her Bolshevism at lunchtime."

"What did she say?" Lothar whispered back to his brother.

"Something about them being Bolsheviks *and Soviets*. If I wanted to talk to her, I'd have to use the proper forms of their titles. This *Soviet* stuff," Manfred winced.

"She's too old, anyway," Manfred tried to console his brother.

"She has something — at least, for me, you know — something attractive," Manfred smiled to Lothar.

"Yes, a leftwing revolutionary assassin. Exciting, no doubt. But, find a nice German girl. An Austrian. The war will be over someday. Find a French girl — from Paris. Someone sophisticated, but refreshing, who's not a killer," Lothar chuckled to his brother.

Manfred motioned with his head to the conference table, where things were about to break up for the day. He and Lothar broke their parade rest stances and stretched with their arms.

"Perhaps you are right," Manfred was glad to talk out loud in a normal voice.

"Yes, it's Friday, right?" Lothar asked.

"Yes, the eleventh of January. Why do you ask?"

"We'll be gone. Well, you'll be testing the new Fokker soon. This woman is no good for you," Lothar laughed.

"Many women are no good for us, but we persist," they heard a voice from behind them. It was Count Czernin.

Manfred, Lothar and the Czernin broke out laughing.

"Well, the Russians ..."

"... the Bolsheviks *and Soviets*," Manfred corrected their friend.

"I'm glad you've learned that, Manfred," Czernin said with mild sarcasm.

"Yes, well, we try to keep an open mind, Otto," Lothar replied for his brother who was laughing again.

"Yes, well, things are coming to a head now. The Soviets don't want to meet our demands," Czernin started to explain.

"Are they in a position to refuse?" Manfred asked.

The Count got agitated as he pulled the brothers aside, out of the hubbub of the post-conference rush for aperitifs.

"Wilson, the American President has thrown his hat in the ring," Czernin started to explain.

"Is this something we can talk about over dinner?" Manfred asked.

"Let's get an aperitif and talk now. Mr. Wilson has our side very riled up," Czernin smiled.

The large salon was more animated than usual. Manfred avoided Anastasia's glances, deciding that discretion in the name of the Fatherland outweighed his desire for human passion. Love and his possible assassination would have to wait. Naturally, the fact that Manfred decided that he wasn't interested in her any longer meant that she kept looking his way throughout the evening.

"I think she's sizing you up for the kill, dear brother. Perhaps a close range shot to the abdomen," Lothar joked. "That is her specialty."

"Well, I'm not a man of letters, but the old poets used to speak of dying in a woman's arms," Manfred smiled as he took a sip of Vermouth.

"They meant something different," Count Czernin again came up behind the brothers.

"We understand that, Otto," Manfred smiled.

"Ah, I remember being young," Czernin began.

"We remember before the war. That was being young," Lothar joked.

"Yes, it was," Czernin began. "But, I want to know. Have either of you heard of the American writer — he's also a medical doctor — Charles Alexander Eastman?"

Both brothers thought for a moment and then shook their heads.

"Charles Alexander Eastman is an American Indian. He was also very educated in the Anglo-European way. A medical doctor and a writer. He has written a book that was translated into German: *Indian Boyhood*."

"You are explaining something to us?" Manfred asked.

"Yes. It will all make sense in a few minutes," Czernin explained.

"This is fine. We want to know what is going on," Lothar focused on Czernin.

"A few years ago there was a conference in London. Representatives came from all over the world. Eastman went as the representative of the American Indians. It was the *First Universal Races Congress*," Czernin went on.

"Was this a good thing?" Manfred asked.

"Actually, I think so. It was the first world conference to promote and study racial understanding. I mean, the differences between all the different groups on earth," Czernin clarified.

"Germans were there?" Lothar asked.

"Someone of German birth helped organize the Congress. He is Felix Adler. Alongside him were Gustav Spiller and another fellow whose name I forget but his last name was Stanhope. And also a New Zealander named Reeves," Czernin took a sip of vermouth.

"What was the outcome of the *Congress*?" Manfred asked.

"Well, you see, this idea that everyone has rights is part of our modern age. It will come to dominate many discussions in the future. Besides, in Germany there is this deep love of American Indian culture. They founded the Club Manitou in Dresden a few years before the war began," Czernin said.

"Yes, I've heard of this," Lothar smiled.

"Part of us in the Central Powers — at least in Germany and some in Austro-Hungary — are fascinated with the American Indian," Czernin went deeper into his point.

"I've seen some people camping in these things they call teepees," Manfred recalled as he was thinking about the German fascination with the American Indian.

"I've read our own Karl May's novels. His Indian characters Winnetou and Old Shatterhand," Lothar added to the discussion.

"Yes, I've read one of your copies of his books, Lothar," Manfred remembered.

"His books are very popular," Czernin pointed out. "So, did you know that the North American Indians have, in the past, sent ambassadors to Europe? They are seeking support against the subjugation the Canadians and Americans are forcing on them. Turning them into worse than medieval serfs," Czernin alternately explained and asked.

"No, we didn't know that. I'm not sure many people do," Manfred answered.

"Well, they have been here in the past asking for help," Czernin assured the brothers. "But, they got none. No help. But, let me ask: did you know we have our own quest for human rights here in Europe?"

"I imagine this is true, but I'm sure neither one of us have thought about this," Manfred spoke for both brothers.

"Yes, the Soviets say they are all about the rights of everyone," Czernin went on after a healthy swig of vermouth and then waving his empty glass at a waiter for some more.

"They hate us," Lothar said.

"Yes, they do. But, let me go on," Czernin agreed with Lothar. "There is this movement for the Slavic peoples. The Pan Slavic movement."

"Sure. I've read about it in *Aunt Voss*," Manfred said.

"No matter what anyone says about it, it is not necessarily a spontaneous movement. A large part of the impetus of this movement comes from Moscow. First Czarist Russia and now Soviet Russia," Czernin was on a roll. "Their motivation is to weaken the Austro-Hungarian Empire because it consists of many Slavs. We also have Magyars and Romanians and German peoples, but, this Slavic thing, the Pan Slavism, is a central part of the Russian interest in destroying the Empire."

"So they can move into Eastern Europe," Manfred finished Czernin's thought.

"Yes, absolutely," Czernin responded.
"I can see that now," Manfred said.

"So can I," Lothar agreed.

"Good. I'm glad you follow. That brings me to the American President, Mr. Wilson," Czernin was getting a little excited.

"What has he done?" Manfred wondered.

"He has just proposed his Fourteen Points," Czernin answered Manfred.

"What are these Fourteen Points?" Lothar asked.

"He is claiming these Fourteen Points have self-determination as their main idea. That America is in favor of self-determination for all people," Czernin began his next part of his lengthy explanation to the two brothers.

"Ah, I think I see," Manfred responds.

"Yes. This is not good. In his many different points, Mr. Wilson has put forward that Poland be independent of Russia and Germany. You see, self-determination. And, Alsace-Lorraine goes back to France. Self-determination. And Austro-Hungary gets split up by the many Slavic groups inside the Empire. Czechs, Yugoslavs, Poles and Romania," Czernin brought the bad news out.

Both brothers were silent, as this puts a very depressing picture of post-war Europe in their minds for the first time.

Finally, Manfred spoke, "Self-determination for everyone?"

"That's how the Americans are explaining this," Czernin looked Manfred in the eye, then Lothar. "But, this is a lie. A sham. A trick with words. Hypocrisy! You see, they aren't offering self-determination to all those peoples who were at the First Universal Races Congress. Not to their own American and Canadian Indians. Not to the American Negro. These are very suppressed groups."

"Yes, you are making sense," Lothar said after a moment of thought.

"And, the British, our friends the British, they are not offering to free India from colonial servitude. Nor the French their colonies in Africa and Asia. Yes, we committed some atrocities in Belgium at the start of the war, but the Entente newspapers use that to cover up Belgian atrocities against the native Africans in the Congo," Czernin was angry.

"Yes, I see," Lothar replied.

"From their point of view, only the German and Austro-Hungarians, along with our Turkish allies — yes, were are the world's oppressors. You see, the Fourteen Points make a false promise to address injustice. They aren't helping a lot of people whom they oppress. What it really does, this proposal by Mr. Wilson, is to insert America into the center of European politics while dismantling Germany and Austro-Hungary. All in the name of rights, of self-determination — which is a lie. The Americans and British do not want to free people. They want to destroy us."

"I don't like this," Lothar concluded.

"Nor I," Manfred added.

"Yes, thank you for seeing. The Entente with their new American friends are demanding too much, but they plan on winning this war," Czernin concluded. "Maybe we should get some dinner now."

Lothar looked at Manfred, who was no longer looking refreshed from their hunting in the ancient forest at Białowieża. Manfred looked like he had the past several months: haggard, gaunt and exhausted.

"What do you think, brother?" Lothar asked.

"We have to be strong. We have to be determined to win," Manfred answered Lothar.

"Indeed we do," Lothar looked his brother in the eye.

Manfred returned his brothers gaze," I don't think I'm going to take that promotion. This is our last stand, brother."

Chapter Twenty-Nine

"Yes, this has potential," Manfred said to himself as he touched down at Johannisthal-Adlershof Aerodrome. He was composing his thoughts as he taxied toward the hangar where some pilots were returning from their flights and others were simply standing around talking. He waved to Anthony Fokker as he got near, with Anthony heartily retuning his wave accompanied by a big smile.

"So, what do you think?" Anthony shouted up to Manfred as he turned off the Mercedes D.IIIa rotary engine with its 160 horsepower.

Manfred thought a moment before he responded. He also was trying to come to grips with his headache and that damn recurring nausea that bothered him for several hours after each flight. It didn't help that he had had his recurring nightmares last night, either. He woke up out of a cold sweat several times—he forgot how many—working himself into a state where he was afraid to go back to sleep. He was on the rocky road in his bare feet, voices were yelling at him to get a move on and then he was at the beach, with corpses sitting up out of their shallow graves. It was ghastly, but Manfred didn't know what to do about it. He was afraid to tell anyone, since he thought they would brand him unfit to fly, which for him would have been the worst nightmare of all.

The General Staff had called for the first of several airplane competitions to see who could make the next and, hopefully, better battle plane. The competition was set for three weeks at Johannisthal-Adlershof right next to Berlin. It began on January 21. The British and French — and soon to be Americans — were proving to be vexing opponents in the air. They had more planes than the Germans and their latest designs were now more than a match for the likes of the German Fokker, Albatros and Pflaz battle planes. If you add to the mix that planes had to fly higher because of effective anti-aircraft fire from the ground, then you could see that the success the Germans had had the previous year, especially during *Bloody April*, was a thing of the past. Air battles had many more planes and took place, quite often, higher up in the sky. *Up there* was literally higher *up there* than ever before. So, the Germans were looking for some mechanical advantage with this competition. There were thirty-one entries with their respective makers hoping that theirs would be judged the best, that would prove to be durable, fast, maneuverable and had a good climb rate.

"Hello, hello, hello!" Manfred exclaimed as he climbed out of the experimental Fokker V.II.

"What do you think?" Anthony was excited to hear Manfred's appraisal of his newest plane.

"Let me tell you, I think we're on to something here," Manfred began.

"Two wings here are better than the triplane, don't you think?" Anthony could hardly contain himself.

"Listen, Anthony. Just listen," Manfred, though feeling sick, was amused by Anthony, who was like a young child with a new toy.

Anthony paused, then waited for Manfred, "Well?"

Manfred deliberately paused, playing with his friend.

"Well?"

"This is an impressive beginning point. But, let me get to it. It's unstable in a long dive. Awkward in a fast descent. Hard to control the direction, which is key, because—well, you know—we dive on our prey. *Falcon tactics* and all that," Manfred explained. "We need to shoot straight, but can't do that unless we can fly straight—you know, in a line."

Anthony looked at one of his fabricators, Reinhold Platz, "I think we can fix this overnight, right?"

"What do you suggest?" Reinhold asked his boss.

"Let me think a moment, but I have a couple of ideas," Anthony looked at Manfred. "Dinner and drinks on me at the Café Sanssouci in Adlershof tonight?"

"Let me get back to the hotel and clean up," Manfred looked around for a ride back to his hotel. "I need a ride … anyone?"

"Here. Take my boat tail," Anthony offered his vehicle to Manfred. "I've got an idea on how to fix the plane. A quick one."

Everyone, the other pilots and representatives from the other companies were listening and wondering what Anthony was going to do. No fool, he ordered the plane into one of the impromptu tents he had put up near the hangar. This was, after all, a competition and Anthony did not intend to give any secrets away. He wanted that fat government contract.

*   *   *

Manfred was standing at the corner of the bar at the Café Sanssouci with a glass of wine in his hand. Any alcohol still bothered his head, but he kept up appearances by taking the occasional small sip. No one ever noticed. He made sure of that. As he looked around, he decided that he liked this place. The Café had an elegance that was far removed from the inhumane conditions at the front. It was a different world. Full cloth settings at

232

the tables, stylish modern chairs, elegant wall paper and someone playing the piano as background music. And driving up to it in Anthony's boat tail was the height of style, Manfred thought. He even let his mind race wild for a few moments, imagining that the war was over, that a younger version of Anastasia *the Soviet* was there to meet him, that the two of them would drive down to the Alps for a two week getaway in some mountain hotel. Hiking, hunting and romance.

"Hey, fellow, where are you?" Anthony had walked in and stood next to Manfred for nearly a minute without Manfred noticing him.

"What?" Manfred was startled.

"Day dreaming?" Anthony chided. "Don't you know, there's a war on? Pay attention, Manfred."

"Oh, just taking in the elegance, Anthony. Nice car," Manfred changed the subject. "People stop and stare at you when   you drive by," Manfred looked around, spotted the waiter and held up two fingers for a table for two.

"Yes, the old girl gets the job done. Great automobile," Anthony was still excited as the two of them grabbed their wine glasses, walked to their table and sat down. "Some of the best money I've spent—that boat tail—and, believe me, I've spent enough."

"I can believe that!" Manfred laughed at his friend's flamboyance.

"Part of it is image, you know. But, it's fun along the way, too," Anthony admitted.

"Enough bragging, Anthony. I'm hungry tonight," Manfred looked at the menu.

"Listen," Anthony began as he reached across the table and pulled the top of Manfred's menu down. "I think we've got it."

"Ready tomorrow?" Manfred didn't expect the changes to come so quickly, but he liked to press Anthony, since not many people could face Anthony down.

"That's abrupt! But, believe me or   not, the answer   is, *of course*. I've thought about one more bay to the fuselage. Simple welding, plus add new material to cover the frame. Easy really."

"Is that all?" Manfred was impressed with Anthony's quickness.

"No. We've decided to add a small fin in front of the rudder. A little extra drag, but much more stability," Anthony smiled, as he looked up at the waiter. "Beef stew for both us, along with green beans and some rolls."

Manfred nodded as the waiter wrote the order down and then went to the kitchen.

"I'll fly it tomorrow morning," Manfred was excited and he was surprised to see Anthony make changes so quickly.

"I will fly it first thing, but you get the next try, *Old Man*," Anthony held up his wine to clink Manfred's glass.

As the two of them were finishing dinner, the owner of the Café approached their table, "I hope everything was satisfactory. Our menu is somewhat limited these days."

"Excellent, as always, Gottfried," Anthony answered. "By the way, this is my friend, Manfred, Baron von Richthofen."

Manfred stood up, shook Gottfried's hand, "Excellent meal tonight, Gottfried. Thank you."

"I'm glad to help both of you. Dinner is my gift to you, to the Fatherland," Gottfried smiled. "No charge, Captain."

Several patrons looked over as Manfred stood up. They recognized Manfred and Anthony. They then   applauded the two of them. Manfred, slightly self-conscious, tipped his head to each side of the room as Anthony, always flamboyant, stood up, waved and smiled.

"I hate to be pushy, but could each of you sign this postcard of the Café Sanssouci?" Gottfried held out a fountain pen with a postcard.

"Of course!" Anthony snatched the card away from Manfred and wrote *Fokker* in large letters on the entire left side of the card.

"Dear Lord, Anthony! No one plays second fiddle to you!!" Manfred snatched the card back and signed *Brn. Von Richthofen* in the upper right.

"Ah, this is wonderful," Gottfried was grateful. "My sons have Sanke Cards of you and Jasta 11, Baron. They will be excited when I tell them you were here for dinner. Thank you. Thank you."

*   *   *

"I think you'll like the changes," Anthony helped Manfred wrap up his flying pants and fasten his belt as he was about to test the latest changes to the V.II.

"We'll see," Manfred was unusually quiet, Anthony thought. He saw that Manfred was preoccupied and looked gaunt.

"You can take her up to six thousand meters, just to let you know. The Tommies won't be able to out climb this one," Anthony became serious as he watched Manfred finish setting his scarf after pulling on his helmet. It was cold. He wondered about Manfred's wound, which, he noticed the night before, was still open to the bone.

Manfred climbed in the Fokker. A mechanic helped him strap in, then they turned the plane by picking up its tail and walking it in a half circle. Finally, the mechanics pulled on the propeller. It started on the first try. Manfred, impatient and wanting to get airborne, taxied to the east side of the runway, looked for the all clear from Anthony and gave the V.II full throttle into the west wind. As the plane accelerated down the runway,

Manfred pulled back on the control stick. He lifted off and proceeded to climb to three thousand meters, which took just fourteen minutes.

Manfred was impressed as he turned left. He felt himself pushed down in his seat as he pulled the turn tighter. He then turned quickly to the right, with the plane responding quickly and lightly. This was an easy plane to fly, Manfred thought. He pulled the stick back and climbed another thousand feet, at which point he pointed the plane into a dive that he pulled out of by executing an Immelmann. He rolled the plane back onto its belly and proceeded to immediately dive and then pull into a loop.

"Yes, this is it. You've done it, Anthony," Manfred said out loud as he was now excited about this new design by Anthony.

Manfred dove the plane, then tried a sharp right turn to see how the plane would do in a simple break off maneuver. As he moved the stick to one side, he felt himself pushed down into his seat like never before. This plane was definitely the best he'd ever flown. But, to make sure, he pushed it into a long dive to see how well it handled the speed with the accompanying shear forces on its four wings. Down he went, faster and faster, with the change in air pressure making him force yawn after yawn to equalize the pressure on his ears.

The stability here was wonderful. Manfred looked over the nose of his plane and sighted in as if he were aiming at an imaginary opponent. He then corrected left, then right, then just slightly up as he dove down. Damn, he thought, Anthony had created one flying machine!

The stall, of course, was another central aspect of battle flying, so Manfred pulled up on the stick to see exactly how the plane carried its nose up in the air so the flyer could fire up at vulnerable opponents above. Manfred was surprised that the Fokker seemed to hang on its propeller, able to keep the nose up as it moved forward, just short of a stall.

As he landed back at Johannisthal-Adlershof Airport, Manfred was elated. He was looking forward to flying this Fokker in combat.

"Yes, the answer is yes, Anthony," Manfred shouted as he cut the engine on the plane and started to unbuckle his belts. "This is the best airplane."

Anthony didn't say anything, but simply beamed.

"Listen, everyone — this plane is something every one of you should fly. Tell Anthony what you think. Our future as a nation is at stake here, comrades," Manfred explained to all the other aces who were there. He wanted to go on and praise the new Fokker's climb rate, higher cruising speed and stability in various linked maneuvers. Moreover, he was ecstatic about the visibility it afforded the flyer, along with its capacity to handle well at low speed. Above all, it was an easy plane to fly, one that immediately obeyed the controls without any eccentricities.

Manfred knew this was the plane for Germany's future and he was going to chafe at the bit until they were delivered to his Schwader.

Chapter Thirty

Manfred felt himself in freefall as the nose of his Albatros was pointed earthward in a steep dive. It was a feeling he never tired of. A wonderful day for the 29th of January, a Tuesday, with the temperature at ground level fifty degrees, a welcome respite from what had been, to date, a brutal winter. As his Albatros accelerated, Manfred pulled back on the controls. He felt his head, spine and bottom pushed back into the seat as the compression from his loop fought against gravity as his plane curved up from its dive. He thought, this was going to be even better in Anthony Fokker's new plane! As he was going straight up and beginning to fly upside down, he looked overhead, which for now, was looking straight down at the ground. Again, at the top of the loop he felt as though he had no weight, which carried over as he again entered the dive phase of the loop until he leveled off at five hundred feet.

On the ground, Manfred's younger brother Bolko looked on with excited pride as his older brother executed this basic but visually exciting maneuver in his battle flier airplane. Bolko was happy that Manfred had flown over Wahlstatt so he and the other cadets at the   Wahlstatt Cadet School could see Germany's hero acknowledge them. On the other hand, Bolko wanted Manfred to land so he and the other cadets could meet him, talk with him and hear some words of inspiration from him. Manfred had

Mamma send a note carrying Manfred's promise to land this coming fall after the crops were harvested and the fields were smooth for a safe landing.

Bolko and the cadets cheered as Manfred did a loop, flew over once again to waggle his wings and then waved goodbye on his way home to Schweidnitz sixty kilometers to the southeast.

Manfred was looking forward to getting home in another twenty minutes, as his engine was acting up, with the throttle slightly laggard in its response. Again and again, he wondered what doing such a flight in Anthony's new Fokker would be like.

Kunigunde was delighted that Manfred was finally coming home for a visit. She knew his approximate time of arrival and was standing on the edge of a small sports field across from their house late in the afternoon. Suddenly, she heard a faint sound far off in the distance. She turned her head this way and that until she located a tiny dot appearing just below the clouds. The dot got larger, turned red and its engine attracted everyone's attention in town. Manfred brought the plane directly down, flared up and landed lightly.

"Hello, Mamma!" Manfred shouted as he climbed down from the plane. "It's wonderful to be home."

"Hello, Liebchen," Kunigunde said warmly as she hugged her oldest son.

"I am starving," Manfred said.
"I imagine so," Kunigunde smiled.

"I did fly over Wahlstatt and did a loop for Bolko and the cadets," Manfred held Mamma's arm as the two of them walked across the field to their house across the street.

"He was disappointed you couldn't land," Kunigunde started to explain.

"Hmmm, I understand. He's a good cadet, I've heard," Manfred replied.

"He idolizes you, you understand," Kunigunde started to go on.

"He'll be flying soon, too," Manfred then changed the subject as he saw Mamma's hidden wince at such a suggestion. "I am starving."

"We found some groats and made a torte. I had a hidden jar of jelly. It's not like we'd want, but I'm sure it's sweet and filling," Kunigunde explained.

They arrived home, with a servant taking Kunigunde's and Manfred's coats.

"I'll carry my bag up after I get some torte," Manfred explained.

Menzke stuck his head in the foyer, "As you wish, Captain. But, your torte is ready in the salon."

"Ah, Menzke, good to see you!" Manfred smiled.

"Yes, we found some groats …" Menzke began.

" … *you* found some groats, you mean, don't you?" Manfred interrupted his orderly.

Menzke, momentarily flustered, didn't know what to say.

"I've got bad news for you, Menzke," Manfred began as he followed Kunigunde and Manfred to one of the tea tables in the salon. "The Albatros is not working properly. We have to make arrangements to have a train carry it to Breslau for repairs."

"Dangerous problem, sir?" Menzke asked.

"Something with the throttle. The engine is uneven at times, but, at least to now, no cutting out," Manfred explained.

"I'll get on the telephone and make arrangements, sir. I'll travel with it to see the job is done properly," Menzke read   his Captain's mind, as he knew Manfred would want the job done quickly and correctly.

"Excellent."

"Will it be flying from Breslau to Berlin, sir?" Menzke wanted to know his Captain's itinerary.

"Yes, this is about three hundred and thirty kilometers — well within the range, don't you think?" Manfred asked Menzke, who he liked to bounce ideas off of.

"Yessir, just remember we have to bundle you up. Today is warm, but it's been quite a cold winter," Menzke saluted his Captain and made his way to the telephone in the study. Manfred started to devour the torte. The maid brought in some acorn coffee. He added some sugar and gulped the cup down.

"Hungry?" Kunigunde laughed at her son.

"We've been busy. I have to go again to a few factories. The Kaiserin Augusta Victoria has even gone out to them. Workers are angry," Manfred started to open up to his mother.

"What do you think?" Kunigunde asked.

"I hate this work. I'd rather be flying at the front. No one has enough food, except the bigwigs in Berlin. People are justifiably angry," Manfred was opening up even more, which was not why he had come home.

"Ah, well, good food is hard, even for us here in the house," Kunigunde admitted.

"Listen, Mamma," Manfred changed the subject.

"I'm listening," Kunigunde answered.

The both looked at each other and broke into laughter.

"It's Lothar. He's not taking care of his ears. He needs to listen to the doctors. Nothing major, you know," Manfred smiled.

"I'll mention it to him," Kunigunde smiled and held Manfred's hand across the tea table.

"I'd love to ride right now. I miss Santuzza," Manfred was beginning to reminisce.

"Oh, she was a jumper and a runner, wasn't she?" Kunigunde was happy to see Manfred let go of the serious and talk about old times at home.

"Maybe I can ride some this summer," Manfred was enthusiastic about the future, at least, for this moment.

Kunigunde handed Manfred a letter from Bolko. Manfred stopped talking long enough to read it.

"Ah, I wish I could've landed, but no real place to do that this time of year—and, I had to get here. Sometimes I have too much to do. I hope he and I can ride together this summer. Maybe even go to an Indian camp," Manfred was wistful.

"I'll tell him," Kunigunde said.

"You know," Manfred had a flash of inspiration. "On my way back from Breslau, I'll drop chocolates for him and the other cadets!"

"Very nice, idea, sir!" Menzke interrupted Kunigunde and Manfred.

"Ah, Menzke. We need some chocolates! By the way, what do you think? Can they get my plane done soon?" Manfred looked at his orderly.

"All is arranged. I will be leaving this evening, sir," Menzke looked sad to be going back to the war effort.

"We've enjoyed you here these past two days, Menzke," Kunigunde raised her coffee cup to him and he returned the favor with a slight bow of his head. "By the way, sir—how was the torte? The *entire* torte?"

"Excellent. I've never eaten quite that fast before," Manfred was, in part, happy, and, in part, thinking about his plane, his return to Berlin and the war effort. Kunigunde could see it in his brow.

"And your head, Manfred. I can still see some bone," Kunigunde observed.

"He is better all the time, if I may interrupt, Madame," Menzke tried to put a good face on what was a continuing injury that had never healed properly.

"Thank you, Menzke," Manfred became suddenly more formal and the furrow in his brow deepened.

"Sir!" Menzke saluted and left the salon.

"Let's go to the study. You said you had some pictures. I'd love to have you tell me about them, Manfred," Kunigunde got up with a mother's concern on her face.

Manfred looked around the salon. It was good to be home. The warm confines of his family house with its well-worn familiarity of elegant furniture, portraits and pictures on the walls, familiar books in the study and his room upstairs. He followed Mamma into the study, where he sat down to show her some photographs from the wartime album he was gradually assembling.

"Let's start with three years ago when I was back in Russia, Mamma," Manfred opened the album to the first page.

"Such lively young men, Manfred. I remember your letters from Russia, the friendships, your enthusiasm," Kunigunde turned a page and recognized Manfred among a group of young fliers he began his flying career with. She looked for a moment and pointed to a smiling fellow.

"Yes, I was, perhaps, naive, Mamma," Manfred replied.

"Who is this fellow?" Kunigunde, again, pointed to a smiling fellow.

Manfred's face darkened, his light mood seemed to fly away in an instant, with his eyes appearing sunken, his brow furrowed and his mood changed, "He is gone, you know. Gone."

"Ah, and this friend of yours?" Kunigunde was searching for some good in all this, in what was appearing to be a mistaken exercise in trying to make her injured son feel good about things.

"He, too, gone. Shot down by the enemy," Manfred said. "And this one, too, Mamma. All of them now gone to the other side," Manfred was now thoroughly depressed, as if the brief respite he had in coming home was, like his fallen comrades, gone.

Manfred, though, steeled himself, stood up, walked to the window, looked out and then turned to his mother, "Let me tell you this, Mamma. Don't worry about me when I'm *up there*. I am the master of the sky, even with my head wound. I hunt and the Tommies scatter, as much as they want to shoot me down."

"Ah, I feel a little better," Kunigunde managed to smile at her son's confidence.

"I've often wondered what would happen if I was shot down on their side. If I had to land over there," Manfred conjectured.

"You are known. I know that much," Kunigunde replied.

"Imagine, well, they'd treat me with some respect," Manfred's mood improved and although he didn't look as light as he did when he was first home, his face was considerably better than it had been a few minutes earlier.

Kunigunde was afraid to follow this line of discussion and was trying to think of something to change the subject.

*   *   *

The very next morning Kunigunde, Manfred and Ilse, who had arrived home later the evening before, travelled to Rankau, near Breslau, to celebrate the birthday of Elfriede, Kunigunde's sister.

On the way, Ilse drove, while Manfred and his mother talked. The drive took just a little over an hour.

"Manfred, you're already known throughout Europe — and, dare I say, even the United States," Kunigunde began.

"Yes, but the fame is not necessarily worth it. Talking in factories, signing those damn Sanke Cards," Manfred laughed.

"Well, you could stop flying. You have sixty-two victories — the most of the war," Kunigunde reasoned.

Manfred was silent as he looked out the window of the Mercedes.

Ilse hit a bump in the road, "Sorry. Really, sorry everyone."

"That's no problem, Ilse," Manfred said softly to his sister.

"It's good to see you, Manfred," Ilse glanced over to her brother. "Mamma's right, you know."

"Yes, and you need to see the dentist. You were telling me about that sore tooth last night," Kunigunde added.

Manfred was quiet. After a few minutes, Ilse looked to the back seat at her mother. The day outside was colder, with the ground covered in snow and frozen puddles of ide from the melted snow the day before when it was much warmer.

"The dentist could help that tooth," Kunigunde quietly brought the subject up in hope that Manfred's mood would lighten.

"Ah, it's useless. There's no reason to go," Manfred seemed to deflate as he sat there in the front seat with his head turned out toward the broad fields of snow.

Ilse directed a furtive glance toward her mother, who was looking at the back of Manfred's head with that damn bandage held in place by the rubber bands.

The three of them were quiet the rest of the drive to Rankau. Ilse was now aware of something that she had been fearing since she first heard of her brother's injury the summer before. Manfred was suffering from his head wound, but, with the pressure of the war, the shortage of good men and the limits of modern medicine, Ilse knew there was no way to fix him, no way to make him who he was before.

Kunigunde, much more limited in her knowledge of modern medicine, was trying to cope with the fact that her son Manfred was no longer the happy and sometimes brash adventurer who enjoyed life to its fullest. She noticed his dark countenance, his sunken eyes, his somber mood.

When they arrived at Elfriede's house, Kunigunde was hoping that her sister's birthday would be a festive occasion, a party that was worth the drive in the dead of winter. Instead, when they got inside the home of Elfriede and her husband Ernst, they found the mood disappointingly subdued, with several friends and relative dressed in black, in mourning for a child, friend or relative who died in combat.

Manfred was glad it was time to catch the train to Breslau.

"I love you, Mamma," he hugged his mother.

Kunigunde kissed his forehead, "Ah, little baby boy — I love you, too."

"Let's not get too sentimental. Let me drive you to the station," Ilse smiled at her younger brother.

"That's what big sisters are for," Manfred managed a smile. Then, he cracked, "Let's not crash on the way, eh?"

"I'll do my best," Ilse saw a welcome twinkle in Manfred's eye.

The way to the station was only a short ten minute drive down the main road into Rankau.

"You know, Manfred, let's be careful *up there*," Ilse began.

"I know what I'm doing *up there*," Manfred reminded her.

"So I've read in the newspapers," Ilse laughed.

"Yes, the same geniuses who had married me off a few months ago," Manfred was sarcastic.

"Well, dear brother — we do want to see you again," Ilse went on.

Manfred was quiet for a   moment, then he replied, "Do you think I would die a meaningless death?"

When they arrived at the station, Ilse insisted, "Let me see you off."

Manfred objected, but relented when he thought he saw that Ilse was about to cry, "You're a hearty woman. You can carry my bag."

"I could, but you'll carry your own bag, thank you very much," Ilse chuckled at her brother.

Manfred got a ticket, then the two of them walked to the platform. Manfred hugged his sister, "I love you Ilse."

"I love you, too, Manfred," Ilse clutched her brother and didn't want to let go.

"I have to get on, Ilse. I'm sorry. There's a lot of preparation. I'll let you in on a secret. We have a big spring offensive. I have a lot of work," Manfred whispered in his sister's ear.

"Come home when you can," Ilse said.

"I will. I'm dropping these chocolates off to Bolko, tomorrow on the way back to Berlin," Manfred smiled as he got on. He got into a car, opened the window and said, "Keep your chin up. Help Mamma, too,"

The train started to pull away and they looked into each other's eyes as they were pulled apart.

Chapter Thirty-One

February and early March were very busy.

Anthony Fokker won the competition in February—much to Manfred's influence—and received the contract from the German government. A very creative designer, engineer and salesman, he worked best alone, which meant that he had trouble putting the Fokker V.II, his successful prototype, into the Fokker D.VII, the mass produced combat ready battle plane the German military was expecting. So, Anthony was forced to come up with the numbers by dividing the production between his own Fokker Works, Albatros and Ostdeutsche Albatros.

Manfred, as commander of Jageschwader 1 and as a man with a fine strategic sense, knew that the remainder of the war was going to be difficult. The British planes flew every day, mostly for reconnaissance, and no matter how many were shot down, the Tommies just kept coming. Manfred eventually wrote a letter to   General Ernst Wilhelm von   Hoeppner, the Commander of the German Air Force. Manfred asked him pointedly, "What about the new Fokker biplanes with the   high compression engines? The new British planes fly so high we can't begin to reach them!" That might be a slight exaggeration, but it indicated a certain deep concern on the German side of things.

The Germans were adamant about winding up the Brest-Litovsk negotiation so they could pull fifty divisions and all their aircraft off the eastern front to ready for their planned spring offensive. Trotsky took over from Joffe as head of the Soviet delegation. The Soviet Central Committee was split on whether or not to accept the harsh German terms. And things on the Central Powers' side was not particularly rosy, as Count Czernin offered the Soviets a separate peace for Austro-Hungary. General Hindenburg told his allies that they would pull every German division off the Austro-Hungarian border with Russia, which would effectively leave the Empire's eastern side unprotected. Czernin withdrew his offer.

The Soviets withdrew from the negotiation in mid-February, a stupid miscalculation. They had thought that the labor unrest in Germany would result in a revolution, which would make further war unnecessary. Nothing of the sort happened. As retaliation, the Germans successfully took a large part of Ukraine, Belarus and the Baltic States. They also sent their fleet toward the Gulf of Finland to take the Russian capital of Petrograd, old St. Petersburg. The Soviets finally relented and the Treaty of Brest-Litovsk was signed on the third of March.

At this point in time, things were certainly far, far away from that idyllic winter day where Manfred and Lothar hunted in the ancient Białowieża Forest outside Brest-Litovsk.

For certain, this was no time for play. Manfred was making sure that proper maintenance was done on his existing Fokker, Albatros and Pfalz battle planes. He inspected things every day and chided his mechanics to be thorough in their work. The last thing they wanted, he would explain, were planes that would fail mechanically and structurally due to improper maintenance.

Manfred was still an inspiring comrade and commander. Berthold Guthmann, one of Manfred's fliers, remarked that their leader was as "an umbrella of fellowship and chivalry for every German pilot." This was in sharp contrast to a rising star in the German Air   Force, Herman Göring, Commander of Jasta 17, who made anti-Semitic remarks about fliers of Jewish ancestry, aces like Guthmann, Willi Rosenstein, Friedrich Rüdenberg and Wilhelm Frankl. Manfred thought this was bad form socially and certainly bad form from the point of view of leadership.

At the same time that Manfred was fair, dutiful and well above competent, he was strange.

Although Ullstein Publishing released his book *The Red Battle Flier* to the soldiers at the front and to the German public at large, Manfred resented having to sign autographs, it seemed, wherever he went.

Menzke noticed it more than anyone, save for Manfred's mother and sister Ilse.

"Yes, you know, Menzke, when I wrote in my book *The Red Battle Flier* that there is no creature more perfect and beautiful than my Great Dane Moritz, I meant what I said," Manfred opened up to his orderly.

"Yessir, I understand. Moritz is a spirited fellow. Each day is like his first. He is always filled with childlike energy," Menzke was comfortable speaking frankly to his Captain.

As Manfred tousled Mortiz's head and neck, he told Menzke, "We're going into difficult times, Menzke."

"Sir, I know you've confided in me the past few weeks," Menzke said as he was folding Manfred's laundry in his quarters in the Château Dejardin at Avesnes-le-Sec. Manfred had been up very early at 4 am, but had come back to his quarters for an unplanned break.

"But, before I tell you what I've got on my mind, I'm feeling nauseous, again. I'd like to take a nap," Manfred curled up like a tiny comma on his cot before Menzke could reply. Menzke began to cover him, as he had been doing now for the past few weeks, but he was interrupted as the alarm went off.

Manfred was up in an instant. He vomited in a bucket, but kept moving as he readied himself to go up in the air once again.

"Sir, should you ..."

"Menzke, I'm fine," Manfred cut his orderly off. "It's morning. The Tommies are coming."

"All the time, it seems," Menzke added.

"Yes. You can stay here and clean, please. I'll lead the Schwader," Manfred jogged out of the Château.

Up in the air, Manfred was resenting his now outdated Fokker DR.I. He was looking forward to Number Sixty-Six on this 18th day of March, but he wanted a better plane for his men. He would, though, make do today. That was certain, he thought. Besides, he knew another victory would be publicized and give the troops in the trenches hope for the offensive that was to begin in the near future.

Jageschwader 1 assembled — this time   with Manfred in Jasta 11 and two more Jastas for a total of thirty-five planes — into a triangle, of sorts, as they spotted the unit they had skirmished with the day before. The Sopwith Camels were proving difficult. Although they were an excellent plane and the British pilots were well trained, they had the disadvantage of flying over German held territory. On their way back to their side of No Man's Land, they had to fly into the prevailing westerly winds over Belgium and northern France.

Manfred tore into a bomber, an Airco DH.4. Because of his innate grasp of the battle environment, he sprung instantly, which caught the Brits off guard. In just one pass, Manfred knew he had damaged the bomber, but he had to cut off his attack as there were two British planes attempting to circle in behind him.

Manfred climbed, wanting to get above the enemy, for he had spotted another squadron of Camels whom he wanted to punish. Although Manfred had taken to heart his father's admonition to be a warrior and not a butcher, Manfred went at it these days with a certain vehemence, a deeper desire to inflict pain upon an enemy who was harming his homeland.

Manfred levelled off and immediately saw a Camel pounce on one of his own. With precision, he dropped down on the fellow, feeling the compression in his back as he pulled up to sight in for a quick pass. He fired just once, pierced the fellow's gas tank and shot the pilot. The Tommie tried to land his plane, but to no avail, as he crashed. Manfred had Sixty-Six just after eleven in the morning. This would make lunch a happier time, Manfred thought.

Manfred then went after the squadron he had tangled with yesterday. With a large group of Fokkers and Albatros battle planes, Manfred and his comrades hit the British squadron, which scattered. It was every man for himself in this melee, with planes dodging, climbing, diving and simply going at it. Two Fokkers were hit and descended, it seemed to Manfred, under some pilot control. Eventually, the British dissolved away back to their side.

Manfred landed back at their aerodrome. Though nauseous and with a headache, he was happy to have Sixty-Six. He was also wondering about his losses today. He taxied to a tent and unbuckled his straps. Menzke came up to help.

"Lothar is alive, sir, but smashed his face pretty badly on crash landing," Menzke had a way of getting all the information out in as few words as possible, something he had picked up from his Captain's direct and honest manner.

"At the hospital? Still in the field, I hope not?" Manfred was upset to hear about Lothar.

"Hospital, sir. He'll be fine, but, as you know, pain for quite a while," Menzke jumped off the wing and took Manfred's hand to help him jump down.

Manfred thought about his younger brother. Such a fine pilot who pulled much more than his own weight. And the time they spent together in the Białowieża Forest was worth a lifetime of vacations! Walking back to their sledge when they spotted the elk. Those tall and flattened horns like giant oaks themselves. It had been so quiet that day, the stillness itself was momentous.

"Sir, are you all right? Sir?" Menzke grabbed Manfred's upper arm and began to shake it. "Sir?"

"Ah, Menzke — very good. Number Sixty-Six today."

"We have the automobile ready to take you to the hospital for Lothar," Menzke pointed to the driver.

Chapter Thirty-Two

The Spring Offensive, now having a real name, the Kaiser's Battle, began on March 21. Manfred was impressed with how well the Germans pushed into Entente territory. In some places they advanced as much as forty miles. And Manfred had advanced as well. Today, April 7 he had two victories, both Sopwith Camels.

As he joked with Menzke, "I'm home for early afternoon *apéritifs.*"

"I'd like to help out, sir, but there is no vermouth, if I remember your preferred drink," Menzke was light hearted about it all, but Manfred knew the lack of vermouth underscored the German shortcoming with its Spring Offensive. Too many causalities — perhaps as many as 200,000 by now on the German side alone — and not enough supplies to sustain soldiers who were advancing far into what had been enemy held territory.

If today were a day to celebrate Seventy-Seven and Seventy-Eight, ten days earlier on Wednesday — and Manfred will always remember it was a Wednesday — the 27th day of March, he had three victories.

"You know, Menzke, I'm piling up the wins, several a day at a time," Manfred joked with his orderly.

"Yessir, I think even Moritz is impressed," Menzke joked while Moritz finally lay at the side of Manfred's cot.

"Very good," Manfred smiled.

"I've left you some tea and a roll, sir. Maybe to settle your stomach in the middle of the night," Menzke saluted his Captain and left.

Manfred was all alone, his windows shuttered, light coming from a makeshift lantern he had made from part of a British plane he had fashioned as a trophy. He had a copy of *The Red Battle Flier* on his thighs as he lay there on his cot with his back up against a pillow against the wall, knees up, having just completed his daily reports and thinking about the offensive that he had just found out, was not amounting to what they had hoped.

Lothar, perhaps, didn't miss a thing, Manfred thought. In the hospital with his jaw broken, wired together by the doctors, having been given enough morphine for a regiment, Lothar was going to make it. Manfred had called Mamma regularly to tell her just that, to let her know along with Ilse and Bolko — all of them — that Lothar was going to be fine.

Manfred looked at his book. He wondered: who was that handsome young man who wrote this flippant account of the war as if it were a sporting event, a steeplechase, hunting in the woods, playing football with schoolmates?

He had a blank sheet of paper and began to write a letter — no, letter — instead, to write his thoughts — his own thoughts about what had taken place in his life. What things had come to.

Manfred's thoughts were a jumble: the makeshift lamp emitted an uneven pattern of light and shadows as it revolved in the imperceptible movement of air in the room. Made from the cylinders of an engine from one of his victories, it was, tonight, unsettling. Manfred started to write, now focused on generating a confessional passage about his thoughts and conclusions at this point in the war.

Manfred looked up at the light and continued to write:

…God knows the light appears eerie and unreal. I have, when I lie like this, a lot to think about. I write it down without knowing if anyone other than my family will see what I thought. I avoid the idea of adding to my book The Red Battle Flyer, for quite specific reasons. Now the war, open on all fronts, has really become a serious worry. There is nothing left of the "fresh, cheerful war," as we used to call our duties at the beginning of all this. Now we have to defend ourselves, desperately, so the enemy won't break into our country. I now have the dark thought--The Red Battle Flyer is really a totally different Richthofen than what the public expects. When I read the book, I smile at my brashness. Now I'm no longer brash. It is not because I imagine how it will be if death one day climbs up my back to sit on my neck — not sure why — although I'm reminded often enough it can come anytime. In fact, someone up the chain of command told me that I should give up flying now, because one day it will catch up to me. I would be miserable, if I now, fraught with fame and medals, would live in retirement while the fellows in the trenches do their duty…

… After each air combat I feel awful. Maybe that comes from the aftereffect of my head wound. When I take my feet off the plane and again stand on the ground, then I make for my four walls, wanting to see no one and hear nothing. I think how it really is. It is not like people in our homeland have imagined, with Hurrahs and a Roar. It is all more serious and grim.

Manfred put down his pen, set his pad of paper next to Moritz, clicked off his light with the switch hanging from the wall and went to sleep.

Chapter Thirty-Three

"I have your orders, sir. In two days you and Lieutenant Wolff can go to the hunting at the Voss lodge," Menzke handed his Captain his travel orders with a smile.

Manfred finished buttoning his shirt and glanced for Menzke to help him slip on his Captain's jacket. Manfred took the orders and looked them over, "Joachim and I will be hunting in three days' time."

"Most welcome, sir," Menzke smiled at Manfred as he held the jacket for Manfred to put arm through first, then the other one.

"By the way, the cool tea and roll helped last night. I woke up once — I think at 2 am," Manfred remarked.

"Excellent, sir. We'll keep up that routine for tonight," Menzke made a point that they were on the right track with helping Manfred control his nausea.

"But, the hunting — this is exciting," Manfred sounded enthusiastic.

"Good news is welcome, sir," Menzke was chatty.

"We could use some good news, eh, Moritz?" Manfred grabbed Moritz and tousled him all over his body.

"Quite a day, yesterday, sir," Menzke opened up the conversation as Manfred had just finished dressing in his new bunker, a far cry from his quarters at the Château in Avesnes-le-Sec.

"We need good news, Menzke. It's been raining these past days and it's been almost impossible to fly. You know, it's no secret I was not happy with our move here to Cappy. This whole four year affair here in the Somme has been an exercise in mud," Manfred explained as he stepped out of his bunker and swept his arm around him. "All of No Man's Land — such a waste."

"Yes, moving the Schwader from Avesnes-le-Sec to here was not exactly your idea," Menzke replied.

"The men have been joking. No more château," Manfred chuckled.

"Yes, well ... there is that, sir," Menzke stuffed Manfred's dirty clothes in a bag and was about to take them to the laundry.

"Moving the entire Schwader over sixty kilometers ... Well, at least we have Cambrai back under our wing," Manfred said. "I'm glad I got to fly here, but you had to travel with the Schwader on the train — and, it was raining, eh?"

"Wet, sir. But we strive," Menzke enjoyed his banter with his Captain. Manfred was a likeable fellow. His men loved him,   he treated everyone fairly and, most importantly, people knew he was suffering with his head wound, but he pulled more weight than several of them together.

"We try to get better all time, Menzke!"

"And two victories late in the day, yesterday, for Seventy-Nine and Eighty," Menzke complimented his Captain.

"I'll be with the men as we await our orders today. Let's hope the 21st of April brings more good tidings, eh?" Manfred walked out of his bunker toward the tents of the Cappy aerodrome. He was waving his travel orders in the air.

As Manfred arrived, the men were in a festive mood, joking and laughing. The men—Schwader Adjutant Karl Bodenschatz, Vizefeldwebel Scholz, Wolfram Scholz, Hans Weiss,   Richard Wenzl, Walter Karjus and

Manfred's new hunting partner, Hans Joachim Wolff—stood at attention and saluted.

"As you were," Manfred sat on a folding chair. Another orderly walked up to hand him today's orders, "Sir, your orders."

Manfred saluted and immediately read the orders, "We are to patrol toward Morlancourt Ridge, along the Somme, the north and western side."

"Toward the bad folks, eh?" Wolfram Scholz joked.

"The very bad folks," Hans Weiss reiterated.

"All of us, sir?" Lieutenant Wolff asked. "I'm looking forward to the fight."

"You and I go to Voss's lodge for hunting in two days," Manfred changed the subject, clearly happy with the short vacation he was afforded. He was up to eighty victories, but could use even a shortened week of leave for the relaxation.

"Great, we get a break for a few days," Wolff was equally happy.

"But not today," Manfred began. "Woodcock shooting in three days, though, Lieutenant. Herr Voss will have some Drillers we can use for the birds. Quite a nice setup over there. He knows the woods and the fields as well as anyone, I'm told."

"My family, we own two Drillers. Both belonged to my grandfather— still excellent shooters—buckshot for hitting birds," Lieutenant Wolff explained.

"And that single barrel rifle underneath for big game," Wolfram pitched in.

"They cook up juicy, those woodcocks," Manfred added.

Manfred noticed the men had been spoofing each other, with one lying on a cot and the other kicking one of the makeshift legs out from underneath it. He held up his hand as if he were going to explain more, nonchalantly walked past the cot and kicked out the leg. As Vizefeldwebel Scholz rolled off the cot onto the ground, the men erupted into laughter.

"The better weather has brought some spirit," Manfred laughed, as Bodenschatz wanted in on the fun by lying on the cot so Manfred could kick the false leg out once again.

Soon Moritz joined the fray, but someone had tied a wheel chock from one of the planes to his tail. Everyone roared as Manfred stood there with Moritz standing up next to him on his hind legs, "What's up with you, Moritz? Those wheel chocks are for planes, dear boy."

"He's game, sir," Lieutenant Wolff chimed in.

"Moritz won't be joining us up there today," Manfred stood there talking as Moritz was perfectly content to pretend, for those few moments, he was human.

"Just begin today with Jasta 11, you five will be fine. Six of us total. We go up and patrol toward Morlancourt Ridge. It's just 10 am, so we level off at four thousand meters to start," Manfred broke off from Moritz, tousled him one more time and headed over to his red Fokker triplane.

"By the way, I see the wind is out of the east today," Adjutant Karl Bodenschatz made sure everyone heard him.

"Very good. We take off down there. Remember that it will be easy to end up on the other side of No Man's Land," Manfred warned. "Vizefeldwebel Scholz and Wolfram on my right. Weiss, Wenzl and Karjus on my left. Wolff, you go later in the day—maybe with me. I may go up twice. For now, dream about hunting!"

Jasta 11 leveled off at four thousand meters, with Manfred serving at the point man in a V-formation. They flew directly east toward Morlancourt, about eight kilometers away, on the northern side of the Somme.

Manfred was looking forward to hunting. He was also sorry that he couldn't take Bolko out of the Wahlstatt Cadet Academy for this coming trip to Voss' lodge. He knew that he would make it up to him this summer by taking him riding and, perhaps, camping. Maybe they could find a tee-pee like the American Indians. Manfred knew that he was fortunate that he was who he was, a national hero, so that he could get over to see Lothar in the hospital every day. Later today he would regale his brother with tales of the grand hunt in the sky over the Somme.

Manfred spied a British squadron attempting reconnaissance over Morlancourt Ridge. Jasta 11 dropped in on them as if by instinct. Manfred felt the compression as he pulled out of his shallow dive to center on a Sop-with Camel. The British scattered, which meant that a one-on-one dogfight might last up to twenty minutes or even longer.

Manfred was intent on getting his next victory. He quickly centered, but couldn't shoot as his gun jammed. He quickly tried with the other gun, found that the bolt released too quickly, which meant he had to pull it back after only a few shells fired. The British pilot, panicking, dove, then broke off to the one side, but edged over No Man's Land. Manfred cut him off, but followed him down even lower. He knew that this poor Tommie was about to get shot down. He turned his head quickly—and he felt a sharp pain in his neck and head—as he saw a Tommie was trying to close in on him. As his prey tried to circle around, Manfred made sure he had cocked his one remaining gun as best he could. The Brit evaded once again, trying to break off with a sharp turn. Manfred was confident that he would now pull him in, center and shoot. Then, he would evade the fellow trying to draw in on him and scoot back home.

As he was reaching for the trigger, he felt a sharp pain in his right side. Manfred almost blacked out. He didn't know he'd been hit through his right rib cage with a British .303 bullet. The .303 tumbled and ripped through his inner torso, to exit around his left nipple. Manfred managed, with the force of will that had kept him going since he was shot on the 6th of July the year before, to land.

Australian infantrymen ran head over heel to his plane. Manfred looked at the first soldier and simply said, "Kaput."

Knowing that they had shot down the Red Battle Flier, *le petit diable*, his conquerors quickly stripped and dismantled his plane for souvenirs.

Everyone on the German side waited for news of Manfred. Late the next day a single British plane flew low over the Cappy aerodrome to drop a note that simply read, "To, the German Flying Corps, Rittmeister Baron Manfried VON RICHTHOFEN was killed in aerial combat on April 21st, 1918. He was buried with full military honours."

Epilogue

Moritz, Manfred's faithful dog, lived into old age on the farm of Lieutenant Alfred Gerstenberg.

Manfred von Richthofen was buried on April 22, 1918 in the village cemetery in Bertangles, France. This was two weeks before his twenty-sixth birthday. Part of his funeral procession was captured on film and is on YouTube. He was reburied in a military cemetery at Fricourt in the early 1920s. Bolko took Manfred home in 1925, but instead of being buried in the family plot in Schweidnitz, the German government gave him a state funeral when they interred him in Berlin in the Invalidenfriedhof (Invalid's Cemetery), a traditional resting place for Prussian military. Manfred was moved in 1975 to a family plot at the Südfriedhof (South Cemetery) in Wiesbaden, next to Bolko, Ilse and her husband.

Albrecht, Baron von Richthofen never got over his son's death and died a depressed man on March 8, 1920.

Lothar von Richthofen worked briefly on a farm after the war, but then married Countess Doris von Keyserlingk in 1919. The two of them had two children before they had their marriage dissolved: Wolf-Manfred (1922–2010) and Carmen Viola (1920–1971). Lothar worked as a pilot in the incipient airline business. He died in a crash on July 4, 1922.

Kunigunde von Richthofen lived until April 2, 1962. She published her wartime diaries as *Mein Kriegstagebuch*, which she intended as an anti-war statement. It was issued in 1937 at the behest of Herman Göring, who had other ideas in mind.

Ilse von Richthofen married Freifrau von Reibnitz on August 28, 1920. He died on July 21, 1929. Ilse lived until February 2, 1963.

Bolko, Baron von Richthofen lived until March 12, 1971.

In World War I, 16 million people died, while 21 million were wounded. There were 9.7 million military deaths and around 6.8 million civilian ones.